Praise for
New York Times and USA Today Bestselling Author

Diane Capri

"Full of thrills and tension, but smart and human, too."
*Lee Child, #1 World Wide Bestselling Author of Jack Reacher
Thrillers*

"[A] welcome surprise….[W]orks from the first page
to 'The End'."
Larry King

"Swift pacing and ongoing suspense are always
present…[L]ikable protagonist who uses her political
connections for a good cause…Readers should eagerly anticipate
the next [book]."
Top Pick, Romantic Times

"…offers tense legal drama with courtroom overtones, twisty
plot, and loads of Florida atmosphere. Recommended."
Library Journal

"[A] fast-paced legal thriller…energetic prose…an appealing
heroine…clever and capable supporting cast…[that will] keep
readers waiting for the next [book]."
Publishers Weekly

"Expertise shines on every page."
*Margaret Maron, Edgar, Anthony, Agatha and Macavity Award
Winning MWA Past President*

STRAIGHT JACK

by DIANE CAPRI

Published by: AugustBooks
http://www.AugustBooks.com

ISBN: 978-1-942633-57-0

Original cover design by: Cory Clubb
Digital formatting by: Author E.M.S.

Published in the United States of America.

Visit the author website:
http://www.DianeCapri.com

ALSO BY DIANE CAPRI

The Hunt for Jack Reacher Series
(in publication order with Lee Child source books in parentheses)

Don't Know Jack (The Killing Floor)

Jack in a Box (*novella*)

Jack and Kill (*novella*)

Get Back Jack (Bad Luck & Trouble)

Jack in the Green (*novella*)

Jack and Joe (The Enemy)

Deep Cover Jack (Persuader)

Jack the Reaper (The Hard Way)

Black Jack (Running Blind/The Visitor)

Ten Two Jack (The Midnight Line)

Jack of Spades (Past Tense)

Prepper Jack (Die Trying)

Full Metal Jack (The Affair)

Jack Frost (61 Hours)

Jack of Hearts • (Worth Dying For)

Straight Jack • (A Wanted Man)

Jack Knife • (Never Go Back)

The Jess Kimball Thrillers Series

Fatal Distraction

Fatal Demand

Fatal Error

Fatal Fall

Fatal Game

Fatal Bond

Fatal Enemy (*novella*)

Fatal Edge (*novella*)
Fatal Past (*novella*)
Fatal Heat (*novella*)
Fatal Dawn

The Hunt for Justice Series

Due Justice
Twisted Justice
Secret Justice
Wasted Justice
Raw Justice
Mistaken Justice (*novella*)
Cold Justice (*novella*)
False Justice (*novella*)
Fair Justice (*novella*)
True Justice (*novella*)
Night Justice

The Park Hotel Mysteries Series

Reservation with Death
Early Check Out
Room with a Clue
Late Arrival

Short Reads Collections

Hit the Road Jack
Justice Is Served
Fatal Action

CAST OF PRIMARY CHARACTERS

Kim Otto
William Burke
Carlos Gaspar
Charles Cooper
Lamont Finlay
Frances Neagley
Marion Morrison ("Morrie")
Petey Burns
Doug Jerzekowski ("Doug XYZ")
Moe Smith
Ray Vance
Andrew Mitchell
Hugh Sullivan

and
Jack Reacher

Perpetually, for Lee Child, with unrelenting gratitude.

STRAIGHT JACK

A WANTED MAN
by Lee Child

There was no point in making a plan. No plan could survive the first exchange of fire. No plan ever did. Except in this case it was impossible to make a plan, anyway. Because there was no information.

CHAPTER ONE

Thursday, May 19
Las Vegas, NV
11:05 a.m. (PDT)

FBI SPECIAL AGENT KIM Otto's plans for the day were
scrapped without notice. She was planning to interview Andrew
Mitchell, a Senior Agent in Charge in the FBI's Chicago field
office. Formerly assigned to anti-terrorism in Kansas City, he
had tangled with Reacher seven years ago. The Boss believed
Mitchell had unreported intel on that operation worth pursuing
now.

The meeting was scheduled and confirmed.

Until it wasn't.

Her partner should have been discharged from the hospital
this morning. She'd arrived to collect him and head to the
airport, which didn't happen.

The doctors said Burke needed more intravenous antibiotics.
Belly wounds were notorious infection risks, they said.

He'd be released tomorrow.

The situation was far from ideal. She shrugged. Nothing she could do about it. When there's only one choice, she didn't bother to struggle against reality. She turned to altering her plans.

Burke, on the other hand, never accepted anything gracefully. He was livid about his forced confinement and wanted to leave the hospital against medical advice.

"The Boss won't like it," Kim said, shaking her head, but she handed over the burner phone that would connect him directly to the man who called the shots where their assignment was concerned.

"I've had worse injuries before. I'm fine. Reacher's got a long head start already. We're losing ground here," Burke argued as he waited for The Boss to pick up. "We need to get to Chicago and then wherever we're going after that."

"You tangled with Reacher last night and lost. So you want another chance. I get it." The Boss was not moved. "But the docs say you're not ready. The last thing I need to explain is a dead agent. You'll stay in the hospital and do what they tell you. End of story. You can hit the ground running tomorrow."

"He came at me from my blind side," Burke growled in defense of his failure to succeed against Reacher.

"I don't have time to argue," The Boss said. "He's been in the wind before. Otto can keep working while you're confined. She doesn't need you to bloodhound Reacher."

Which was true.

But The Boss's suggestion that Kim could succeed where Burke had failed ticked him off again. He jabbed the button, ending the call without signing off.

Kim tried to cheer him up for another ten minutes before she gave up. They'd been partnered six days, and she didn't know him well. But she'd learned that FBI Special Agent William Burke could be one touchy dude, as prickly as any wild beast when his skills were questioned.

She couldn't really blame him for that. She didn't tolerate that kind of disrespect, either.

"I'll get busy. We'll touch base later. And I'll pick you up in the morning. A twenty-four-hour delay before we hit Chicago won't matter, just like The Boss said," she told him on her way out, ignoring the thundering anger on his face.

At the hospital parking garage's exit kiosk she lowered the window, paid five dollars for an hour's parking, and rolled the big Lincoln Navigator out into the sunlight.

Away from downtown and the tourists who flocked there, traffic on the boulevard was lighter and moved along at the speed limit.

She'd already chosen a solid investigatory target. To make the most of the unexpected free time, she needed a good place to start. The Boss had access to all the resources and she had none.

Kim punched the call button on The Boss's burner phone and turned left on the boulevard toward her hotel on the Las Vegas strip.

The phone's ringing echoed through the speakers in the empty cabin.

Kim slowed behind a line of traffic stopped at a red light ahead. The suburban Las Vegas boulevard was lined on either side with business establishments of all sorts. She counted eight of the usual fast-food joints on one corner alone.

Burgers, chicken, Chinese, Mexican, noodles, sandwiches, frozen yogurt, and pizza.

The shapes and sizes were familiar because fast-food spots populated the country these days, the way diners once did.

Recurring repetitive brands made most suburbs in America seem more homogenous than they actually were.

They also made grabbing a quick lunch a lot more predictable.

Kim noticed a drugstore chain on the far corner of a strip center, anchored on the other end by a Walmart. Both were good places to pick up new burner phones and a few other things, like maybe snacks for her room back at the hotel.

She grinned. Kim didn't mind giving The Boss a heart attack when she presented her outrageous minibar bill. But the selection of junk food and drinks in the room was too limited for an extended stay.

The Boss's phone had been ringing for a solid five minutes at least. She gave up and disconnected. He'd call back when he felt like it.

Meanwhile, she was on her own here. Again.

When the red light changed, she rolled through the intersection and turned into the parking lot of the strip center on her right. The shopping center filled the whole block. The open lot was about half full of vehicles and a few people heading into and out of the stores.

Smaller eateries perched on the corners at the strip mall's entrances. There was a drive-up ATM located in the center of the pavement, about halfway between the boulevard and the stores. On one side of the lot was a row of six electric vehicle charging stations, three of which were in use.

Kim shook her head and murmured, "If you've seen one strip mall in America, you've seen them all."

She didn't often agree with him, but The Boss had made the right decision back at the hospital. Right for Burke and right for her, too.

Reacher had bested Burke last night when her partner was at full strength and well-armed. He'd left Burke writhing in pain, bleeding after a knife fight.

If they tangled again before Burke was fully recovered, Reacher could easily kill him.

She cocked her head as one true thing ran through her mind again.

Reacher could have killed Burke last night. But he hadn't. Kim wanted to know why.

So far, the answer to that question and several more had eluded her. She turned her attention to locating a parking spot for the big Navigator.

"It's like driving a bus," she murmured, seeking a place to park with plenty of room on all sides.

For convenience, shoppers had left their vehicles near the various stores in the strip center. Most were parked at the other end, near the Walmart.

Kim turned toward the drugstore, hoping she could complete her shopping faster there. Those big box stores usually had busy checkout lines of shoppers longer than the never-ending queue of screaming fans at a Beyoncé concert.

The burner phone rang, startling her. It was The Boss, returning her earlier call.

"Otto." She picked up, then added a little snark to her reply. "Nice of you to call me back."

"I'm busy," he snapped in return. "What do you want?"

She shook her head as the SUV rolled past an elderly Asian couple standing at the ATM. They must have been dropped off or left their car parked nearby and walked up. Both were tiny and bent almost double with age. A strong wind might have blown them over.

The old guy was facing the ATM's screen, peering through his bifocals, slowly and deliberately punching the buttons, holding a deposit envelope in one hand. The old woman peered over his shoulder, coaching him through the process.

Kim's attention was diverted from the couple when she spied a parking spot near the drugstore entrance and headed in that direction.

She replied to The Boss, "Petey Burns is the best lead I've had for a long time. We know he was traveling with Reacher. I might gather some useful intel if I had a solid place to start."

Before he had a chance to reply, she glanced into the rearview mirror and caught an odd movement in her periphery. She turned her head to get a better look.

CHAPTER TWO

Thursday, May 19
Las Vegas, NV
11:25 a.m. (PDT)

A MAN WEARING A surgical mask, sunglasses, and a ball cap that shaded his face ran up behind the old man at the ATM. He snatched the envelope and shoved the old man to the ground.

The old woman screamed a torrent of words in a language Kim didn't understand and grabbed the mugger's arm. She held on, refusing to let go as the two engaged in a savage tug of war.

The mugger attempted to shove the old woman aside, but she didn't release her hold on his arm. She kept screaming while her husband struggled to stand.

If the mugger managed to break free of her hold, he'd fling her to the ground. Her fragile old bones would easily shatter when she hit the pavement.

When he couldn't shake her off, the attacker reached behind his back with his free hand and pulled a pistol from his belt.

The old woman continued the stream of incomprehensible

words and turned her face away. But she didn't release her two-fisted grip on his arm.

When the old man looked up from the pavement and saw the gun, he began to yell, too.

Conditions were evolving quickly. The situation had turned from a simple snatch-and-go assault toward a possible double homicide.

Kim steered the big SUV out of the driving lane, slammed on the brakes, and slid the transmission into park.

"What's going on?" The Boss demanded.

"Attempted robbery. The victims aren't capitulating. He's got a gun. Call for help." She unlatched her seatbelt, opened the door, and slid onto the pavement, running the moment her feet hit the ground.

The old man had managed to get up onto one knee, struggling to push up with his cane. The robber kicked him viciously, knocking him to the ground again, while the scrawny woman continued her valiant tussle.

Kim shook her head. The old girl was stronger than she'd first appeared. Which was escalating this thing well beyond reason.

The mugger moved the pistol around his torso and brandished it close to the old woman's terrified eyes. He snarled something, but Kim couldn't hear the words.

"Stop!" Kim yelled.

She sprinted to reduce the gap between her SUV and the mugger, but she wasn't close enough to stop him. Nor did she have a clean shot from here. The three were engaged in a deadly dance, tangled and inseparable.

The attacker pointed his gun directly at the old woman's face. He couldn't possibly miss her if he fired from that distance.

Kim attempted to distract him long enough to save the old woman's life.

"Stop!" she yelled again as she poured on more speed. "Leave her alone!"

This time, the mugger heard. He glanced up, startled.

He saw Kim running straight at him.

He shook his head, confused, trying to sort out the situation. He seemed to realize he had precious few seconds to make up his mind.

Not enough time to kill all three.

Should he shoot the screaming crazy old woman or apply his gunfire to the interfering young one rushing toward him?

His instant of indecision proved disastrous.

While he was distracted by Kim's approach, the old woman lunged forward, bent her head, and chomped a huge bite from his cheek. She held a patch of his bloody skin in her teeth.

The mugger howled and shook the old woman's hold from his forearm, slapping the envelope he still held in his left hand toward his face to stop the blood that gushed from her bite.

The old woman fell on top of her husband. They were piled in a heap of fragile, tangled limbs on the hot pavement under the glaring sun.

The outraged robber roared and raised the pistol to shoot them both.

A moment before he squeezed the trigger, Kim leapt forward and kicked his torso swift and hard.

He bent over and grabbed his belly as she rushed to capture his gun.

Faster than she'd expected, his body flooded with adrenaline, the attacker raised his gun and struck Kim's left clavicle a solid blow.

When the strike landed, her momentum caused her to stumble.

Intense pain shot through her shoulder, running down her arm to her fingertips.

She staggered to keep upright, giving him the brief opportunity he needed to dash away.

Kim regained her balance and gave chase, ignoring the pain in her shoulder.

The attacker ran ahead of her, five strides out of reach. His legs were longer, but she was a faster runner. She was in better shape, too.

She narrowed the distance between them just as a black sedan came speeding up and slammed to a stop a few feet ahead of the mugger.

An accomplice.

For the first time, Kim realized the attacker was not operating alone.

The sedan's passenger door flung open. The driver yelled, "Get in! Get in! Let's go!"

The robber pumped his arms and ran the last distance flat out, with everything he had, desperate to reach his getaway.

He was almost there.

He slowed to place the hand still holding the bloody envelope atop the sedan's door to steady himself.

He lifted one leg, preparing to jump inside, gasping for breath.

It was all the advantage Kim needed to close the space between them. She jumped forward and landed a strong shove on his ass with the force of her full weight and knocked him to the ground.

The driver of the sedan realized his buddy wasn't getting up.

He peeled out, tires squealing and smoking.

The sedan sped toward the exit while Kim caught her breath.

She pulled her phone from her pocket and snapped a few photos of the escaping sedan and its rear license plate.

Kim heard sirens in the distance, coming closer, moving fast. At least one police cruiser and one ambulance. Maybe more.

Between big gulps of air, she directed him, "Stay put, pal. You're not going anywhere."

He drooped and laid his undamaged cheek against the pavement.

She flipped his cap off his head and jerked the mask and sunglasses away to snap a few shots of his face before she slipped her phone into her pocket.

Kim didn't have a set of handcuffs. Which was okay because less than a minute later, the first police cruiser pulled up and two officers got out to take charge of the scumbag.

While the first officer dealt with the mugger, the second asked for her ID. She supplied it, along with a brief statement about the incident.

The officer nodded and thanked her. She shrugged off his appreciation.

"ATM robberies have been a problem all over the Vegas area lately," the officer said. "Seems like we might have a theft ring going on. This is the first one we've caught. So thank you for that."

"I guess it's easier than robbing a bank," Kim nodded, dusting the parking lot grime from her clothes. "But ATMs usually have all kinds of security and sensors and cameras. How do the thieves get away with it?"

The officer shrugged. "Around here, ATM robberies tend to fall into two camps. They take the whole machine, cart it off, and bust into it somewhere to steal the cash that's inside. Or they attack the customers, either before they make a deposit or after they get their cash out."

"Do they get enough money to make the thefts worthwhile?" she asked, straightening her clothes. She tucked a stray lock of hair into the tight bun she wore at the base of her neck.

"Each ATM can hold about two hundred grand when they're full," he said, nodding. "And people make sizeable deposits sometimes."

"Well, maybe you can break this guy and figure out how to put a stop to it. He doesn't seem like a criminal genius."

The officer shook his head. "We don't catch the smart ones."

Burke had said something similar to her not long ago. She'd argued with Burke but didn't bother explaining to this patrolman just how successful law enforcement could be against the smart ones.

"These sorts of theft rings tend to hang together," Kim said, nodding toward the attacker. "You'll have solid DNA from this guy, thanks to the woman's quick thinking. Run the DNA before he lawyers up. Could help find the driver of that sedan. He could be listed as a known associate in the databases."

She went over to check on the old couple. The paramedics were already well into triage. They would be okay, he said. Cuts and bruises and injured pride, mostly.

"They're lucky it wasn't a lot worse. That guy could have killed them," Kim replied.

"These folks own the Chinese restaurant over there," the EMT nodded, pointing to one of the restaurants on the corner. "The robber tried to take the week's deposit. To them, the money to pay their employees and their other bills was worth dying for, I guess."

Kim shook her head and watched a few moments more as the first responders did their jobs before she turned and made her way back to the Navigator. She still needed her supplies.

She was headed back to her room when her phone rang. She recognized the number. Only one man ever called from that number, and he rarely called.

Lamont Finlay, Special Assistant to the President for Strategy, the highest-ranking civilian responsible for Homeland Security and Counterterrorism. One heartbeat away from the US Commander in Chief.

No watchdog kept tabs on him. He reported seldom and only through verbal briefings. No paper trail so much as named the missions he'd undertaken.

Everything she'd learned about Finlay marked him as dangerous. He deployed unspecified unique skills in service to her country on unidentified missions. Like nuclear power, when properly harnessed he might be useful. But she'd found nothing restraining him, not even his own word.

Was he friend or foe? Wiser to assume the worst, Gaspar always said.

She answered the call. "Otto."

He chuckled as if he was mocking her business-like attitude. "I heard you had a bad night. How's your partner?"

"Thanks for checking in," she replied, meaning it. "He'll be okay. They're examining him now. He'll be released tomorrow morning. Then we're headed to Chicago."

She found it oddly comforting that Finlay kept tabs on her, even though Gaspar was suspicious and didn't trust him. Before this assignment was over, she had the unsettling feeling that she would need all the friends in high places she could muster.

"Why Chicago? Does Cooper think Reacher is likely on his

way to meet up with Neagley again?" Finlay said, clearly skeptical.

"Possibly." Kim had reached the parking lot. She parked and turned off the ignition. "He didn't say that, though. We're interviewing another FBI agent. One who crossed paths with Reacher a few years back."

"What sense does that make in Cooper's twisted head?" Finlay asked.

"No clue." She heard someone call to him in the background. He rarely had more than five minutes to give her.

"Watch your back, Otto. Cooper doesn't have your best interests top of mission here. Never forget that. I'll be in touch," he said before he disconnected.

And just like that, she had something else to worry about.

CHAPTER THREE

Thursday, May 19
Las Vegas, NV
7:05 p.m. (PDT)

INSTEAD OF REJOINING THE manhunt for Petey Burns early this morning as planned, Kim had ended up working the phone and her laptop all day. She had precious little to show for her efforts.

She stretched her sore neck and shoulders and walked around the room working out the kinks. Running through a hot parking lot and tackling a mugger to stop a robbery in progress had left her with mild residual muscle complaints that a hot shower and a good night's sleep would easily handle.

The blow to her clavicle would take a few days to resolve. Could have been worse.

The delay in Burke's medical discharge had left her with extra time on her hands. When she'd returned to the hotel, she extended her room reservation for another night. She worked out in the hotel gym and then showered the grime from her body, letting the hot spray soothe her aches.

After that, she ordered a bite to eat and turned to the old-fashioned detective work she hoped would help locate Reacher. She'd lost him twice in the past week. She didn't want to strike out after a third miss.

The Boss had told Burke she would find Reacher again. Which was a certainty. Luckily, he hadn't imposed a hard deadline to accomplish the task.

The best place to start was with Petey Burns. He and Reacher had been traveling together for several days. They'd been seen the night before, right here in Vegas.

Burns was with Reacher when Burke was injured.

Burns had been driving, which seemed to be half of his expertise. The other half was stealing German luxury cars equipped with enough anti-theft protection to defend the Pentagon.

By all accounts, Burns was charming and chatty and goofy and fun to be around, too. As one witness had put it at his first trial on grand theft auto charges, *Burns could charm the pants off a preacher's wife.*

Apparently, he'd done exactly that more than once. Then he'd stolen the preacher's BMW. The rest, as they say, was history.

Kim grinned and shook her head. She was looking forward to meeting Petey Burns, although he seemed an odd partner for Reacher.

At this point, Reacher's contribution to the duo's adventures remained unknown. But she could make a few educated guesses. Reacher had supplied the brawn, for sure. He might also have identified the targets.

Question was, where were they heading next?

The Boss had supplied the entire criminal database of reports on Peter Allen Burns, and she'd skimmed the files, looking for anything that might lead her to Burns's current location.

Burke called. "I'm bored. Catch me up."

Kim filled him in on the attempted ATM robbery first, then recited certain items of interest from the Petey Burns files aloud.

"Born in Georgia... Orphaned at age seven when his parents died in a house fire... In and out of foster care and then various jails."

She flipped through the arrest reports and picked up again. "Until he ended up in the Bolton Federal Correctional Facility after his tenth grand theft auto arrest."

"Anything illuminating in the Bolton records?"

"Not really. Burns's time served there was relatively short because he escaped during last week's prison break."

"So he didn't have enough time to get into trouble," Burke said.

Kim sat back on the bed, stretched out, and opened a bottle of water. She swigged directly from the bottle and listened to Burke as she mulled things over in her head.

"Let's recap," Burke said. "Burns joined up with Reacher after the prison break. We don't know exactly where or why, but they connected somewhere between Mount Rushmore and Duncan, Nebraska."

"They were together last night and probably still are." Kim hoped. Because Petey Burns should be a hell of a lot easier to find than Reacher.

As if he'd read her thoughts, Burke said, "Yeah, well, Burns is a fugitive from justice. His face is plastered everywhere. There are BOLOs out for him around the country,"

Kim nodded, even though he couldn't see her. Every federal, state, and local cop within a three-thousand-mile radius of

Bolton, South Dakota, should be looking for Petey Burns.

Every traffic camera, security camera, and satellite feed could be accessed.

Every car rental, airline, train service, and bus station employee would have Burns's photo next to their checkout counters.

All of which meant Kim could trace Petey Burns in ways Reacher could not be followed. With so many jurisdictions involved and the general lack of communication between agencies, the process of piecing things together would take longer than it needed to.

But she could find Burns, which would lead her to Reacher.

She just had to be methodical about it.

Burke said, "I've got to hang up. They're taking me down to another department for more labs."

"Problems?"

"Definitely not. I'll be ready to go in the morning, as planned."

"Okay. Sounds good," Kim replied and he disconnected, leaving her wondering whether he'd be ready or not. He wouldn't admit it if he weren't ready. No point in dwelling on the unknown.

Several hours ago, she'd called her former partner, Carlos Gaspar, with a wish list of requests. He hadn't called back.

But he would. As soon as he'd found the needle in the haystack she'd asked him to locate.

Kim ordered room service and then picked up the burner phone that would connect her directly to Gaspar. She placed the call, pacing the room like a caged tiger, while she waited for her food and for him.

Forced inactivity wasn't her idea of a great way to spend her time. It wasn't likely to help her find Burns or Reacher, either.

She needed to get out in the field. The flight to Chicago had been rebooked and the interview rescheduled. If Burke wasn't released tomorrow, she would leave him here. He could catch up later.

Gaspar picked up the call. "Good evening, Suzy Wong. I was just about to ring you."

"Great. Did you find Petey Burns yet?" She heard the hopeful tone in her voice. He'd hear it, too.

"Actually, I did," he replied.

She imagined his big self-satisfied grin.

She stopped pacing. "Excellent. Where is he?"

"Let me rephrase. I don't know where he is right at this moment."

"Great," she deadpanned.

"Look, it's not that easy. Do you know how many cameras there are in Las Vegas? Not to mention the satellites and drones and cell phones." Gaspar paused to slurp something from a cup. Probably his sweet Cuban coffee. He might as well mainline that stuff. "But I found him after checking about a zillion traffic cams. Finally."

"What's he driving? Where was he headed?" she asked, pacing again.

"Keep your panties on, Sunshine. Don't you want to know how I found him?"

Kim ran a palm across her face. From long experience, she knew he wouldn't be rushed. But she was out of patience.

"Chico, I definitely want to hear the blow-by-blow. But first, just tell me, is Reacher still with him?"

"Yep. Reacher was in the car."

She stopped moving, stopped breathing for a moment, too. "How do you know?"

"Check your secure server. I just sent you a few stills from different angles," Gaspar said. "Images are fuzzy. I cleaned them up as much as I could. But it's him. Or rather, both of them."

Kim opened the laptop and connected it to her server. She downloaded the images and flipped through them one at a time. After a few moments, she realized she'd been holding her breath.

Gaspar was right. The images were definitely Petey Burns and Jack Reacher. No doubt about it.

She grinned and took a big gulp of air. "Chico, you're a genius."

He laughed. "You say that like my brilliance is a revelation. Surely you already knew that."

Kim plopped onto the bed, grinning like a fool. "Well, prove me right, then. Where are Burns and Reacher now?"

CHAPTER FOUR

Thursday, May 19
Gaucho, NM
9:05 p.m. (MDT)

"TWO ROOMS, PLEASE. MY buddy needs his beauty rest, so put him on the end. I don't want to walk that far. Make mine a few doors from the office," Petey Burns said politely as he pushed cash across the counter toward the clerk at the Gaucho Motel.

The countertop was sticky, like it hadn't been cleaned in a while. Which was okay. They'd chosen the place precisely because it wouldn't become more popular overnight. They'd be gone tomorrow.

The Gaucho Motel had seen better days, probably sometime early in the last century. The tan block building was laid out like old motels everywhere, resembling a figure seven.

The office was on one end facing the road, with an attached cover across the driveway so patrons could drive through to unload.

A single-story line of rooms ran perpendicular to the office. The room layout was designed to protect against the sounds of traffic. Except there shouldn't be any road noise. The old road probably carried fewer than a hundred vehicles a week these days.

Each room's door opened onto a covered sidewalk abutting the parking lot, which was essential. Petey never knew in advance how quickly he'd need to get out.

"Spell those names, please," the clerk said as he keyed the names into the computer. He palmed Petey's extra fifty bucks, sliding it into his pocket without so much as a blink.

The man was maybe forty. Big but paunchy in the way of an aging high school football hero. His head was oversized. Long, greasy hair parted in the middle to frame a broad face with a wide nose and fleshy lips. Narrow brown eyes with sleepy lids barely glanced up.

Petey grinned. Just the kind of guy he liked. Odd, dumb, and slow. He'd take the bribe and forget about Petey altogether. Perfect.

"Sure." Petey spelled out Ben Franklin and John Q. Adams.

The clerk didn't crack a smile as he typed the fake names. He handed over the keys to rooms six and fifteen, waving toward the sidewalk, and turned again toward the old movie showing on the television mounted behind him.

Petey pushed through the glass door and strolled into the cool evening air. He'd parked the car in the lot out of view of the clerk, just in case the dude was more alert than he seemed.

Doug had told him this place was perfect, and so far, it was.

Petey strolled across the pavement toward the dusty white Volkswagen Tiguan SUV to grab his duffel. The vehicle was six years old and showed every inch of its mileage. It had crashed at least twice in its lifetime, too. He planned to replace it as soon as he had the chance.

His oversized traveling companion had climbed out of the Tiguan and was stretching his legs while he waited for Petey to return with the keys. They pulled two duffels out of the back and headed toward their rooms.

"It's not the Taj Mahal, but there's a bed and a shower," Petey said as he tossed the key to room fifteen. The hulking giant caught it with one hand and kept walking.

Petey had plans tonight, and Jack Reacher was a light sleeper. The farther his room was from Petey's, the better.

He watched Reacher's retreating back move past the cubbyhole with the ice machine and on toward the end of the row. Beyond the last room, a bum slept upright on a bench, waiting for a bus or something.

Petey called out, "We'll hit the road again early in the morning."

Reacher said nothing. He unlocked his door and went inside room fifteen.

Petey watched him disappear, shook his head, and murmured, "That is one strange dude."

He unlocked number six, pushed the door into the room, and flipped the light switch.

The room wasn't the Ritz, to be sure. Hell, it wasn't even a Motel 6. But it was a damned sight better than his last prison cell because he could leave whenever he damned well felt like it.

Still, the place was way overpriced.

The brown carpet was buckled and worn and smelled disgusting. He hoped the bed sheets were reasonably clean because he wasn't sleeping on top of that dirty bedspread. Not even for a minute.

The heating and cooling unit was tucked under the big window that faced the sidewalk. He pulled the curtains closed and punched the max setting on the unit to draw outside air, hoping to freshen the stench. The place smelled like more than one rodent had died in here.

He tossed his duffel on the bed and stretched to work the tension from his muscles.

Reacher didn't drive. Claimed he wasn't good at it. Never even had a driver's license.

Petey found the idea preposterous. How could any red-blooded American male not have a driver's license?

Also, this made Reacher less useful than Petey had hoped for when he picked him up hitchhiking back near Mount Rushmore. Petey liked hitchhikers for three reasons. Obviously, to help with the driving, which on a long haul like this one, could get tedious. Second thing was to provide interesting conversation. With Reacher, he'd struck out on both counts.

But the third thing? Petey liked a guy who could handle himself when trouble came calling.

Reacher had proven way more than competent on that score.

All things considered, Reacher was a keeper. For a while longer, anyway.

Since last night, they'd been traveling on the back roads across the desert from Las Vegas. The interstate would have been a lot faster, but Reacher didn't seem to care and Petey wouldn't risk it.

Traffic cameras and speed traps were more likely along the major highways. Since he'd escaped from the federal prison in Bolton, South Dakota, last week, Petey's face showed up everywhere. Every newscast, every newspaper. The feds had "be on the lookout" orders for his mug circulating in all fifty states.

He had to be careful. He liked being out of prison. He didn't plan to go back.

Not that he worried about it much.

Petey grinned. Cops were idiots. He'd been evading police almost as long as he'd been alive.

Sure, every now and then one of the Barneys got lucky and scooped him up. But Petey never stayed in jail for long.

He was a lover, not a fighter.

Fortunately, he was cute and lovable, so women were easy to get. He liked fast cars and he had a talent for stealing them. His preference was German luxury vehicles. German driving machines were far superior to everything else he'd stolen over the years.

Plus, he liked the challenge. The tech on the damned things was complicated. Petey was way smarter than he pretended to be.

He lived simply, although he enjoyed what he thought of as the good life. Which meant, every now and then, he needed to acquire some serious money.

This was one of those times.

Which was why he'd come here.

He glanced at the clock on the bedside table. He was meeting Doug in a nearby bar in an hour. And he needed a shower first.

His dirty clothes were so stiff he thought they might stand up on their own when he shucked them off.

He'd been wearing a baseball cap to shield his face from cameras. When he tossed it onto the bed, he ran his hands through the matted mess of hair on his head. Man, he hated hats.

Petey kept his shoes on as he walked naked across the bedroom to the bathroom. He flipped a switch by the door that controlled the light over the tub and also started the raucous overhead fan.

The damned thing was loud enough to wake the dead.

No way to have the light on without the fan and it was too dark in there without the light. So he left both running.

After a moment, he noticed the stench rising from the toilet. Smelled like something had died in there, too. Recently. He flushed twice and watched the iron-rich brown water swirl in the bowl, but flushing didn't improve the odor.

He wrinkled his nose and breathed through his mouth. He wouldn't stick around in here long.

One shower. One night. He could live with this place that long. He'd survived worse.

Petey pushed the opaque plastic shower curtain back. It had concealed an old porcelain tub, scratched, gouged, chipped, and brown-stained by hard water.

The tub might have been scrubbed sometime in the past month. Maybe. Impossible to tell.

He reached over and turned on the water. The pipes banged inside the wall like the midget who lived in there was pounding them with a hammer. Half a minute later, the showerhead sputtered and spit and sprang to life.

Brown-tinged sludge plopped from the rusty pipes. He waited a few minutes until it cleared a bit, pushing some of the clogs through the holes and improving the flow.

Then Petey shrugged out of his shoes and stepped into the still-sputtering spray, allowing the warm shower to scrub the road filth from his body.

On the edge of the tub, he found one of those small bars of soap that cheap motels seemed to acquire by the gross. Stuff was strong enough to melt your skin right off your bones.

He unwrapped the soap and rubbed the bar all over his body until it melted into a sliver and then disappeared.

No more than ten minutes later, the hot water ran out.

He turned the shower off and pushed the beige shower curtain aside. Instead of twelve rings holding the plastic on the metal rod, it had three. Which allowed the curtain to gap and water to leak onto the floor.

Petey pulled a threadbare towel from a rack above the toilet and used it to dry off. The towel had been white once. The brown water had stained it a dingy shade of rust. Same as the floor of the tub and eight inches up along the bottom of the plastic shower curtain.

He wrapped the thin terrycloth around his waist, slipped his wet feet into his shoes, and traipsed across the grungy carpet to the bed.

He rooted around in the duffel and removed his new clothes. First, he pulled on a pair of clean cotton boxers. He followed them with the new twill pants and rough cotton shirt, which he buttoned and tucked into the waistband. He pulled his belt from his dirty jeans and slid it through the new pant loops.

He'd acquired the new duds at an Army surplus store somewhere in Arizona this afternoon. Reacher's idea. And a damned good one. The new togs changed his appearance a bit, which would help with the BOLOs, maybe.

When he was dressed, Petey took a quick look in the mirror. He'd added seven days of reddish beard. Though it itched like crazy, he hoped the beard might obscure his identity a little. His blond hair was shaggier than usual. He combed it with his fingers and left it to air dry.

Overall, not too bad, he thought. Not gonna attract any hot women, but there weren't likely to be many ladies around tonight, and he didn't have time for that anyway.

In Petey's experience, hot women cost money, too. He didn't have any of that, either.

Until he got paid.

Then he'd buy all sorts of new stuff, and the women would flock to him, and he'd buy them stuff, too.

He glanced at the clock again. Time to go. Doug was waiting.

CHAPTER FIVE

Thursday, May 19
Gaucho, NM
10:05 p.m. (MDT)

PETEY BURNS MUSCLED THE door closed, stuffed the key in his pocket, and looked down the row of rooms. On his right, the motel's office lights were off now. The dimwitted clerk must have gone out.

He looked left. At the end of the row, Reacher's room was as dark as the others. The bench beyond the motel was empty now, too. The bum had moved on.

Satisfied that he wouldn't be seen, Petey stuffed his hands in his pockets, left the crappy Volkswagen in the parking lot, and set out on foot. A warm breeze caressed his skin as he walked three blocks along broken sidewalks into downtown Gaucho, New Mexico. Such as it was.

He was alone in the dark. He didn't pass another soul, dead or alive. No animals scurried away in the darkness.

No cars drove along the road. The few remaining Gaucho residents seemed to have tucked themselves in for the night.

Petey always wondered why people stayed glued to places like this. The reasons, whatever they were, made zero sense to him. But people did live here. Not many. They didn't even have a gas station. Just enough folks to require a watering hole and a place to buy a few necessities.

What kind of life was that? Petey had been locked up in jails and prisons that held more excitement than Gaucho, New Mexico. He'd rather be dead than holed up in such a lonely place.

Gaucho's main street was only one block with a few sad storefronts on either side. All the buildings had been constructed during some economic boom or another a hundred years ago. Like every boom, a bust or three followed, sure as night follows day.

Now, several of the buildings were abandoned and the others were falling down on their foundations.

He strode past a decrepit dry goods store and a worse-looking drugstore, both closed up for the night. Neither had felt a paint brush for a decade, at least.

In the middle of the block was the place he'd located when he drove through town an hour ago. A lighted sign in a small window proclaimed it *Delgado's Bar*.

Shaped like a cracker box, Delgado's adobe façade was twenty feet wide and probably ran all the way from the main street straight through to an alley. Could have been parking in the back, since there were only a handful of angled spots near the front.

Petey pulled the heavy door open and stepped into the cool, dim interior, giving his eyes a moment to adjust.

There was a long bar on the left and a row of tables on the right. Way in the back, he saw a pool table and a dart board. Four guys were standing around holding longneck beer bottles while two others racked the balls and held their cue sticks, prepared to shoot.

From this distance, they looked young enough, fit enough. Clean enough. Sober enough.

Pathetic. Petey shook his head. Six guys hanging around a pool table in Delgado's Bar. Probably the whole damned male population of Gaucho, he figured as a rustle on his right caught his attention and he turned his head.

Doug Jerzekowski sat alone at a four-top table in the corner, back to the wall, facing the door. He was finishing up a plate of greasy food that made Petey's mouth water.

He offered a one-fingered wave and Doug nodded and Petey headed over to the bar to grab a beer.

"Can I get a burger and fries?" Petey asked as he paid for the beer.

"Yeah, sure. I'm alone tonight. Might take a minute. That okay?" the bartender replied, chewing on a wooden toothpick, sizing him up like he was worried.

What the barkeep was worried about, Petey couldn't guess. He had never started a fight in his life. Never won one, either. He didn't plan to change his luck on that score tonight.

"I'll be over there," Petey pointed the beer toward Doug's table. "Let me know when you've got it ready and I'll come get it."

"Will do," the bartender said, moving the wooden toothpick around with his lips like tooth picking was an Olympic sport.

Petey gave him a nod and headed across the narrow space. He took the chair on Doug's left side, which put his back to the wall, too. He'd watched Reacher sit like that everywhere they went for the past week. He figured there was a good reason for it. Reacher didn't do things just for the hell of it.

"How ya doin', Doug?" Petey said, lifting the beer to take a long swig.

He'd met Doug XYZ, so-called because his surname was unpronounceable, during a short stint in jail back in Georgia a few years ago. They'd lost touch the way guys do until Doug got word to him back in Bolton Prison. Said he was sorry to hear about Petey's troubles and when Petey got free, to call him and Doug would hook him up.

So he'd called. Doug said he had something going on and to meet him here tonight, at Delgado's Bar.

Now here he was. Not exactly sure why. But maybe something good was headed his way. Petey was an eternal optimist.

Besides, Doug XYZ was the sort of guy who brokered opportunities. Petey needed a profitable opportunity.

He'd been free of prison for a whole week now, which was some kind of record, and he'd figured out he liked it. The freedom. The room to move. Choosing his own food and his own beds and his own stuff. He'd started to enjoy himself on the outside.

Course, nobody gave him a clean bed, three square meals a day, or did his laundry now. Which were chores that consumed way more of his time and energy than he'd expected.

Petey didn't want to keep running and shopping at the surplus stores forever. Which meant he needed money. After he filled his wallet to a nice, fat, comfortable level, he'd figure the rest out.

Which was why he was sitting here in Gaucho at the same table as Doug XYZ.

Doug eyed him and swallowed the last of his burger before he said, "Took you long enough. I was expecting you yesterday. You didn't show up tonight, the plan was to drop your ass from the team. Where you been?"

"Yeah, sorry. I meant to get here sooner. Had to take a detour to Vegas."

"Vegas? What the hell for? You ain't got no money." Doug frowned and swigged from his own beer bottle. "You in some kinda trouble already, Cuz? I can't handle the heat. Not right now. Got too much goin' on for that nonsense."

Petey looked him straight in the eye and said the only thing he could say. "Naw. Ain't nothin' to worry about."

The bartender brought two more beers and Petey's food to the table. He said, "I set you up with a tab. Figured you might have a few more before you leave."

"Thanks," Petey replied, although he'd barely sipped the first beer and he only had forty bucks in his pocket. Even cheap clothes at the Army surplus store cost more than he could afford at the moment. Which was why Reacher had paid for them.

The burger smelled great. Petey hadn't eaten for a long time. He dug in. Greasy food was only good while it was fresh and hot.

Doug watched him for a while before he said, "This is a huge operation. We got big guys at the top holding the controls. Can't screw it up. Screw it up, and we die."

Petey nodded. Sounded perfect to him. The bigger, the better. He didn't plan to screw anything up.

Doug asked, paying close attention. "I saw you drive into town. Looked like there was someone with you in the car."

The question startled him. Petey's big mouthful of burger got caught in his throat. He swigged the beer to wash it down, which gave him a second to think. "Yeah, I'm alone. I mean, I picked up a hitchhiker. That's all."

"A hitchhiker?" Doug asked, staring intensely like the question was important.

"I figured he could help with the driving, you know?" Petey said, chewing and swallowing and trying to act like Reacher didn't matter. He didn't. Not really. They weren't partners or anything. Reacher barely even talked. Petey knew next to nothing about the guy.

Unless Doug needed muscle for the new job. In which case, Reacher would be an asset, for sure.

"He's been with you all this time? The whole week?"

"Yeah."

"What do you know about him?"

"Whaddaya mean?" Petey said, eating the fries, slower, a few at a time.

"You were in a car with him twenty-four-seven for a week. He musta told you something about himself," Doug said, sounding annoyed. "Does he have any skills? Would he be useful?"

"He doesn't talk much. He's an army vet, like you. Good training. Knows how to handle himself. Pretty self-sufficient," Petey replied.

"What else?"

"His name is Jack Reacher. Honorable discharge a while back." Petey shrugged. "What do you want to know? Just ask me. If I know, I'll tell you. If I don't know, you can ask him yourself."

"Maybe I'll do that. Where is he now?" Doug asked, cocking his head.

"I left him over at the motel. Room fifteen. On the end," Petey said. "Can't say for sure that he's still there."

Doug cocked his head. "Why wouldn't he be?"

"Hell, Doug. I don't know. I didn't marry the guy. I gave him a ride. Maybe he's sick of me. Maybe he didn't want to stop for the night. Who knows?" Petey said, annoyed himself now.

He didn't want to talk about Reacher. He wanted to know about Doug's opportunity. And to move on. This burger was the last thing he could afford to buy. He needed cash. Clothes. A better place to sleep and then a place to live. Sooner was better.

Doug cocked his head and narrowed his eyes and swigged the last of his beer. He stood up. "Order me another beer. I'll be right back."

"Where are you going?"

"Check out your hitchhiker. See if he's worth adding to my unit. Maybe we can use him. You stay here. We'll talk about everything when I get back," Doug said before he headed toward the door.

He fished a cell phone from his pocket and made a call on his way out. Petey couldn't hear the conversation.

CHAPTER SIX

Thursday, May 19
Gaucho, NM
10:35 p.m. (MDT)

DOUG XYZ LEFT THE bar, moving purposefully toward the motel. Long strides got him there quickly.

The place looked closed up. The desk clerk wasn't the brightest bulb in the pack, but he was smart enough to know that nobody else would be looking for a room tonight. Hell, he'd be lucky if he got another tenant this week. Or this month, even.

Doug pulled a key from his back pocket. He'd checked out of his room earlier. He'd kept the key just in case he needed it.

He'd been here off and on for two weeks, getting his unit together. All the rooms were the same. He was familiar with operations and personnel.

The front desk clerk was a creepy dimwit named Roland who slept in the back of the office most of the day. The kind of guy who watched kiddie porn all the time and believed it was okay.

Doug wagged his head. Lowlife.

Roland employed one maid, his sister Rhonda, who was about half as smart as he was. She had a kid and lived in a single-wide across the main road and down in the valley. Doug liked her a little bit. They'd spent some time together. Two weeks, off and on, was a long time for a guy to do nothing in a place like Gaucho.

Rhonda cleaned all the motel rooms in the morning. When she finished, she left the curtains open over the one big window next to the doors. If the curtains were open, the room was vacant. She was done by mid-afternoon when she left to pick her kid up at school. She never came back to work until the next day.

The place had quirks. The iron water that stained the toilets, tubs, and sinks. Noisy pipes that vibrated and banged and sounded like a foghorn from an ocean liner when they started up. Or the filthy carpet and stained bedclothes that gave them all nightmares about bed bugs and head lice.

And he knew all the rooms unlocked with the same key.

The plastic key fobs were shaped like a plastic diamond and marked with different room numbers. But the keys and the locks they opened were all the same. Which Doug had discovered when Rhonda accidentally walked in on him in the shower once.

Nobody ever bothered to check the keys they got at the desk to see if they'd open the other doors, Rhonda said. Why would they?

Doug had checked out, planning to move the unit on to the next stop after Petey Burns arrived tonight. He hadn't left his key on the bedside table.

The plate-glass windows were as cheap as the rest of the Gaucho Motel's construction. From the driveway, Doug saw the curtains were closed on room thirteen, so Roland must have had somebody else show up. There were no lights on inside, which meant the renter was probably sleeping.

Doug walked past room thirteen and then past fourteen and slowed up as he approached fifteen, in case Reacher had ears sharp enough to hear him coming. Although the rattling air conditioner units under the windows overwhelmed just about every sound out here in the quiet desert, so he wasn't too worried.

Room fifteen's curtains were closed, meaning the room was occupied, as expected. The interior lights were on in the bathroom and the dressing room. He flattened his ear against the glass. Reacher's shower was running.

Doug pulled a pistol from his waistband and attached the sound suppressor before he inserted the key into the doorknob and turned it to unlock the door.

He flattened his back against the exterior wall, just in case Reacher was not actually in the shower.

Doug was a careful man.

He pushed the door into the room on silent hinges and stood aside, half expecting a bullet to whiz past where a real visitor would normally have been standing.

He got lucky. No bullet.

Doug turtled his head around the doorjamb to peer into the dimly lit bedroom.

The sounds of running water from the noisy old shower pipes and the clattering ceiling fan over the tub were unmistakable. Steamy air wafted through the open bathroom door.

Stealthily, Doug made his way across the sticky brown carpet toward the bathroom, avoiding mirrors that might reflect his image and staying in the shadows.

When he reached the open bathroom door, he turtled again and stared into the steam.

Behind the opaque beige shower curtain, he saw the shadow of a hulking giant facing the wall, hands on his head, which was bent under the spray to wash his hair.

Doug changed his stance, took quick aim, and fired through the shower curtain into the man's body.

Three silenced shots pierced the plastic and hit the mark.

The big man shouted with pain and fell back against the plastic shower enclosure, sweeping the shower curtain to one side and pulling it off the rod. He lost his footing on the slippery porcelain and plopped down into the tub.

He landed hard, giving the tub a solid bounce with enough force to snap the old, rusty pipes, disconnecting them from the drain.

On his way down, his face thumped onto the porcelain with a hard splat to his nose and then a bounce to his temple. Blood spurted and ran from his ear.

If the bullets hadn't killed Reacher, that blow would have finished the job.

A folding toothbrush lay near the sink beside a used razor, an open tube of toothpaste, and the wrapper from a ridiculously small bar of soap supplied by the motel.

Doug stepped into the doorway of the small steamy room.

He took a good look at the body. No need to touch him to know he was dead. Or close enough.

Blood mixed with the iron stains in the tub swirled down the busted drain along with the water. For half a second, Doug wondered where the bloody water would end up.

He grabbed a tissue to conceal his fingerprints, turned the water off, and stepped out of the bathroom. Last thing he needed was a flood that might cause an alarm. He pulled the door closed and hurried to the bedside table where Reacher had dumped the contents of his pockets.

Doug shuffled the guy's few possessions. A little bit of cash and a few coins and bits and bobs of pocket lint.

No driver's license. No ID of any kind.

Doug shook his head, pocketed the few folded bills Reacher had tossed on the table and turned to go.

He took another quick look around to be sure he hadn't missed anything important and left the room, locking the door behind him.

Room thirteen remained as quiet as it had been before. Only one other room had the curtains pulled closed across the window. Room six. The one Petey Burns had rented.

Doug used the key to unlock room six and went inside. He saw a pile of dirty clothes on the floor and not much else. Quickly, he collected Petey's few possessions and tossed them into the duffel on the bed.

He picked up a Volkswagen key from the bedside table. Then he carried the duffel outside and locked the door behind him.

Petey Burns wouldn't be coming back here.

Doug crossed the parking lot and used the Volkswagen key to unlock the beater. He tossed the open duffel inside and slammed the hatch to lock it. Then he locked the car and turned for one last look toward room fifteen.

"What a place to die," Doug murmured, shaking his head. "Alone. A seedy old motel's crappy bathroom. Desolate place like this. Jeez."

He pressed the redial on his cell phone. After three rings, voicemail picked up. Doug waited for the beep. He left a two-word message. "It's done."

He disconnected, slipped the phone into his pocket, turned, and headed back toward Delgado's Bar.

About halfway there, he tossed the Volkswagen key into a stand of brush and kept walking.

CHAPTER SEVEN

Thursday, May 19
Gaucho, NM
11:35 p.m. (MDT)

PETEY BURNS HAD FINISHED his food and was nursing his
second beer when the front door at Delgado's Bar opened, and
Doug strode inside. He walked over to the bar and tossed some
money toward the bartender. He waved toward the guys in the
back who were still playing pool. Then he walked over to
Petey's table.

"Come on. Let's go," Doug said.

"Go where?" Petey replied, wondering what the hell was
happening.

"We've got a job. I thought you wanted in," Doug said. "But
if you don't, that's no problem."

Petey nodded. "I do. I think. What is it?"

"I'll fill you in on the way."

"What about Reacher? Is he coming?"

Doug shook his head. "Said thanks, but no thanks. He's not

interested. I left him the keys to that piece of junk Volkswagen so he'd have a ride outta here. Seemed like the decent thing to do."

"Right. He'd have a long walk to find another ride, for sure. And I can always steal something better," Petey said, not mentioning again that Reacher didn't drive. What would be the point?

Doug turned and walked toward the back exit.

Petey thought about it for a nanosecond before he stood and followed.

It's not like Petey had planned to partner up with Reacher forever, anyway. He'd come to appreciate Reacher and his talents. But if the big guy didn't want in on Doug's opportunity, that was okay, too.

They covered the distance to Delgado's back door quickly enough. Doug pushed the door open and went outside. Just as Petey had guessed, there was a parking lot out back.

A black panel van was already idling, with the side door open. Two of the guys he'd seen playing pool earlier were already inside. One was in the driver's seat.

Doug climbed into the passenger seat and Petey stepped over the running board to settle into the big captain's chair near the right side door, behind Doug. The driver pushed a button to slide the door closed and they were rolling almost before Petey realized it.

"Moe Smith, Ray Vance, this is Petey Burns," Doug said by way of introduction, jerking his left thumb toward the driver and then over his shoulder.

They murmured greetings and then Doug said, "We got a full unit now and a long way to go."

The van smelled of the Delgado Bar's stale beer and greasy

burgers, which wasn't surprising. Petey probably smelled the same as the others.

Moe said, "As long as we find a better rack than that damned Gaucho Motel, I'm good. Never slept in such a dump in my life."

Ray replied, "I second that."

Petey hadn't slept there, but he nodded agreement just the same. Truth be told, Petey had slept in worse places. But no need to get off on the wrong foot with his new unit by bringing that up.

"Where are we headed?" Ray asked.

"Oklahoma. We can run on the Interstate. Shouldn't take too long to get there. Six or seven hours. I got a place set up where we can go over the details," Doug said.

"When are we doing the job?" Ray asked.

"Tomorrow night is the first one," Doug replied.

"The first one?" Petey asked.

Doug said, "Three in all. First one's small potatoes. Second one's bigger. Third one, we'll all be set for life."

"Sounds good to me," Moe chimed in.

"We need to practice. Get our system down," Ray said.

Petey figured Ray was one of those guys who needed to plan everything down to the last detail. No room for improv.

It wasn't the way Petey preferred to work.

But what he wanted was money, and three jobs were more likely to give him a big payoff. So he was good with it.

"How about you, Burns?" Moe asked.

"If one's good, three's better, right?" Petey replied easily, flashing a goofy grin that none of them could see in the dark.

"That why we are doing the first one in Oklahoma?" Ray asked. "For practice?"

"Yeah. Exactly. Work the kinks out. Make our mistakes where it don't matter much," Moe said, nodding as if he approved already. Maybe he knew the plan.

Petey felt like this wasn't the time to ask more questions. He'd learn the details soon enough.

Moe drove the van north to I-40 and then turned east toward Oklahoma City.

The bags in the back slid to one side as Moe took the cloverleaf a little faster than the boxy van was comfortable with. But once they got on the highway and things settled down again, Petey leaned his head back and closed his eyes.

Might as well catch some sleep since he never got any back at the Gaucho Motel. His eyelids felt gritty like the desert sand had rubbed them raw.

Briefly, he thought again about Reacher. They'd ridden together in the same vehicle for a solid week. Petey liked the guy.

Sort of.

Reacher didn't help with the driving, and he didn't talk much, but he was low maintenance, and he'd helped out with expenses.

Having the guy around wasn't boring, for sure.

Too bad Petey didn't get a chance to say goodbye. Maybe their paths would cross again someday.

Probably not, though. They were both moving on. Which was as it should be, he supposed. He'd planned to leave Reacher behind at some point, anyway.

After the three jobs with Doug's unit, Petey would have more than enough money to head down to Costa Rica. He'd always wanted to go there. He could live like a king. Maybe meet a woman he liked well enough to settle down.

Petey liked kids. He was good with them. His mother always said it was because Petey was just a big kid himself.

He supposed that was true enough.

The three amigos he'd joined up with didn't talk much, either. Petey was fine with the silence for a while. He was tired. He'd had a lot of excitement this past week. Escaping from prison, then hanging with Reacher.

Man, whenever Reacher showed up, all hell broke loose. People shooting guns and fist fights and explosions. Way more excitement than Petey was used to, for sure.

He grinned as he recalled their adventures. It was kind of like hanging out with the really cool kids when you're just a younger brother. Story of his life, actually. Except he never had any cool kids to hang with. No older brothers, either.

But he knew the feeling anyway. He was always the tagalong, never the leader, and he didn't really mind. Petey wasn't interested in taking any responsibility for other dudes. Every man for himself, that's what Petey wanted. He liked to do things the easy way.

The low hum of the van's tires on the interstate and the gentle rocking of the captain's chair lulled him into a drowsy slumber and then into deeper levels of unconsciousness.

The next thing he knew, the van had stopped moving.

The stillness awakened him. He opened his eyes and looked around. It was well past daylight. Moe had pulled into a motel parking lot and turned off the engine.

"Welcome to Oklahoma," Doug said as he opened the door and stepped outside. "I'll get the rooms. You wait here."

CHAPTER EIGHT

Friday, May 20
Las Vegas, NV
7:15 a.m. (PDT)

KIM COLLECTED BURKE AT the hospital entrance. He had been discharged from the hospital without further delay. He looked worn and tired but otherwise fit enough for the job.

No one ever sleeps in a hospital. Like he'd said, he'd been injured before. He knew how far he could push his damaged body. She wasn't his nurse and he didn't need her to be.

He climbed inside and fastened his seatbelt. "Where are we headed?" he asked as she turned toward McCarran International Airport.

"How are you feeling?" she asked.

"What are you, my mother?" he snapped harshly in response.

She arched her eyebrows and turned her attention to the driving. After she'd pulled out of the parking lot and blended into the traffic, she answered his original question.

"We're headed to Gaucho, New Mexico. We'll pick up new wheels in Albuquerque and drive about forty-five minutes south."

"Why?" Burke asked.

"Petey Burns is there. Reacher, too."

Burke stared at her as if she'd said they were meeting a colony of Martians.

"And you know this how?" Burke demanded. He was wearing sunglasses against the morning glare. They concealed his eyes, but not the frown.

Kim gave him a side-eye behind her sunglasses. She'd cut him some slack because he'd been hurt and stuck in a hospital for two days. But she wouldn't put up with his short-tempered disposition forever.

"Digital legwork, mostly," she said. "I was awake half the night staring at computer screens, piecing their movements together from various camera footage along the way."

"Catch me up." Burke leaned his head back against the headrest and kneaded his forehead with his fingers.

Kim explained the work she had done with Gaspar to locate and trace Burns from Vegas to Gaucho. She told him about the images captured from various cameras—everything from ATM cameras to traffic cams to satellites.

They had traced Burns from the warehouse where she'd last seen him with Reacher to the parking garage in Henderson where he'd dropped the red SUV and stolen a Mercedes black G-550 from a shopping mall parking lot.

"Is he still driving the G-550? Or has he ditched that one already, too?"

"He traded it for an old white Tiguan when they left Nevada," Kim said.

"What the hell is a *Tiguan*?" Burke said, his tone making it plain that he didn't approve.

"Volkswagen SUV. Introduced in 2009, I'm told. *Tiguan* is a made-up name, of course. It's supposed to be a cross between the German words for tiger and iguana." She pulled the Navigator into the airport's rental return lot, slid the transmission into park, and shut the engine down for the last time.

Burke was still frowning.

She flashed him a grin. "Try to keep up, okay? I don't want to have to get you a day nurse."

"In your dreams," he replied with a grin, but she didn't hear as much of the Burke braggadocio in his tone as usual.

"Man, you're cranky. Did they not bring you coffee this morning?" She climbed out of the Navigator, collected her bags, and left the keys in the drop box on her way to the terminal.

As they walked into the terminal, Burke's expression looked like he'd unexpectedly swallowed a frog that would cause long-lasting heartburn. "And you know where Burns and Reacher and the *Tiguan* are now, I assume?"

"Yeah. They stayed mostly on the back roads and away from cameras for the drive, but they had to pick up gas and supplies along the way. They bought clothing at an Army-Navy surplus store. Otherwise, they drove straight to a motel where they stopped for the night."

"You're telling me they're still there? Doesn't seem likely, does it?"

"Maybe." Kim shrugged as they waited for their turn at the security checkpoint. "The Volkswagen is still there. Gaucho isn't the kind of place where they could've left the car and then hitched a ride out. So they might still be there, too."

"Sounds a little too easy, doesn't it?" Burke said.

"You say that because you weren't the one burning the midnight oil doing all the work," Kim replied. "But even if Burns and Reacher are not there now, they were there last night and should be easier to find."

He cocked his head. "Why? You've failed before, Nancy Drew. Why should this time be different?"

"You surprise me, Frogman. Nancy Drew? I didn't think you could read," she tossed back his jive-talk with a grin.

He rewarded her with a deeper scowl. "Seriously. Why do you think we'll find them this time?"

Truth was, she didn't know for sure. But she had a good lead. And she wasn't about to let it slip away.

Not that she'd tell Burke any of that and listen to him tell her five thousand reasons she could be wrong, especially since he didn't seem to have anything better to offer.

She was the lead agent on this assignment. His job was to follow and stop griping about it. Simple as that.

Instead, she arched her eyebrows and joked. "Hard to hide that particular Mutt and Jeff trudging on foot in the empty desert without their camo gear, don't you think?"

Kim moved ahead of Burke toward the scanning devices and flashed her ID at the TSA officer standing ready. One at a time, passengers stepped into the puffer, raised their arms, and submitted to full-body scans for explosive residue.

The Boss had cleared their duty weapons for concealed carry in the plane's cabin. Which was absolutely against every rule there was. Kim never asked him how he got the clearance because she didn't care. The simple fact was, she wouldn't get on the plane without her weapon. So The Boss made it happen.

After a few minutes, the TSA officer waved them through, and they went straight to the departure gate.

They boarded the Boeing 737 and stowed their bags. The flight lifted easily into the air, right on time, well before eight o'clock. Weather was clear and cool. Perfect morning for flying, the pilot said over the speaker from the flight deck.

Which, surprisingly, turned out to be true.

The flight sailed easily from departure through landing in Albuquerque, on time and without turbulence or delays. Moving from the Pacific to Mountain time zones seemed like losing an extra hour, but they'd spent only eighty-five minutes in the air.

That was plenty of time as far as Kim was concerned.

Frequent flying was one of her least favorite parts of the job. Couldn't be helped, though. She had no desire to drive across the country and she damned sure wasn't planning to take the bus.

Jets were better than other flying contraptions and a quick up-and-down was exactly the kind of trip she preferred.

Although most airline disasters occurred on takeoff or landing, spending long hours strapped to a seat inside a steel tube hurtling through the atmosphere while inhaling recycled air held zero appeal. A quick up and down was the lesser of all the other evils.

It was true that thousands of flights landed safely every day, even though none of the media outlets ever reported that bit of news.

They stopped in the restroom at the Albuquerque airport, collected their bags, each grabbed coffee and a breakfast burrito, and trudged to the rental lot.

Kim approached a brilliant blue metallic Mercedes GLC, opened the driver's door, and retrieved the keys from the front seat. She used the fob to unlock the hatchback.

"Fancy," Burke said, nodding toward the mid-sized SUV. "Is this bait for our expert German car thief or something?"

Kim shrugged. "Can't hurt to tempt Petey Burns a little should the occasion arise."

"He's not like a mouse you can lure with peanut butter and shove into a cage when he comes sniffing around, Otto," Burke warned, wrapping his torso with his forearm as if his wounds were still fresh and tender. They probably were.

"Uh, huh," she said, focused on getting the vehicle set up so they could get on the road.

"Burns is a clever thief with the conscience of a psychopath. Which is to say, none. And he's traveling with Reacher, who's not all that softhearted either," Burke said. "Believe me. I've got the sore belly to prove it."

She nodded. "I hear you."

"Otto!" he said loudly.

She looked up to meet his gaze.

"If Burns wants to steal this SUV, then let him have it."

"That's exactly my plan," she said, lifting her bag into the cargo compartment. "There's so much tech in this thing that we could track him from anywhere if he were driving this puppy."

Burke shook his head and lifted his travel bag with his left hand instead of his right. Behind his sunglasses, it was impossible to see him wince. But she heard a little puff of air escape from his lips as if the exertion pained him.

He must've realized she'd noticed because he reached up and pushed the hatch closed as if he had something to prove.

"You know that's motorized, right? Just push the button, and it closes by itself," Kim said sweetly, pushing the fob into her pocket and heading toward the cabin. "You want to drive, Frogman? Or shall I?"

Since she'd met him, Burke had insisted on driving except when he had a strategic reason to be the passenger. Like the time she drove while he used a rifle to try to take down a private jet.

Her question was a small test. He knew it, too. If he were really capable of taking on Reacher again, he'd want to drive.

So, was he at one hundred percent? Or not?

Burke didn't respond to her question, but he walked around to the left side and settled himself into the driver's seat.

Kim nodded and opened the passenger door and slid inside, still unsure.

Maybe he was genuinely okay. She hoped.

While he adjusted the mirrors and the seat and buckled up, she punched the address for The Gaucho Motel into the GPS. Then she sat back in her seat while Burke pulled out into traffic.

Kim applied a bit of advice from her former partner. "Sleep when you can," Gaspar often said.

She dozed off behind her sunglasses and when she opened her eyes again, Burke was approaching a jarring display of red, blue, and white flashing lights atop four official vehicles.

She counted three squads and an ambulance in the dirt parking lot.

"What the hell is going on here?" Burke murmured.

CHAPTER NINE

Friday, May 20
Middletown Village, Oklahoma
10:45 a.m. (CDT)

THE FRONT DOOR OF the van closed, startling Petey more fully awake. He'd slept longer than he'd expected to. His body was stiff and he had to pee. Where the hell were they?

It was daylight again, and he guessed maybe eight hours since they'd left Delgado's Bar, give or take. From his seat, he watched Doug approach the front entrance of another motel and go inside.

This place was about a thousand times nicer than The Gaucho had been. It was newer, for one thing. Painted a clean beige. The parking lot was surrounded by actual landscaping. Grass, flowering bushes. Stuff like that.

The kind of cookie-cutter franchise place his mother would have liked because it felt familiar. Not that she'd ever traveled anywhere in her life or stayed in a motel, either, for that matter.

This one was two stories instead of one. The roof was green

shingled and looked like it wouldn't leak. The same basic figure-seven shape as a zillion other motels. Two rows of rooms, one stacked on top of the other, ran north from the main office.

Reminded Petey of that old song lyric his mom liked about one man's ceiling being another man's floor. He grinned.

All in all, a big improvement, Petey noticed, moving his tongue around inside his mouth to work up some saliva for his parched throat. No way he could pay the rent on a place like this for a single night. Not unless Doug gave him an advance on his share of the take from whatever they were expecting to collect tonight.

After shopping with Reacher at the army surplus store and buying the burger and beers at Delgado's, Petey had less than two bucks in his pocket.

Moe had leaned his head back against the driver's seat and closed his eyes.

Ray seemed wide awake.

When Petey glanced his way, Ray said, "I hear you're a good driver. That, true?"

Petey nodded. He sensed it was not the time to be modest. "Yeah."

"I hear you're good with tech, too."

"Some tech. Cars, mostly," Petey said. "I'm very knowledgeable about the tech in cars."

"What kind of cars?" Ray asked.

"My specialty is German luxury vehicles."

"Car thieves have specialties now?" Ray frowned.

Petey grinned. "This one does."

"Why?"

Petey shrugged. "God gives you a talent. Why in the world wouldn't you use it?"

Ray's frown deepened to a scowl. "Doug says your expertise is bypassing computerized security systems."

"Yeah, I guess. Partly," Petey replied. He was hearing this idea for the first time. He'd never focused on what his skill set was in that way before. But sure. Cars had computerized security systems. German cars were wicked tight with the damned security. So yeah. What Doug said made sense.

"What do you mean by that?" Ray was sounding way too grouchy.

Petey didn't want a fight with his new unit before he got paid. "Well, I mean, sure, I have to get around all the tech security they cram into a two-hundred-thousand-dollar car. It's quite a challenge. Those German engineers are experts, you know?" Pete said with another wide grin. "But then, I have to drive the car, too. And not get caught. That's another whole skill set, right?"

"It is. Moe here's an expert driver. Never been inside. Not once." Ray's expression remained grim. He was agitated. He flexed his hands into fists and pounded on his thigh for punctuation. "You were in prison when Doug met you. You been inside several more times. Just got out a week ago on a fluke. How good can you possibly be?"

"Knock it off, Ray," Moe warned in a deep voice from the front seat, like a father exasperated with his kid. "This is Doug's unit. He wants Petey on it. End of story."

"Yeah, well, we need a guy who knows what the hell he's doing. Not some dumbass who can't even keep himself out of jail," Ray said, getting in the last word before he turned his head away from Petey and said no more. The flat of his fist continued the steady, angry rhythm on his thigh.

Petey kept to himself for a bit, but after a while, he tried conversation again. He liked to talk. Everybody knew that. "Where are we, anyway?"

Moe replied, "Middletown Village, Oklahoma. Maybe thirty miles from Stockton. Give or take."

Petey grinned. "And where the hell is that, exactly?"

"Where the money is, dumbass," Ray growled under his breath.

But Petey heard the warning. He stopped asking questions. He was just being friendly. He didn't really care where they were. He wanted to get started because the sooner he started, the sooner he'd be done. He was hungry and the two bucks in his pocket wouldn't even buy a sausage biscuit at McDonald's.

He'd already spent more time with Ray than he cared to. Petey had been around guys like Ray before. They started out cranky and they got worse over time. The situation was bound to end badly.

Which meant Petey needed to get started on a Plan B. Sounded like Doug brought Petey in to help Moe. If the money was good enough, maybe they could do without Ray. More for everyone that way. He wondered what Ray's specialty was. Whether it was something Petey could do better.

Doug came back to the van five minutes later. He pulled the door open and climbed in, pointing. "Drive straight ahead. Our rooms are down there, at the end of the row, on the first floor. Guy said we can order food delivered. There's a diner, but we need to stay out of sight. The fewer people see us while we're here, the better."

Moe put the transmission in gear and drove down the parking lot to the end of the building. He parked in front of the fourth room from the end.

Should there be any nosy nellies paying too much attention,

the van would block their view. It wasn't much protection, but it was better than none.

Petey climbed out of the van and stretched his legs. The rough clothes Reacher had paid for were wrinkled and uncomfortably scratchy now that he'd lived in them a while. Petey shrugged. Nothing he could do about that at the moment.

Ray stepped out on the other side of the van.

Doug handed out the room keys. Moe had the room closest to the van and Ray's room was farthest away, at the end of the building. Which was just fine with Petey. The farther he was from Ray, the better. Nothing worse than an angry man with a weapon, in Petey's experience.

Doug and Petey took the two rooms in the middle probably because the team didn't trust Petey yet. He wasn't planning to give them any reason for regrets. He wanted to do the job, do it well, collect his money, and get the hell out.

Ideally, before Ray decided how he planned to prove his low opinion of Petey's value to the team.

"Drop off your stuff and meet in my room. Give me an hour. I gotta make a phone call and get a shower. I'll order food and go over the plan for tonight," Doug said to the others as he headed inside.

Ray and Moe walked away while Petey unlocked his room and ducked in. The door closed automatically behind him.

"You seen one seedy motel, you've seen them all," Petey reminded himself as he took a quick look around.

This room was newer and cleaner but laid out pretty much like the one he'd left behind in Gaucho. Maybe a little smaller footprint. Petey guessed it at a fairly standard thirteen by twenty-five feet. Bigger than a prison cell. Not quite large enough to move around comfortably.

Two full-size beds, a bedside table between them, a lamp mounted on the wall above the table, and a telephone. Across from the bed was a low dresser with a television perched on top of it.

Next to that was a small refrigerator with two bottles of water inside and a sign that read, "Free for our guests."

"Like people break in here to steal the water?" Petey shook his head at the silly sign, snagged one of the bottles and screwed the top off, and took a long swig. He hadn't realized how dry his throat was. He emptied the bottle and tossed it into the trash.

Directly opposite the entrance, a mirror ran across the back wall, above a sink and a laminate countertop. He walked through.

On the right of the sink was an alcove with a bar to hang clothes on, if he'd had any. On the left was a door. Inside the small room were the toilet and tub. Both were in much better shape than the last place he'd showered, but not even as nice as the bathroom in his mom's single-wide trailer when he'd lived at home.

On the countertop beside the sink, the motel offered a cellophane-wrapped toothbrush and toothpaste, another small bar of soap, and plastic drinking cups. He used the toilet first, then washed up, brushed his teeth, and used the mirror as he combed his fingers through his hair.

"That's as good as it's going to get, dude. Let's get this freight train moving," he murmured to his reflection.

His blood was buzzing in his veins, ramped up with anticipation. Whatever Doug had going on, it was big. Petey could feel it. Soon, he'd be able to buy better clothes. And a lot of other things.

He took a quick look around to be sure he hadn't forgotten

anything essential before he remembered that he'd had nothing to bring inside with him.

Petey shook his head and grinned as he pulled the door open and left to join the others in Doug's room next door. He was hungry enough to eat a horse.

CHAPTER TEN

Friday, May 20
Gaucho, NM
12:45 p.m. (MDT)

THE ENTRANCE TO THE Gaucho Motel's parking lot was blocked at the road by the county sheriff's vehicle. The light bar was flashing. There were two more squads parked near the motel's office.

An EMS unit had backed up to the end of the row of rooms. The back doors of the ambulance were open.

Two EMTs rolled a gurney from the motel room into the ambulance.

Kim couldn't see his face. But even from her vantage point two hundred feet away, she could tell that the patient was a big man. His body covered every inch of the gurney and his feet hung way off the end.

He wore heavy brown work boots, scuffed and grotty—the kind of boots she'd seen before on Reacher's big feet.

A spike of electricity shot up Kim's spine. A small gasp escaped her lips.

One of the EMTs hopped inside with the patient while the other closed the doors and ran around to the driver's seat. He flipped on the siren and sped away, heading north toward Albuquerque.

Indecision gripped her. Kim's churning gut urged her to speed after the ambulance. She'd acted on crazier impulses. But instinct held her back, too.

What would she say to Burke? "After those boots!"

She kneaded the sudden headache that had popped into the space between her eyebrows. If Reacher was on that stretcher, he wasn't walking away any time soon.

She had a little time to figure out what the hell was going on here instead of chasing the ambulance based on nothing more than a guess, really.

Burke nodded toward the flashing lights headed north. "He needs urgent care, or they wouldn't have rushed out of here like that. Which means he's not dead yet, whoever he is."

Kim nodded, taking a few deep breaths. She reached into her pocket for an antacid and placed it under her tongue to make it last longer.

"There's the SUV Burns was driving," Kim pointed toward the only unofficial vehicle in the parking lot. A white Volkswagen Tiguan covered in dents and dust like it had crossed the desert floor to get here. Maybe it had.

"You're sure?" Burke replied as he pulled off the road onto the shoulder and parked.

"A Tiguan isn't that common out here," she said, deliberately sidestepping his meaning.

"Yeah, we've covered that," Burke said. "Hell, a Tiguan's not that common anywhere, is it? I haven't seen another one since we landed in Albuquerque. Can't be more than this one hanging around this hamlet."

"That's my guess." Kim had last seen the Tiguan captured by the security camera at a gas station west of Albuquerque when Petey Burns filled the tank.

The same video feed had recorded Reacher as he walked into the store and returned with two large coffee cups. He'd been wearing brown work boots at the time. He'd handed one coffee to Burns, and they'd headed south again.

The license plate had been obscured on the CCTV images and she couldn't see it now, either. But she'd lay strong odds that this was the Tiguan Petey Burns stole back in Nevada.

Why would he have abandoned it here? Unless he didn't. Maybe he was still here. Hell, if Burns was here, Reacher could be, too.

"Let's find out what's going on." Kim released her seatbelt and stepped out of the SUV into the cool, dry afternoon. Burke joined her and they crossed the dusty lot toward the motel's office.

The familiar buzz of activity around a crime scene felt palpable in the still dry air.

Both of the deputies were inside the motel office. One was standing behind the counter, staring at a computer screen.

The other seemed to be looking for evidence of something. He glanced up and saw Kim and Burke approaching, so he hurried outside.

"Sorry, folks. The motel is closed. You'll need to get a room somewhere else," he said kindly.

"Is there another motel in Gaucho?" Burke asked.

The deputy shook his head and pointed. "Closest one is fifty miles south."

Kim pulled her badge wallet from her pocket and showed it. "We're FBI. Special Agents Otto and Burke. Tell us what happened here."

The deputy's eyes rounded. "FBI? We didn't call you guys. Not that we don't need the help. But why are you here?"

"Are you the sheriff?" Burke asked as if that made all the difference to his response. Which, of course, it did not.

The deputy shook his head.

"Deputy Evan Lark," he said, tilting his head toward the end of the sidewalk where the ambulance had been a few moments ago. "Sheriff George Carpenter is down at room fifteen where we found the victim."

Kim arched her eyebrows. "Victim?"

"Isn't that why you're here?" Lark replied.

"Manhunt. Looking for two guys." Burke pulled his phone out and found the photos of Burns and Reacher. He showed them to the deputy. "The younger, goofy-looking one escaped from the federal prison up in Bolton, South Dakota. You heard about that, right?"

"Yeah. We heard. Got the BOLOs posted everywhere." Lark looked at the photo of Burns and shook his head. "I haven't seen him, but we work the whole county. I haven't been here in Gaucho for a weeks. No reason to. Nothing much ever happens here, and whatever does happen is pretty much done by the time we get to it. You should ask Sheriff Carpenter, though."

"We will," Burke replied, flipping to the best of the grainy photos of Reacher they'd pulled from one of the traffic cams. "What about this guy? Have you seen him?"

Lark took the phone and enlarged the photo for a better look. "This guy sort of looks like the attempted murder victim we found back there in room fifteen. Shape he was in when I seen him, it's hard to tell."

Kim's breath caught in her throat. She was barely able to squeeze the words past her vocal cords. "You're sure someone tried to murder him?"

"Shot three times while he was in the shower. We'd call that attempted murder around here. You?" Lark said, returning Burke's phone.

"Yeah, sure seems likely," Burke replied, nodding. "I take it he didn't have a gun handy so he could shoot back?"

"Big guy. Heavy. Smashed his face up pretty good when he fell." Lark shook his head without acknowledging Burke's comment. "He was still alive when we responded, but barely. He'll likely be dead soon enough."

The second deputy emerged from the gloomy office, squinting against the bright sunlight. "What's up, Evan?"

"This is Deputy Tom Snow." Lark nodded again. "These two are FBI. Otto and Burke. They're looking for two escaped cons. Could have been staying here, I guess. You find anything in the registrations, Tom?"

"Maybe. It looks like a few of the rooms were occupied yesterday. Five singles. Three checked in a few days ago and checked out yesterday," Snow replied, pointing as he talked. "Two more, including the guy in room fifteen, checked in last night around nine o'clock. I was just heading to see if the second guy is still here since it seems like these last two arrived together. That's probably their beater parked over there."

"Did they give their names?" Burke asked. "Pay with credit cards?"

"All cash transactions, according to the books," Snow said, shaking his head. "The last two registered as Ben Franklin and John Q. Adams. The others weren't quite as obvious, but probably still fake because there's no ID in the files. I'll get you the names if you want them."

"So who was in room fifteen at the end?" Kim asked.

"Adams," Snow replied. "Franklin was assigned to room six."

"When we find him, we'll ask," Lark replied. "He's in the wind at the moment. But his SUV is still here, and there's not a lot of places he could be. Gaucho's not big enough to hide anyone or anything for very long. When we start looking, we'll find him."

Burke said, "No train, bus, nothing like that goes through they could've jumped on earlier?"

Lark and Snow shook their heads simultaneously.

"Any CCTV here?" Kim asked, nodding, even as she realized the question was probably as ridiculous as the fake names.

Snow shook his head again.

"What does the desk clerk have to say?" Burke asked.

"New guy on the night shift. Only on the job a few weeks. We haven't met him yet," Lark replied. "Chris Rudy. Lives a couple of towns west of here. He didn't answer his phone. We're trying to find him."

"You know the guy?" Kim asked. Both deputies shook their heads. "Got any intel on him at all? Could he have been the shooter?"

"Possible. But nothing we know about him says he's been violent before." Lark shrugged. "Suspended driver's license. Driving under the influence. Spotty attendance record. Shows up to the job here off and on, when he feels like it, the maid said."

Lark replied, "Sheriff told us to wait here until he's done in room fifteen. We're shorthanded. Sheriff will call in the State Police once we know what we're dealing with."

"It was the maid who discovered the victim?" Kim asked. "Has she been questioned yet?"

The sheriff walked up in time to hear the question. "I'm Sheriff George Carpenter."

"FBI Special Agents Kim Otto and William Burke, Sheriff. We're looking for two fugitives." Burke showed his ID and gestured toward the Tiguan. "We have reason to believe they arrived driving that Volkswagen last night. One of them might be your shooting victim."

Sheriff Carpenter cocked his head. "And the other one maybe was the shooter. That what you're thinking?"

Not even close.

CHAPTER ELEVEN

Friday, May 20
Gaucho, NM
1:45 p.m. (MDT)

AFTER THE SHERIFF SENT his deputies off to secure the crime scene and call in the state police, he remained behind. "I've got to get to work. You here to help? Or not?"

Kim asked, "Who was the man on the stretcher, Sheriff?"

"Don't know yet." Carpenter shook his head and stuffed his hands in his pockets and looked down at his dusty cowboy boots. "He was in the shower when he was shot. His face was a bloody pulp. Damage caused by landing hard on the bathtub's edge when he fell would be my guess."

"No wallet or anything in the room?" Burke asked. "No jewelry, like a wedding ring or a watch?"

"I didn't want to disturb the crime scene, but I took a quick look around and didn't see any ID anywhere," Carpenter replied. "No wallet. No car keys. Nothing. Just a bunch of smelly old clothes on the floor."

"Sounds like there will be plenty of DNA for the techs to analyze," Burke said. "We'll know who he is soon enough, assuming they can match someone already in the databases."

"Or maybe we can just ask him," Kim suggested.

"Not today, we can't," Carpenter shook his head. "He'll be in surgery for a good long while. They've gotta remove three bullets, repair the damage there, and deal with the head trauma. Then he'll be sedated for a few days, at least. We won't be asking him anything until sometime next week, at the earliest. Whoever shot him will be long gone. And honestly, I'm not sure the poor sap will make it."

Kim nodded. "Did you take pictures of him?"

Carpenter cocked his head. "Why?"

"We'd recognize him if he's our guy."

Carpenter nodded. "I snapped a few quick shots of the crime scene and some close-ups of his face after they got him on the gurney. Best I could do. The EMTs arrived immediately and they were in such a damned hurry to get him out of there while he was still alive."

Kim pulled her phone and found the most recent photo of Reacher. She showed it to Carpenter. "Is this the victim?"

Carpenter studied the image and finally shook his head again as he returned the phone. "Hard to say. Your photo's not clear. And the victim's face was pulverized and bloody. I don't know. Could be the same guy. Or not."

Kim slipped the phone into her pocket. "Can we see your photos, including the crime scene?"

Carpenter pulled his phone, found the photos, and handed the phone to her. She flipped through quickly, pausing a long moment to view the man's face. Then she emailed the photos to herself and handed the phone to Burke.

Carpenter said, "Is it him?"

Kim shook her head. "Can't tell. Maybe."

"Like I said, his face is a mess," Carpenter agreed.

While Burke was studying the photos, she said, "Let's go talk to the maid."

"There's a break room in the back of the office. We left her there. Rhonda Delgado. She's local. Her ex-husband runs the one and only bar in Gaucho," Carpenter explained as he walked toward the office with Kim. Burke followed behind, still examining the photos. "I'll be heading over to Delgado's Bar next if you want to come along."

"What about the daytime desk clerk? What's he got to say?" Kim asked.

At the office entrance, Carpenter stopped to glove up again. "Roland Meeks. Rhonda's brother. Took the day off, Rhonda said."

Kim reached into her jacket pocket and retrieved a pair of gloves. Burke did the same.

Carpenter was careful not to touch the handle where a visitor might have naturally grabbed it. He yanked the door open and stood aside. With a mock bow, he said, "After you."

Burke walked inside without a backward glance and Kim followed.

Sheriff Carpenter walked through the office into the break room, which was small, square, windowless, and way too warm.

A six-foot laminated countertop ran along one wall. A small round table and two plastic chairs occupied the center.

Kim could walk around the table if she moved the chairs aside first. She scanned the room in a single glance and focused on the witness.

Rhonda Delgado was seated in one of the cheap plastic chairs at the plastic table, nervously drinking black coffee from a twelve-ounce Styrofoam cup. She was probably thirty-five and looked sixty-five. Average height, scrawny, with stringy hair and skin that had been exposed to the harsh desert for way too many years.

She'd bitten the Styrofoam around the rim of the cup to create a scalloped pattern with her teeth. Her eyes were jittery like she wanted to cut and run.

A tender, sensitive woman wouldn't have survived out here. Or wanted to. But Rhonda Delgado had done both.

Kim took everything in and reached the only reasonable conclusion.

This wasn't the kind of woman who would crumple at finding a dead body in the shower. Something else had her spooked.

"Hey, Rhonda. Rough morning, eh?" Sheriff Carpenter asked as he leaned against the open doorjamb.

Kim caught the implication. Carpenter knew the woman. Interesting that he hadn't mentioned that before. She shot a glance toward Burke to be sure he'd caught it, too.

Rhonda nodded. "Morning, George. Yeah, not the way I prefer to start the day, you know?"

"You recognize the victim?" He slid inside and leaned casually against the counter as if his questions were of no real importance.

Rhonda shrugged and sipped the coffee from the one spot where she hadn't bitten into the rim.

"Tell me what happened. Then I'll follow up on anything that's unclear," Sheriff Carpenter said as he pulled the Bunn flask from the warmer. He poured coffee into Rhonda's cup first, then filled a cup for himself. The whole process was easily within his arms' reach.

He cocked his head and waited for Rhonda to talk.

"Roland told me he'd be late today, so I was the only one here. Set up my cart. Made some coffee. Checked the guest roster. We had two rooms occupied overnight, six and fifteen. And we had three that were vacated yesterday after I'd already finished cleaning. Made five rooms I needed to clean today, in all," she said, her dry, husky voice breaking.

She took another swig of the coffee, which she raised to her mouth using both shaking hands.

"I cleaned the rooms in order, starting nearest the office. Took me a while. Fifteen was last on the list. I got down there, let myself in. Went toward the bathroom." She paused to wet her throat with the coffee again. "Found him. Checked for a pulse and he was still alive."

She spent a few moments chewing the skin off her dry lower lip. The sheriff didn't interrupt, just waited for her to start talking again.

Rhonda cleared her throat. "Then I came back outside and called you. Someone from your office must have called the ambulance. That's it. That's all I know."

Sheriff Carpenter nodded. He drank his coffee. He nodded toward Kim and waited for Rhonda to get used to talking in response to questions from the strangers.

"What else can you tell us about the victim?" Kim asked, more gently than Carpenter had. Rhonda was tough, but she was shaken, too. Nothing would be gained if she got more spooked than she already was.

"Big man. His clothes looked like he bought them at the surplus store. I figured he was a vet. Mostly vets do that. Like they feel comfortable in those sturdy fabrics or something, you know?" Rhonda said, raising her eyebrows. "I feel sorry for them. They come through here from time to time, like they've got nowhere in the world to be, nowhere to go, no one to get home to, you know?"

Sheriff Carpenter said, "So he was a vagrant? Just passing through?"

"Dunno." Rhonda shrugged. "He was in no shape for conversation when I found him."

"So he didn't say anything to you?" Burke asked, and she shook her head.

Burke showed her the photo of Reacher on his phone. Rhonda studied it for a while.

"Coulda been him, I guess. Kinda hard to say. His face was…" she shuddered and stopped talking. Burke took the phone back.

"Had you seen him before this morning? Maybe hanging around town?" Carpenter asked.

Rhonda shook her head. "Not that I remember."

Kim said, "All the other rooms you cleaned today, nothing out of the ordinary?"

Rhonda shook her head again.

"You didn't find the shooter's gun in any of the rooms?" Kim asked.

Rhonda's gaze met Kim's. "No. I didn't find any kind of gun in any of the rooms. But I wasn't looking for guns, either. Guess that's something else George's deputies should be doing."

"And we'll do that. First, tell me about the other guests. The ones who overstayed their checkout yesterday," Carpenter said. "We didn't find any record of them in the computer registration records out front."

Rhonda shrugged. "Roland does that sometimes when he

needs extra cash. Guys just passing through, he pockets the money. Says Uncle Sam will never miss it."

Burke asked, "Did you know those guys, Rhonda? Ever seen them before?"

Rhonda kept her gaze down, watching the coffee, running her finger over the scalloped edges of the Styrofoam cup.

Sheriff Carpenter glanced at Burke and Kim and then left the room to talk to his two deputies. Burke stepped out after him.

The sheriff's office was definitely going to need help on this one.

But not from Kim and Burke.

Unless the victim was Reacher.

Or the shooter was.

Kim lingered behind until Carpenter and Burke had time to get outside. Then she sat down next to Rhonda as if to suggest that the women needed to stick together. "You knew the other guys, didn't you? They were here a few days, you said. You must have seen them, talked to them."

Rhonda shrugged, but she didn't deny knowing them.

"Are they gone now?" Kim asked.

"They were at Delgado's Bar last night, Luis said. Luis Delgado, my ex. He said they left around midnight, I guess," Rhonda said quietly as if she were testing the story and couldn't quite believe it.

"Do you know when the man was shot, Rhonda? Was it before midnight?" Kim asked.

"I don't know. Could have been any time after he checked in and before I found him, I guess." Rhonda shook her head slowly. "They couldn't have shot this guy. They were already gone. He and his buddy checked in at nine last night. The others checked out long before he even got here."

Kim nodded, wondering why Rhonda was worried about the shooter. "Anything else you noticed that might help us here?"

"The guy was in the shower. Naked, you know? No way to defend himself." Rhonda refused to meet Kim's gaze and shook her head. "He had a lot of scars on his body. Looked like war wounds to me. Like he'd been a war hero, maybe. Another reason I thought he was a vet."

"Seems like he should have been able to fight back if he'd had that kind of training," Kim replied.

"Guy who shot him was a coward. Like shooting fish in a barrel." Rhonda shook her head slowly, miserably. "He didn't have a chance. He should be dead. Fact he's not is a fluke."

"Yeah. Sure seems like it," Kim said.

Her stomach had begun to settle down as she'd heard Rhonda's story. A glimmer of possibility had opened up.

Staring into the cold black coffee, Rhonda said, "Why would anybody shoot a guy like that? Makes no sense. No sense at all."

Kim disagreed. The shooting wasn't random. It wasn't frenzied. It was calculated and executed with precision. Organized, the profilers called it.

And the shooter got away.

All of which meant there was a motive here, and Rhonda seemed to be worried about what that motive was. She knew why the guy was shot. Or thought she knew. But she wasn't saying.

Kim pulled a business card from her pocket and handed it to Rhonda. "If you think of anything else that might help us, my number's on the back."

Rhonda nodded.

Kim left the tiny room, feeling like she was escaping Rhonda's life filled with the kind of desperation no one ever wanted.

But Kim felt better. Her stomach snake had stopped its constant thrashing. Several things Rhonda said suggested Reacher wasn't the victim or the shooter.

Whatever the motive for this crime, there had been one. Someone came into his room and shot him with the intent to kill him. That wasn't a random thing.

Reacher hadn't been in Gaucho long enough to give someone a reason to shoot him.

And shooting a naked guy taking a shower wasn't the sort of thing Reacher would do. Nothing she knew about Reacher suggested he would.

But if Reacher had shot the guy with intent to kill, the man would be dead. For sure.

So Reacher probably wasn't the shooter.

On the flip side, getting shot while he was naked in the shower was not something Reacher would allow, either. He had lightning-fast reflexes. He'd trained himself to notice every threat and defend himself against it.

Reacher wouldn't just stand there naked under the running shower and let some guy break into his room and shoot him.

Not under normal circumstances, anyway.

Which logically meant Reacher hadn't been the shooter, and he wasn't the victim, either.

Did Petey Burns shoot the guy? Possibly. His motive was an open question. And where would he get a weapon with a silencer?

The bigger question was where Burns and Reacher were now.

She could be totally wrong, of course. What she needed was confirmation. Nailing down the exact time when the shooting happened would go a long way in the right direction.

Kim slipped her sunglasses on and left the motel office through the big glass door. She walked toward Burke and Carpenter, who were still talking in the parking lot.

CHAPTER TWELVE

Friday, May 20
Gaucho, NM
2:45 p.m. (MDT)

AS SHE APPROACHED, SHERIFF Carpenter said, "My deputies are searching for the gun, starting with the rooms. We'll broaden the search if we don't find it. We've got the State Police and crime techs on the way. Not much more we can do here for now."

Kim agreed. The shooter was probably long gone, as Rhonda had said. Probably left not long after he did the deed.

Burke said, "Have you heard anything from the hospital in Albuquerque? Got an ID on the victim?"

Carpenter shook his head. "We've collected a few fingerprints off the shower. If Rhonda's right that he was a veteran, he's probably in the databases somewhere. The military's been collecting DNA on members for a long time now. Maybe we'll get a hit soon. Otherwise, we need to wait for the techs to finish. Or we might get lucky like you said, and the victim will wake up and tell us everything we need to know."

"What about the Tiguan?" Kim asked, tilting her head toward the SUV. "The gun could be inside."

"Could be. I'm tempted to search it. But the vehicle is locked, and that little flashing red light suggests the alarm is set. No exigent circumstances exist at the moment that would allow us to break into it," Carpenter replied.

Burke said, "The license plate's probably stolen. Vehicle, too."

Carpenter nodded. "We're running the VIN now."

Time and distance and lack of manpower were some of the most vexing problems he had to deal with today. Seemed like the resources he had access to were running slower than he'd like.

Carpenter said, "We looked in the windows. There's an open duffel. It looks like it's full of clothes. The gun could be in there, too. But if it is, we can't see it."

Deputy Snow stuck his head out of one of the rooms and flagged Carpenter. "I'll be right back," he said as he headed off.

When Carpenter was out of earshot, Burke said, "If Reacher is the gunshot victim, our work may be completed. He dies, and we're done. Or he lives, and we've got him. Either way, we need to know whether it's him."

Kim cocked her head. "You want to drive to Albuquerque and see if you can confirm? The Boss might be able to help with that if he had a better photo. He could run it through facial recognition. If it's Reacher, he could get a hit, even though the guy's face was damaged."

Burke's eyes were hidden behind his sunglasses, but Kim felt his level stare all the same. "You don't want to come along?"

"If it's Reacher, I'll come up, too. But Rhonda said the other men were at Delgado's Bar last night. She thinks that gives them an alibi for the shooting. Maybe it does. But she's worried about it. I'd like to know exactly what happened," Kim said quietly, for his ears only. "And I'd like to know where Petey Burns is, too."

"If Reacher's not the victim or the shooter, then why do we care about any of that? This shooting isn't our case and we've got bigger fish to fry," Burke replied. "And if Reacher is the victim, we should be there to make sure he doesn't walk away when he wakes up."

Kim kicked the dirt with the toe of her boot. Carpenter was walking toward them and she didn't want him to overhear. "Go to Albuquerque. Find out if he's Reacher. I'll finish up here. It'll be faster if we split up."

Carpenter approached and said, "Rhonda's ex, Louis Delgado, owns the only bar in town. If those three guys were staying here, along with your two escapees, odds are they were at Delgado's place last night when our victim was shot. Nowhere else in this town where they could have been."

"Sounds like a solid theory," Burke said.

"I'm on my way over there. You wanna come or not?" Carpenter asked.

Kim gave Burke one last glance and said, "Yeah, I'll come along. Burke's going to Albuquerque to check on the victim. We need to know if he's the guy we're looking for."

"If he is one of your fugitives, you figure the other one was the shooter?" Sheriff Carpenter arched his eyebrows above his sunglasses. "Be nice to wrap this up. The FBI has plenty of time and resources to throw around. Maybe this is really your problem, and you can handle this whole thing."

"I'll let you know what I find out," Burke said, shaking his head as he trudged to the SUV.

"I'm with you, Sheriff," Kim said, watching Burke turn the vehicle around and head north.

Man, that was a good-looking SUV. You don't live in and around Detroit your whole life and fail to have an appreciation for cars and trucks.

She understood Petey Burns's preferences in driving machines. She came from a long line of German Americans. Quite a few of them were proud automotive engineers. She could hear her father's voice in her head, wistfully listing the GLC 300's many fine attributes.

As Burke drove away, Kim turned back to Sheriff Carpenter. "Where is Delgado's Bar? Could those guys have walked there from here?"

"Easily," Carpenter replied, heading toward his SUV. "But we'll take my squad. We might want to go somewhere else afterward instead of coming back here."

"The first three guys weren't registered as motel guests. But Rhonda knows who they are," Kim said, buckling her seatbelt for the brief ride.

"Yeah. No point in pushing her just yet. That woman is as hard as they come," Carpenter replied. "Easier to find out something we can use. Then confront her when we've got some solid intel."

Kim nodded. It was a reasonable plan. "What about her brother? Roland, is it?"

"Two-bit crook. Rips off the tax collectors and anybody else he thinks he can get away with. He'll steal himself a quick trip to the graveyard one of these days," Carpenter nodded. "Not the sharpest knife in the drawer, either. If he were, he'd be living somewhere else."

"Which means you don't think he's the shooter, then?" Kim asked as Carpenter navigated to the slight right turn onto Main Street.

"Possible. But not likely."

Six minutes later, he parked in one of the vacant angle parking spots on the deserted street in front of Delgado's Bar and shut the engine off. He opened his door and stepped out.

Kim followed suit. She took a quick look around, which was all the time required to absorb the dilapidated buildings, empty storefronts, cracked sidewalks, and busted pavement that summed up Gaucho, New Mexico.

Perhaps the town had been prosperous once, too long ago to matter.

She didn't see a single CCTV camera. Given the lack of anything worth watching, she wasn't surprised.

As she surveyed the terrain, only one thought ran through her head. What the hell were Petey Burns and Jack Reacher doing in this place?

She'd assumed they were passing through and stopped for a meal and shuteye. The existence of the shooting victim didn't change her analysis much.

The timing suggested, more likely than not, Burns and Reacher were involved in the shooting somehow.

Reacher was a trouble magnet. The dead and maimed seemed to show up with distressing regularity wherever he went. The situation could have been as easy to explain as that, although it still felt weak to Kim.

And why leave the Tiguan in the motel lot? Burns changed vehicles like other men changed shirts. He didn't go shirtless for long. It was hard to believe he'd found a better ride parked in the Gaucho motel lot, though.

Which meant what, exactly?

Carpenter hadn't found the Tiguan keys. Burns might still have them. Or not.

What she had now were more questions than answers. Nothing to do but keep moving forward.

The next step was the same as the last one.

Find Reacher.

He was in the wind again, which meant he'd found wheels. Likely, another vehicle had been stolen in the past twenty-four hours. It seemed like the kind of thing the local bar owner might know about.

Sheriff Carpenter had walked from the parked SUV toward Delgado's Bar and yanked the front door open. Kim followed him through into the cold, dark, beer-soaked stench. Her nose wrinkled against the assault.

A guy with an allergy to yeast would probably die just breathing in here.

The building was narrow and deep. The actual bar and a grill were on the left, tables on the right, games in the back. From here, she could see a pool table and a dart board. Farther back was probably at least one restroom, a cleaning closet, and the back exit.

She could pace off the entire length of the place in less than a minute.

There were no patrons here now. The only person she saw was the bartender. She wondered how popular the bar had been last night.

Kim stood to one side, trying to picture Petey Burns and Jack Reacher having a meal or a drink here. The idea tracked. Reacher seemed drawn to dives like this one.

Reacher had a big appetite. They'd arrived late and he would have wanted to eat.

Delgado's Bar felt exactly like the kind of place he might have come to, even if he'd had options. Which he hadn't. This was the only place to get prepared food in the whole town.

No CCTV cameras in here, either, she noticed.

"Afternoon, Delgado," Carpenter called out as he approached. When he reached the bar, he leaned against it, as if the visit was casual, not official. "This is FBI Special Agent Otto."

The bartender's gaze swept past the sheriff and lingered on Kim. "Suppose you're here about that shooting over at the motel. I'll save you some time. I don't know the guy."

"Hard to say for sure, though," Carpenter replied. "The guy's face was so messed up he's unrecognizable."

"I don't need to see him," Delgado shrugged. "Rhonda called me. Said she'd found the guy. Big dude, shot in the shower, banged himself up as he fell," Delgado shook his head. "Said she'd never seen him before. If Rhonda don't know him, I don't neither."

Kim nodded. "So he wasn't here, in your bar, last night?"

"No."

"Which means you know everyone who *was* here last night, then," Kim stated flatly. "You won't mind giving us their names."

CHAPTER THIRTEEN

Friday, May 20
Fort Meade, MD
3:05 p.m. (MDT)

HUGH SULLIVAN WAS NOT assigned an official office at National Security Administration Headquarters in Fort Meade, Maryland. Yet, his workspace was palatial. He was the Special Assistant to the Director of National Intelligence.

He'd held the job for two decades, although his title had never existed on any organizational chart. Which was more than okay with him.

The last thing he ever wanted was to have politicians, bureaucrats, and bean counters crawling all over his turf. He needed room to move.

He identified his own operations and completed missions according to his own rules. Results were all that mattered. His system suited him and the Director. Neither had plans to change.

NSA work had become more essential to national security

every day since the end of the Second World War. Sullivan understood the so-called need for oversight.

But he couldn't, wouldn't work with idiots who demanded the intelligence community do the nation's most important job while wearing a straightjacket.

Congressional hearings, subpoenas, policy directives, demands from the White House. Pure theater. All of it. Ridiculous.

The United States had friends and enemies. If you weren't a friend, you were an enemy, as far as Sullivan was concerned.

Friends stepped up and carried their fair share of the load. If they didn't do that, they were an enemy.

There was no room in his world view for "allies" pretending to be friends while sticking their hands out. Friends didn't need a handout. They had their own assets. Otherwise, "allies" were worthless to him.

He was willing to bribe enemies. Try to bring them over to his side, even temporarily. But bribing allies was a bridge too far. They were either with him or against him. Simple as that.

Even worthy bribes had to be funded. Hell, all of the work he did had to be funded. Nobody had ever knocked on his door offering a multi-billion dollar check. Damned sure they never would.

Sullivan's operations were never a line item on the NSA budget. Funding was his responsibility.

Always had been. Always would be.

None of the politicians, bureaucrats, and bean counters wanted to know where the money came from or how he spent it.

That knowledge would have made them accountable, and none of them wanted that.

What they wanted were results they could flog in the press to help them keep their jobs.

That suited Hugh Sullivan just fine. From the minuscule payments to welfare recipients all the way up to the highest State Department boondoggles, government funding came with strings attached.

He had never been a puppet. Nor would he ever be.

This weekend's work, after he pulled it off, would be a gift that kept on giving for a long time. A few billion over the next few years, if all went well, would free up his time for more worthy operations.

The problem was always the caliber of those he was forced to depend upon, both inside and outside the US Government. The reliability of the players varied, which meant more hands-on effort was required from him.

Sullivan shrugged. Couldn't be helped.

By Monday, he'd have more cash in his war chest than he'd had since his days of working directly with the Saudis. Good times back then. Funding had never been a problem as long as the Saudis were counted among his friends.

But those days were gone.

Doug XYZ, as he called himself, and his unit should be in place for Phase One tonight. Sullivan had never worked with Doug before, but he'd come highly recommended, and Sullivan didn't have as many operatives he could trust in the field these days.

Doug swore he could do the job, and Sullivan planned to watch him closely. With such a large-scale operation, and so many moving parts, one small cog in the wheel could derail the whole train.

Sullivan would not let that happen.

He rummaged through his desk and found one of the burner

phones he'd stashed in the back of the bottom drawer. In his world, burners were good only for a single use. Which meant he accumulated burners the way some people collected airline miles. Couldn't be helped.

Hugh Sullivan had learned many things the hard way during his tenure with the NSA. More than one call on a burner increased the potential for tracking exponentially. It was the kind of mistake a man committed only once in his line of work.

He shoved the burner into his pocket and went for a walk.

The population around Fort Meade was dense enough to provide plenty of cellular traffic to mask the brief call he planned.

A mile from his office, Sullivan fired up the burner and let it connect to a commercial cell tower in the middle of a busy shopping district. It was Friday afternoon and the weather was warm. Kids were out of school, parents were off work, and tourists were pouring into the city.

Perfect conditions.

Sorting through mountains of cell traffic data would require weeks of work from any agency. Amid such crowds, it was fairly easy to get lost long enough to avoid detection.

You just needed to know the weak points in the systems.

Anyplace where hordes of civilians with cell phones existed was one such weak point.

Sullivan took a seat at one of the plastic tables in the outdoor food court. He was surrounded by two groups of grade school kids and several packs of high schoolers.

He glanced around the shops. Most were busy. People were standing in line. Others were coming and going.

More than half the people he could see were using their cell phones.

He smiled as he dialed the number he'd memorized when he delivered the phone. After two rings, his contact picked up.

"Yeah. I'm here. What's up?"

"Are you on schedule?" Sullivan asked.

"Mostly. Got off to a slower start than planned."

"Is he dead?" Sullivan asked.

"No guy should survive three gunshots and head trauma. Working on confirming that now."

Sullivan inhaled deeply. "Not good enough. We must be certain."

"I'm aware."

"When will you know?"

"Soon."

"Keep me informed."

Sullivan hung up.

This operation had been too long in the planning to let something as stupid as a cell phone call screw it up.

He dropped the burner on the concrete and stomped it with his heel, busting the cheap plastic into shards. He collected the pieces and dropped them into several trash bins along the street on his way to his center of shadow operations. He tossed a few pieces down a sewer grate, too.

With a long weekend of work ahead, the big payoff was within his grasp. He could feel it.

CHAPTER FOURTEEN

Friday, May 20
Gaucho, NM
3:45 p.m. (MDT)

FROM HIS POSITION BEHIND the bar, Luis Delgado cocked his head and narrowed his gaze as if Kim were an unusual specimen of some sort.

"I can't give you those names," he said.

"Why not?" Carpenter asked, already pulling his phone from his pocket so he could record. "We're gonna chase them all down, one way or another. I'd rather not spend the whole friggin' day doing it. No reason you can't help us out, is there?"

Delgado leaned against the back counter, hands in his pockets and ankles crossed. "What the hell are you playing at, George? You know everybody in Gaucho as well as I do. Go ask them yourself. Won't take long. There's not that many of us."

Kim had brothers who would do anything to protect her if they thought she needed protecting. Maybe Delgado held similar affection for his ex-wife.

She tried a personal appeal. "Rhonda seemed very upset."

"Of course, she was upset. She'd found a man mowed down in a bathtub. Why wouldn't she be upset?' Delgado said tersely.

"I've interviewed a lot of witnesses over the years, Mr. Delgado. Rhonda didn't impress me as a woman who upsets easily," Kim replied patiently. "I had the feeling she *did* know the victim. And she's worried that she knows who the shooter was, too."

"That so," Delgado snapped. "You should be talking to Rhonda, then. Not me. And before you ask, I didn't shoot the guy. Whoever he is."

Kim nodded her head toward a photo hanging on the wall behind the bar. "That's you and Rhonda. And the boy is your son?"

"My kid is none of your business," Delgado said coldly.

"Maybe not. But he is your concern. Rhonda's, too. And if one or both of you ends up in prison for attempted murder, how will your son deal with that?" Kim asked.

Delgado's face flushed. His nostrils flared and his eyes widened. He snapped, "Rhonda didn't shoot nobody. I told you I didn't neither. You're barking up the wrong tree."

"Maybe. But in that case, you want to help us find out who did the shooting, don't you? Because otherwise, we might get confused and focus on the wrong suspect," Kim replied evenly. "Which could be a problem for both of you."

Delgado stood upright, anger close to exploding. "What do you want?"

"We want to know the names of everyone in the bar last night. Let's start there. Couldn't have been that many. Give me a quick list," Sheriff Carpenter said.

Delgado said nothing.

"Or we can take you into custody now for obstructing justice and lying to federal agents because you definitely know more than you've admitted to. We'd interview you at the closest FBI Field Office, which is Albuquerque," Kim said as if she was offering the alternative and thinking it through. "Take us a while to get there. And it's late. You'd need to stay over the weekend. Monday, too, probably. You'd have to close up the bar for a few days while we check things out. Would you prefer that?"

Delgado looked ready to come over the bar and strangle her. He might have tried if he'd had the chance. But he was interrupted.

The back door opened and bright sunlight flooded the dark corridor. Two young boys came inside. From Kim's vantage point at the front of the bar, they looked about twelve or thirteen.

They were at that scrawny, awkward, exuberant stage boys go through before puberty and before they discover the need to be cool, no matter what. Horsing around, bouncing off the walls, high-fiving each other, laughing.

When they reached the pool table, one called out. "Dad! We're gonna shoot some pool, okay?"

Delgado raised his voice to be heard, "Yeah, sure. But stay back there. We're talking here."

They racked the balls and chose their cues and soon were engrossed in their game.

Kim said, "So that's your son. What's his name again?"

Delgado paused as if he might not answer, but then he shrugged. "Benny. His friend is Oliver. They come here most days so I can keep an eye on them after school while Rhonda's working."

"They seem like nice kids," Kim replied.

The balance of Delgado's options had just shifted in her

favor. She'd seen the dynamic a hundred times. No dad wants to be handcuffed and stuck in a sheriff's squad in front of his kid. Delgado would calm down a bit now that Benny was on the premises. He'd be more reasonable.

Sheriff Carpenter remained poised to record notes on his phone. "I could use up my shoe leather by running all over town to chase these guys down. But what's the point in that? Three or four of the local guys are probably in here every night, Luis, right? Let's start with them."

Delgado's attitude didn't improve, but he offered a staccato list of four names. Carpenter nodded as if he knew each one, which he probably did.

"That's a good start. What about the names of the strangers?" Kim asked.

"What strangers?" Delgado snarled.

"Rhonda said five strangers were staying over at the Gaucho Motel. They had to be here last night. Nowhere else to go. So who were they?" Kim asked, fudging Rhonda's facts a bit. It wasn't a crime for a federal agent to lie to a witness or a suspect. Delgado should know that.

Delgado pursed his lips and said nothing.

"One was this guy," Kim said, pulling out her phone and showing him the photo of Petey Burns.

Delgado nodded imperceptibly.

Kim swiped the photo and showed Reacher next. "Another one was this guy."

Delgado's eyes widened and his pupils dilated when he recognized Reacher's image.

Bingo. Reacher had been here just as she'd thought. Delgado didn't seem like the kind of guy who wanted any trouble with the law, either.

The boys took their pool shots and knocked the balls along the felt and into the pockets. The balls made soft colliding sounds as the game progressed. Mostly, the kids talked quietly. Kim couldn't make out their low-pitched conversation.

"Were the five strangers all together?" Sheriff Carpenter asked, looking worried now. A single shooter might have been a manageable case for his small department. Five guys on a crime spree were not manageable at all.

"No." Delgado shook his head, watching his kid. "Three of them came in earlier in the day. They'd checked out of the motel and they were just hanging here. The first guy she showed me—the blond—he joined them later. I figured they'd been waiting for him. The four of them left together around midnight."

"What about the other man I showed you?" Kim asked. "He never joined them?"

"Reacher? He came in later. He looked around like he was trying to find somebody. Then he walked straight through and out the back," Delgado said.

"Like he was looking for the four that had already left, you mean?" Sheriff Carpenter asked.

CHAPTER FIFTEEN

Friday, May 20
Gaucho, NM
4:45 p.m. (MDT)

DELGADO NODDED. THE BOYS had finished their game, complete with whoops and cackles. It sounded like Benny had won. After exchanging high-fives, they pulled the balls from the pockets and racked them again for a second game.

Kim cocked her head. She ran what she knew along with Delgado's story like a fast video through her mind.

She'd thought Petey Burns and Reacher ended up in Gaucho by happenstance. But Petey had come to Gaucho specifically. For a reason. To meet up with those three guys, who had already been here a couple of days.

Burns met up with them either here or at the motel. At that point, they were all together.

Without Reacher.

They left as a group, all four of them, before midnight.

Then Reacher came in. When he didn't see Petey or the others in the bar, he went out the back after them. They were already gone.

She nodded. Up to that point, the scenario tracked with what she knew about the players. And it made sense.

Other issues were not as clear.

But when Reacher arrived at Delgado's, had the guy at the motel already been shot in the shower? When exactly did that happen?

And Reacher had given Delgado his name. Which meant some conversation between the two must have taken place.

What did they talk about?

"You said Reacher went out to the back parking lot to find Burns and the others, but they were already gone. Reacher came back inside, didn't he? He wanted to talk to you," Kim said. "He came back because he had questions. What did he ask you?"

Delgado's discomfort had escalated when they started talking about the strangers. A thin film of sweat had popped up on his brow and his upper lip. Now that she was asking specifically about Reacher, Delgado's anxiety bumped up a few more levels.

Sheriff Carpenter said, "Come on, Luis. Just spill it. We're not leaving until we get the whole story. Or else we're hauling your ass to Albuquerque like she said before."

Delgado's mouth worked for a while as if he was thinking deeply or something before he supplied the facts in a rote manner. "He said his name was Reacher. He was looking for the blond guy, Burns. Said Burns came to meet a buddy for a drink. Asked me where they were."

Kim nodded. "And what did you tell him?"

Delgado shrugged. "I said they left. About twenty minutes earlier. He wanted to know where they were headed. I told him I didn't know."

Sheriff Carpenter said, "But you did know, didn't you, Luis?"

Delgado lowered his head and kneaded his brow with one knuckle as if he was seriously thinking about which lie to tell. Then he simply abandoned the effort. "Hell, I don't owe Doug nothin'. My kid likes him. My ex likes him. But he's trouble. Knowed it from the start."

"Who's Doug?" the sheriff asked.

"They call him Doug XYZ. I don't remember his last name. Couldn't spell it if I could say it, which I can't. He dates Rhonda off and on. Been hanging around the past few days, waiting for Burns, before they took off last night."

Kim asked, "Where were they going?"

Delgado shrugged. "Ask Rhonda."

"Maybe I'll ask Benny. He probably knows," Kim said, glancing toward the teens. "Benny! Can you come here for a second?"

Benny raised his head when he heard his name. "Sure," he said, trotting over, pool cue in hand.

Delgado's face looked like he might punch her out. It could make things interesting if he tried.

Benny reached them before Delgado had the chance to do anything else stupid.

Kim said, "Benny, we're looking to catch up with Doug XYZ. You have any idea where he went?"

"Chicago." Benny smiled at Kim, who was probably the best-looking woman who'd ever spoken to him like a grownup.

At twelve, Benny was as tall as she was. Which meant he

could look directly into her eyes. She smiled back at him. He blushed.

"But they had some stops to make along the way." Benny's voice cracked when he replied. He blushed and cleared his throat and tried again. "He didn't say where they were stopping. Or why."

"Thanks. That's all I needed," Kim nodded.

Chicago.

She should have guessed. The Boss had ordered her to Chicago, too. He always knew more about Reacher than he admitted. Destination Chicago. Definitely not a coincidence.

Delgado said, "Grab yourselves some sodas and get back to your game now, son."

Benny nodded. "I left my soccer ball in your truck. I need it for practice, and I didn't see the truck in the back lot."

"We'll talk about this later, Benny. Soon as I'm done here," Delgado said with an indulgent smile.

After Benny snagged two cans of soda from the cooler behind the bar and walked away, Kim asked, "Did you tell Reacher those guys were headed to Chicago?"

Delgado shoved his chin forward. "What if I did?"

"What did he say?"

"First, he ordered two big cheeseburgers with fries and a gallon of coffee. Man, that guy can pack it away," Delgado shook his head and cracked a smile. "After he ate, he gave me a very generous tip."

"And then what?" Kim pressed, noting that Reacher didn't seem to be in any particular hurry. If he'd just shot a guy, wouldn't he have wanted to get going instead of filling his gut?

Delgado took a deep breath and exhaled. "He asked to borrow my truck."

"Well, that's a hell of an ask. The guy's got balls. I'll say that for him," Sheriff Carpenter replied. "What did you say?"

Delgado shrugged. "Told him the keys were already in it, and I'd wait until tomorrow to report it stolen."

"Why the hell would you do that?" The sheriff's mouth went slack.

"Figured if I said no, he'd just take it anyway. No point in resisting. The dude's twice my size and looked three times as mean," Delgado said with a shrug. "I thought if I loaned it to him, he might bring it back. If he doesn't, insurance will sort it all out."

"You figured Reacher for a car thief and decided not to resist. That's your story? You seem a lot more proactive than that to me." Kim cocked her head, still looking pointedly at the boys playing pool. "You had another reason to let him take your truck. What was it?"

"Doug XYZ is a sonofabitch." Delgado gave her a belligerent stare. He'd made a choice, and he was pretty damned proud of the way he'd made it. "Told him to stay away from my kid, but he wasn't gonna leave Benny alone. He knew it, Rhonda knew it, and I knew it, too."

"So you're hoping Reacher finds Doug and makes sure he never comes back here," Sheriff Carpenter said. "Did you pay Reacher to take care of Doug and the others, Luis?"

"Didn't need to. Reacher was pretty hot about Doug already. Got a distinct impression all I needed to do was to point him in the right direction," Delgado replied, chin jutted forward. "Nothing criminal about that."

"You think not? If Reacher finds Doug and hurts him, that's aiding and abetting at the very least," Sheriff Carpenter said. "You may end up living in the county jail for a while. See how you like it."

Kim gnawed inside her lower lip. Delgado's story tracked. Everything about it made perfect sense, actually. In the way of all things Reacher.

"Are we done here?" Delgado asked belligerently.

"One other thing," Kim said. "So Burns came in, sat down with Doug. The other two guys with Doug were playing pool. Burns and Doug talked for a while."

"That's what happened," Delgado snarled.

"Almost. But not quite. One of the four left for a while and then came back. Which one?" Kim said. She guessed, but the timeline made sense if the motel shooting happened before the fab four left at midnight.

"Doug was gone for maybe thirty minutes. Maybe less." Delgado shrugged. "I figured he'd ducked out to go say goodbye to Rhonda and Benny."

Sheriff Carpenter shot her a side-eye.

Kim nodded. It could have happened that way. Or not.

The veteran was shot in Reacher's shower. Hell, Reacher might have offered him the room for some reason. It was the kind of thing Reacher might do if the guy was a vet and seemed down on his luck with no place to go.

Maybe Doug went in and shot the guy, possibly thinking he was Reacher, but maybe not.

When the vet was most vulnerable. When he couldn't defend himself.

Then Doug bugs out.

Where was Reacher when all of this was happening?

No evidence on that had surfaced yet. But Kim assumed Reacher had found out about the shooting, at the very least.

Reacher would have concluded that he was the intended target. After all, he was the one who should have been in that shower. It was a fluke of fate that he wasn't the guy who took those bullets.

Maybe he saw the shooter. Maybe he just assumed the shooter would head toward the bar.

Either way, the whole thing probably pissed Reacher off. Offended his sense of justice or some such thing.

Which meant Delgado had called it correctly when he gave Reacher the keys to his truck.

Reacher went after Doug.

Doug would be forced to defend himself when Reacher found him. And he'd fail. They always failed.

"Tell me the make, model, and color of your truck. Include the VIN and any other details you've got." Kim pulled out her phone to make notes. "And if you've got a photo of the truck, I'll take that, too."

Delgado didn't respond immediately.

"Or I can just look it up. Take me five seconds," Sheriff Carpenter's tone conveyed that he was tired of the nonsense.

Delgado smirked and spilled the intel. Kim put it in an email and sent it off via secure satellite with a request to her former partner.

It shouldn't take Gaspar too long to find Delgado's truck.

With any luck, Reacher would still be driving it.

"I need to make a call, Sheriff. I'll meet you outside," Kim said as she walked toward the exit.

She reached for her sunglasses and slipped them on before she emerged from the bar's cool darkness into the still too bright desert sunlight. A notification on her phone showed a fourteen-second voicemail from Burke.

The message was terse.

"Otto, hang tight. I'm on my way back. Nothing more I can

do here. Reacher was in a darkened hospital room, his face all bandaged. A few minutes later, he was dead. Call me when you get this. I'll fill you in."

What the hell? Kim cocked her head and played the message twice more.

Burke's message made no more sense the third time through.

She'd felt so certain that Reacher wasn't the man who was shot in the shower.

Which meant Reacher wasn't the guy in the hospital, either.

Dead or alive, the shower guy wasn't Reacher. She'd bet on it.

What was Burke blathering on about, then?

What had she missed?

CHAPTER SIXTEEN

Friday, May 20
Gaucho, NM
5:45 p.m. (MDT)

KIM HAD CALLED GASPAR with the intel on Delgado's truck. "If he's driving on the interstate, you should be able to find him."

"Yeah. And since Reacher's not much of a driver, he might stick to the main roads. I'll do what I can," Gaspar said and signed off.

He didn't elaborate on his methods and she didn't ask because hacking government satellites was a crime. The less she knew about it, the better.

The sun was headed toward the horizon, but it was still daylight for at least a couple of hours. Gaspar should be able to get an unobstructed view of the truck in the clear, cloudless late afternoon. He might even be able to give her Reacher's exact location.

She stood a few moments longer, thinking about Burke's

message and Delgado's statements. Initially, reconciling them seemed impossible. One missing piece was the timing. When did the motel shooting take place?

Sheriff Carpenter came outside, squinting as he patted his pockets for sunglasses. He slipped them onto his face. "You finish your call?"

"Yeah. And I had a voicemail from Burke. He said your shooting victim died," she replied.

Carpenter sighed and ran a palm over his hair. "Swell. Attempted murder was already a tough case. This makes things a lot more difficult. Were they able to identify the victim?"

Kim shrugged. Gaspar's all-purpose gesture.

Carpenter said, "Look, it's likely that Reacher was either the shooter or the target."

"Why?"

"Makes sense. A stranger rides into town, trouble ensues. Usually, the stranger is the cause, one way or another."

"Possibly," Kim replied. "There were at least six strangers in this town last night. One of them shot one of the others."

The question was, who did what to whom? And why?

"I've got to get back to the motel. State police are on the scene. They need to know the victim has died," Carpenter said, moving toward his squad. "Maybe they can put a rush on those fingerprints and the DNA. We need to know who this guy was. You coming?"

"Yeah. I'd like to talk to Rhonda. See if Doug did come over to see her before he left town last night like Delgado said." Kim glanced up and down the deserted main street again as she sent a quick text to her partner and then slipped her phone into her pocket. She slid into the passenger seat. "Burke's on his way back. He can pick me up there."

At the Gaucho Motel, the driveway was still blocked by the two sheriff's squads. The state police vehicles were parked close to room fifteen. She counted six vehicles in all. They seemed to have the crime scene well covered.

Carpenter parked in front of room ten, probably to keep his vehicle out of the way. "I'm headed to room fifteen. Rhonda's still in the breakroom. Let me know what she says about Doug."

"I'll join you in a few. Anything they can do to narrow down the timing on this shooting will help," Kim said as they climbed out of the squad.

"Not sure how they'll be able to do that, given the lack of physical evidence. If the victim had died here, the coroner might have been able to establish the time of death." Carpenter said.

Kim nodded but said nothing. At the moment, she didn't have any bright ideas. Carpenter strode toward room fifteen and Kim headed in the opposite direction.

At the motel's office, Deputy Snow was still manning the desk, running through the computer systems. He looked up when she walked in. "Agent Otto. What's up?"

"Is Rhonda still back there? I've got a few more questions for her." Snow nodded, and Kim walked past the desk to the break room.

Rhonda hadn't moved much. She held another cup of coffee. No bite marks on this one. She didn't seem quite as fidgety, either. Maybe that meant she'd managed to find some self-control.

When Kim entered the room, Rhonda didn't seem to notice.

"Hey, Rhonda." Kim scootched around the plastic table to the counter and pulled a Styrofoam cup off the stack.

Rhonda looked up and nodded.

"We've been over talking to Luis," Kim said.

When she lifted the flask, the aroma of stale coffee was nauseating. It smelled like the thick sludge had been evaporating from the pot for a dozen hours. It probably had.

She put the cup back and sat in the second plastic chair. "Luis says Doug XYZ is your boyfriend. Is that true?"

Rhonda shrugged.

"Luis says Doug has been your boyfriend for a while. Long enough to become friendly with your son."

Rhonda didn't meet Kim's gaze, but she said, "I guess."

"Doug was one of the three men staying here at the Gaucho Motel for the past few days, wasn't he?"

Rhonda lifted her chin defiantly. "So what if he was? No reason he can't rent a room, is there?"

"Which also means you know his two buddies. Who are they?"

Rhonda shrugged and returned her gaze to her cup. "Just a couple of guys. Never met them."

"What are their names?"

"Doug didn't talk about them much," Rhonda replied.

"Luis says Doug left the bar last night before midnight. Says he was gone about half an hour. Thinks Doug came to your place. Maybe you two had some quick, passionate goodbye sex."

Rhonda glanced up again. Her eyes widened. She shook her head. "That's a lie. No fooling around in the house when Benny's home. Luis and I agreed to that a long time ago."

"So when was the last time you saw Doug?"

"About six o'clock. He came for supper. Then he left. I swear."

Kim nodded. Her story could be true. Luis was protective of Benny. No reason to believe his mother wasn't just as protective of her son.

"But you're worried about Doug now, aren't you, Rhonda?"

Rhonda gnawed her lips and said nothing.

"You're worried that Doug shot that guy in room fifteen, aren't you?"

She shook her head violently. "Of course not! Doug wouldn't do that! What a vile thing to say!"

Kim nodded, watching Rhonda closely. "Yes, you're worried about that, for sure. Did Doug have a gun?"

Rhonda shrugged. "Lots of guys around here have guns. Nothing strange about that."

"Luis says Doug and his buddies were headed to Chicago. What are they planning to do there?"

Rhonda stood up abruptly, knocking the plastic chair to the floor with a clatter. "How the hell should I know? Luis seems to know so damned much. Why don't you ask him?"

She swiveled and dashed out of the room. A few seconds later, Kim heard a door slam in the back and a noisy engine start up. Rhonda floored the old vehicle and sped out of the parking lot.

CHAPTER SEVENTEEN

Friday, May 20
Gaucho, NM
6:15 p.m. (MDT)

KIM REMAINED SEATED FOR a few minutes, thinking about Rhonda's situation. If she was telling the truth, which was a big question, then Doug could have shot that guy in room fifteen last night. No doubt about it.

He had a gun. He had the opportunity.

But why would he do it? Did he know the man? Or had Doug thought the guy was Reacher? Was he right?

The man was dead now. Burke had seen him and said he was Reacher.

Something about that idea still didn't gel for Kim.

If Doug left the bar and shot the guy and then came back to Delgado's to connect with his unit, then the guy wasn't Reacher. Because Reacher was walking around after that. Or at least, that's what Delgado claimed.

Kim stood and stretched her muscles. She was tired and sore

and hungry, and there were no answers to her questions in this small room.

She walked to the lobby where Deputy Snow was still sitting at the desk.

"Sounds like you and Rhonda had words," he said.

Kim took his statement to be a question.

"Saw her high-tailing it outta here in her truck."

"Yeah. She knows more than she's telling," Kim replied.

"About what?"

"Everything, probably."

Snow nodded. "Sheriff Carpenter said to come down to room fifteen when you're done here."

Kim walked through the front doors into the early evening sunshine just as Burke pulled into the dusty lot. He parked near Sheriff Carpenter's squad, got out of the SUV, and stood waiting for her.

When she approached, he said, "Reacher's dead. We're done here. We can head back to DC in the morning. There's a red-eye out of Albuquerque tonight."

Sheriff Carpenter was standing on the sidewalk outside room fifteen. A few state police officers were talking with him.

"Well, about that. I'm not so sure," Kim said.

Burke scowled. "I saw him. Dead as they come."

"Yeah, you saw the guy, and he was dead. I believe that," Kim replied. "What I'm not sure about is whether it was Reacher you saw."

"Why the hell not?" Burke demanded, seriously annoyed. "I've met Reacher. Talked to him. More than once. That's one of the reasons I was added to this assignment. So I'd recognize Reacher when we found him."

"Okay. But while you were gone, we interviewed a witness

who says Reacher was alive after midnight last night. He borrowed a truck and went after Burns," she said.

Burke stared at her, jaw clenched, lips pressed into a firm line, as she told him Luis Delgado's account of Reacher's actions. She followed up with a quick report on Doug XYZ, too.

"So you're saying what, exactly?" Burke's tone had softened a bit, but not much. He didn't want to believe Delgado and Rhonda. That much was clear. But why?

"I'm saying that we need to know the timeline on that shooting. If the guy was shot before midnight, Reacher could have been the shooter, sure. But he wasn't the victim." Kim summarized her conclusions, but she wondered why Burke was so resistant. "Which would mean Reacher wasn't the man who died in that hospital bed."

"So the shooting happened after midnight, then after that Reacher left Delgado's bar. So what?" Burke said, unwilling to let his version go. His bullheaded behavior was exhausting.

"Then where is Delgado's truck?" Kim asked.

Burke worked his mouth and shook his head. "Could be anywhere. Hell, maybe his kid stole it, and Delgado is sending us off on a wild goose chase."

"Possibly. We'll get the locals to chase down the alternatives."

Burke nodded, still frowning.

"But if the shooting victim wasn't Reacher, that means we still need to find him. And whether he's driving Delgado's truck or not, he's got a significant head start," Kim finished. "Let me bring Carpenter up to speed, and then we'll get going. I'll be right back."

Burke fell into step beside her, and they walked toward the small knot of cops handling what had become a homicide when the victim died.

CHAPTER EIGHTEEN

Friday, May 20
Middletown Village, Oklahoma
7:05 p.m. (CDT)

THE BURGER HE'D EATEN earlier had left his stomach long ago, and Petey Burns was hungry. And he still had no money. After the planning meeting in Doug's room, he'd stretched out on the bed, leaving the window curtains open. It was still an hour before sunset, at least.

Doug's orders were to stay in the room until dark. He'd chosen this motel because of its distance from the target. Should they be unlucky enough to see tonight's theft, witnesses would be less likely to connect them to the motel. Which should slow down law enforcement efforts to locate the thieves. In theory, anyway.

Petey understood the precautions. It was good of Doug to keep him on the unit, given the increased risk. Petey had escaped from prison. There were "be on the lookout" orders for him across the country.

Doug had said, "Somebody recognizes you, and we're all screwed. The operation's effectively over. We'll be lucky to get out alive."

Ray sent a steely-eyed glare straight through Petey's head and delivered a hard threat. "If any of that happens, you don't have to worry about going back to prison. You're a dead man."

Petey had nodded, but the truth was that Ray didn't scare him. Ray took his orders from Doug. Doug wanted Petey to drive and be backup to Moe on the tech for all three jobs this weekend. Ray wouldn't dare screw any of that up.

Which meant Petey had a couple of days to figure out how to handle Ray, at least.

Meanwhile, his stomach growled like a ravenous beast.

Petey looked at the digital clock on the TV. Tonight's job was set to happen just after midnight, six hours from now. He couldn't possibly wait that long to eat.

He glanced through the window again and saw movement in his periphery.

He watched as a car came into view with a pizza delivery sign on the roof. The driver looked like a kid. Eighteen, maybe. He pulled up in front of a room two doors away, shut off the engine, and climbed out of the sedan.

The kid's thick body was dressed like a goth, which Petey thought had gone out of style a while ago. Guess not in Stockton, Oklahoma.

Black jeans, tight black T-shirt, pointy black boots with thick heels. His hair was dyed black and spiked up all over his head. He had four piercings in one eyebrow and a silver bar through his fleshy nose. His fingernails were gnawed below the quick and painted black.

Petey grinned and shook his head. The kid looked more like a prison inmate than Petey did.

The kid hustled around to the passenger side, opened the door, bent over, and rummaged inside. He backed out, holding two large pizza boxes. He yanked the tight T-shirt down to cover his butt crack.

Petey couldn't smell the pizza from his room, but the visual cues alone started his stomach rumbling.

He had delivered pizzas when he was a teen. He'd have six or eight in the car at one time. The routine was to deliver those and then go back to the store for more. If this kid had the same system, Petey's dinner was within reach.

He watched until the kid shuffled off toward his delivery address, a room closer to the main office. Then Petey jumped up, propped his door open with the folding lock slide, and dashed outdoors. The kid was three doors north, rushing along, looking at the numbers on the doors, not finding the one he wanted.

Petey hurried toward the car, opened the passenger door, reached in, and grabbed a pizza box. He considered grabbing two. It smelled that good. He was that hungry. But it was too risky.

He turned, closed the car door, and hustled back to his room.

He slipped inside, threw the deadbolt and the lock slide, and plastered his back against the door. His breath came in rapid gasps. Had the kid noticed him?

Petey kept his back to the wall and reached for the cord to close the drapes. He pulled the cord and the heavy drapes slid across the window.

He waited another few seconds. When he heard nothing from the kid outside, he relaxed enough to toss the pizza box on the dresser and open it up.

The scent of fresh pizza wafted up to assault his senses and threw his stomach into an absolute frenzy. Petey grinned. He grabbed a slice and took a big bite and swallowed it practically whole, where it stayed in his throat like he'd swallowed a baseball.

He opened the mini-fridge and grabbed another bottle of water. He twisted the cap and washed the pizza down. It landed in his stomach with a satisfying thud.

Petey gobbled the rest of the slice, careful to chew it first this time, and reached for another. Before he could take a bite, an angry fist pounded rapidly on his door.

The kid yelled, "Hey! You! Give me back that pizza!"

Petey stood still, not moving.

If Doug heard the kid, he'd be pissed as hell. Which absolutely couldn't happen. Not now. Not when he was so close. All he had to do was stay on Doug's good side until Monday. Then, he'd be set for life.

The kid would give up and go away, surely.

The pounding continued. "Hey! Open the door!"

Petey had to make him stop. But how?

He looked around the room for a weapon of some kind. Doug kept all the guns in his room. He said he'd pass them out later.

Petey didn't have anything more dangerous than a flimsy plastic toothbrush. It wouldn't have made a decent shiv, even. He couldn't threaten the kid with that.

The kid kept pounding and yelling. Petey got the sinking feeling that he wasn't going to stop unless Petey opened the door.

So he wiped his hands on a towel, moved to the door, and pulled it open.

The kid stood there, fist raised to keep pounding, mouth open to yell again. He was a little shocked when Petey stood before him.

"Hey, man, quiet down," Petey said, grinning. "You're gonna wake the baby."

The kid blinked. His eyes rounded. Whatever he'd been expecting the pizza thief to say, Petey's non-existent sleeping baby wasn't on the list of plausible excuses.

"I need that pizza back. My boss will skin me alive if I don't deliver it. I'm on probation, dude. I've screwed up a dozen times this week. You gotta give it back to me." The kid's eyes watered and Petey thought he might cry.

Petey shoved his hands in his pockets and tried to look ashamed. He tilted his head toward the open pizza box. "I'm sorry, man. I'd give it back, but I already ate it."

The kid's mouth went slack. He blinked a few more times. Then his nostrils flared and his face reddened. He stuck his hand out and shoved the door wide open. "Then you gotta pay me for it. Fifteen twenty-nine. Right now."

Petey shook his head. "Sorry. I don't have any money. That's why I stole the pizza."

"Seriously?" the kid shouted. "You expect me to believe you're staying at the most expensive place in Middletown, and you don't even have fifteen bucks to pay for a pizza?"

Petey shrugged. "Wish I did. Sorry."

"Stop saying that!" the kid yelled and pushed Petey's chest with both hands. He knocked Petey backward. With his hands in his pockets, he lost his balance and scrambled to stay upright. No luck. The next thing he knew, he was flat on his ass on the carpet.

The kid came inside and pushed the door closed. He looked

like a raging bull. He lifted his left foot and gave Petey a vicious kick with one of the pointy black boots.

Petey scrambled to get out of the way, but the kid landed two more kicks before Petey managed to make it to the bathroom and slam the door. The room didn't have a separate lock. He held the door closed with his entire body.

Petey's hard breath caught on sharp pain in his side when he tried to inhale. It was a pain he recognized. *Crap!* The kid had bruised his ribs with those damned boots.

The kid pounded on the bathroom door now, yelling like a madman. "Come outta there, you pussy! You're gonna pay me for that pizza!"

"Look, man. I'm sorry. All the money I have is on the dresser. Take it," Petey shouted as loud as he could, given how painful it was to breathe.

The kid wouldn't stop. He acted like some kind of crazy lunatic. He was kicking the door with his boots and yelling that he'd break the door down if Petey didn't come out.

And then he said, "You think I don't know who you are? I've seen your picture on every news station since you broke out of prison, Pete Burns."

The words shocked him like an ice cold shower. His body went slack. The kid's next hard kick shoved the door open. He came straight through and kept pushing. The door and Petey slammed against the wall, mashing Petey's body between the wall and the door like a panini.

The doorknob jabbed painfully into Petey's stomach. His ribs hurt. He couldn't breathe. His vision went dark around the edges.

He was about to die in a cheap motel bathroom, stomped to death over a stolen pizza. After all the near-death experiences he'd survived, how moronic was that?

Petey's body slumped. He stopped pushing on the door. His head turned sideways a moment before the door would have smashed his face into his skull and straight back into the sheetrock.

Gravity pulled him down. He felt himself sliding toward the floor. The kid was still pushing, still yelling, but Petey barely heard.

He was almost unconscious. He floated into the easy space between awake and asleep.

So this was the end. This was how it felt to die. Not so bad, really. Nothing like what he'd expected. It turned out life was way more painful than death. Huh. Who knew?

And then, from what sounded like a great distance, Petey heard a new sound, one he recognized. Three rapid gunshots from a silenced pistol.

The kid screamed in pain after the first shot. The second one, too. But not a whimper after the third.

He'd slumped against the door, which continued to hold Petey almost upright.

Doug said, "Hang on. I've gotta move this kid to get you out of there."

When Doug moved the kid away from the door, Petey's body pushed the door forward and he fell onto the cold tiled floor. Slowly, the edges of his vision cleared and he came back to reality.

He heard Doug dragging the kid's body backward, across the tile, into the dressing area, where the sink and the metal clothes rack were the only furnishings. He heard the body hit the back wall.

Doug pushed the door open and said, "Can you get up?"

"Yeah. Yeah, I can do it. I think the little shit bruised my ribs," Petey said, wincing as he put both hands on the toilet and pushed himself up. "I was hungry. It was just a pizza, for cripes sake. Why'd he have to do all that?"

"I told you to stay in your room. What the hell, Petey?" Doug demanded, waving the gun he still held in his right hand. "This is a disaster. The kid recognized you. You compromised the whole operation. I had to kill him."

Petey looked at the kid's body, crumpled in the corner, dead eyes staring.

"Yeah, Doug. Course. No other option," Petey said, holding his ribs as he stumbled toward the bed and plopped down on it.

Doug glared at him for a few seconds. Then he shoved the pistol into his waistband and headed toward the door. "Get yourself together. You're driving tonight. And you'd better be good at it."

The kid had backed the car into place, which seemed to please Doug.

"Help me get this pile of crap into the car."

Petey stared at Doug as if he'd sprouted horns. He realized Doug wasn't joking.

He and Doug struggled to move and lift the kid's body. Every muscle in Petey's body screamed with the effort, even as his bruised ribs took his breath away.

At the threshold, his hand on the doorknob, Doug said, "Wait until I open the trunk. Then we'll take him out and toss him in there. Do it quick. Every minute we're out there, someone could see us."

Doug searched the kid's pockets for the keys, grabbed them, and hurried outside. He opened the trunk and came back.

"Lift him up. That trunk's at least a couple of feet off the ground. And it's full of crap. But we've got to get him in there on the first toss," Doug said.

Somehow, they managed. No one screamed or seemed to notice. Doug slammed the trunk and turned to Petey.

Doug pushed Petey toward the open door. "Lock up here. Go wait in my room. We're leaving early."

Petey hurried inside and locked the door. He fell back on the bed and moaned, the aroma of pizza raising bile in his throat.

CHAPTER NINETEEN

Friday, May 20
Middletown Village, Oklahoma
7:45 p.m. (CDT)

DOUG SLAMMED THE DOOR to Petey's room behind him
and stomped over to the kid's pizza delivery car. He slid behind
the wheel and jabbed the keys in the ignition.

He shook his head.

The kid had been as dumb as a box of rocks, which boosted
Doug's mood.

The little goth had been too stupid to live another day. Who
knew how many others that kid would have stomped or beat up
or done even worse things to?

Doug had actually saved innocent people from that stupid
kid. No doubt about it.

Yep. A public service homicide, that's what he'd done. They
ought to give him a medal.

He turned the key. The starter whined and groaned and

finally sparked to life. He pushed the accelerator to give the engine enough gas to keep it running.

He slipped the transmission into gear, pulled out of the parking space, and headed toward the back exit. He pulled into the alley, fished his phone out of his pocket, and pressed the redial.

Moe answered right away. "Yeah."

"Don't tell Ray or Burns. Get in the van. Go out the back exit. Turn west in the alley. I need you to pick me up in the back of the Walmart parking lot. The one we passed on the way into town," Doug said.

"On my way." Moe hung up. He didn't ask questions.

The kid's wheels were not even good enough to be crushed for scrap. The engine sputtered and skipped and behaved like it had cat piss in the gas tank. The shocks were shot, and so were the springs, so the damned thing bounced whenever it hit a shallow dip in the pavement.

Doug felt like he was riding a bad-tempered bronco the whole twenty minutes to the Walmart parking lot. He pulled around back and left the car near a dumpster in the corner behind some trees.

When he got out, he yanked the damned pizza sign off the roof and tossed it into the back seat. Then he locked the car and threw the keys into the open dumpster. If somebody wanted those keys, they'd have to trudge through the slime to find them.

The kid and his ride had been handled.

The thought lightened his mood, but only slightly.

The only problem now was he might have told someone about Petey and their van. It was a small risk.

The goth kid didn't seem like he'd have had many friends.

But it was a risk Doug didn't want to take. Not now. Not

when they were mere hours away from Phase One of the operation.

He pulled his baseball cap low over his face, stuck his hands in his pockets, and meandered toward the front of the store just as Moe turned the black van into the lot from the main road. He pulled up in front of Doug, waiting near the entrance, and Doug hopped into the front seat.

"Where to?" Moe asked.

Doug opened the glove box and pulled out a fresh burner phone enclosed in a hard plastic bubble. He stabbed the bubble with a sharp key to tear it and then ripped the plastic apart.

"Drive to the other end of the lot and park out of sight. Leave the motor running. I've gotta make a call," Doug said.

Moe nodded and followed instructions, like always. He was a reliable soldier. He rolled the van along the parking lot until he found an empty spot between two trucks. He pulled in and shifted the transmission into park.

"I won't be long." Doug slid out. He pushed the door closed and walked toward the road, dialing the burner as he moved.

The man who called himself Patton picked up right away. It wasn't surprising. The closer they came to the first heist, the more concerned he'd be about unscheduled communications.

"What's the problem? Everybody okay?"

"Everybody's fine. We need a different van. This one's developed a mechanical problem," Doug said, still moving, weaving in and out of the parked cars as if he'd lost the one he'd arrived in.

"That's not something I can help you with at the moment, given your remote location. Not enough time," Patton said evenly, but Doug could tell he was pissed off. "Can you make do until you get to Missouri?"

"Maybe. If not, we'll find another one ourselves. Just letting you know we could be driving something unexpected when we get to Missouri tomorrow," Doug said.

"Okay," Patton replied. He paused and then warned, "We've built in redundancies. I'd rather not be required to use them."

"Got it," Doug said again, understanding that he meant Doug's unit could be replaced.

It might have been true. Although they'd been training for this job for several weeks, and there were other units already set up, too.

Patton might have had unlimited qualified personnel at his disposal, but somehow, Doug doubted it.

Doug said, "Don't worry. It's under control. We'll figure it out."

Patton disconnected. Doug crumpled the cheap plastic phone and walked back. He climbed into the van and closed the door.

"Where to?" Moe asked again.

"First, we need to find a different van. Then, we'll go back to pick up Ray and Petey. Get food. Then, we get to work," Doug replied.

"Where do we get a different van?" Moe asked as he reversed out of the parking spot and turned toward the exit.

Good question. The best places to steal a vehicle were locations that allowed overnight parking. Usually, airports, hospitals, apartment buildings, hotels, suburban residential neighborhoods. Places like that. If they got lucky, the owner wouldn't know the vehicle was missing until they were far down the road.

But Middletown Village was barely more than a crossroads. The population was small and the people who lived here drove into Stockton for almost everything. Which Doug absolutely could not do. Driving to Stockton to steal a van for tonight was out of the question.

The motel parking lot might hold a viable option. But stealing a van parked there wouldn't be the smartest thing, either.

"I passed an auto shop on the way here. Looked like it was closed up for the night. There were a few vehicles parked out front. One was a black minivan," Moe said, casting a glance toward Doug. "Probably a tight fit for all of our equipment. Could work, though."

Doug sighed. *Damn Petey Burns.* "Show me."

Moe nodded. He drove five miles and pulled into the auto shop parking lot. The black minivan was still there.

Doug shook his head. "Looks too small. We need to find something bigger. Drive around back. See what they've got back there."

Moe, as always, did as he was told. The narrow side street led to an alley behind the building. The back lot wasn't fenced and he didn't see any CCTV cameras. Crime was probably not all that rampant in Middletown Village. Two poles casting yellow light cones stood at the back corners of the lot, which seemed to be all the place needed to deter local thieves.

Doug saw two possible candidates. Both were parked in near-total darkness out of the flood lights. Two cargo vans, same vintage, one white, one green. The green one was in better physical shape. Neither one was likely to have rear seats, which was less than ideal.

"Why are we changing to a new van today instead of tomorrow?" Moe asked.

Doug shrugged. "There's a problem with this one."

Moe nodded. He was a good soldier. He understood the chain of command. "Let's take the white one. Less conspicuous.

There are white panel vans everywhere."

"Okay. Can you get it started?"

"Probably."

Moe pulled up next to the white van and climbed out. He had the vehicle open and running in less than three minutes. The man was a genius.

Doug slid over into the driver's seat and drove the old van out of the parking lot. Moe followed in the stolen white van.

All they needed to do was transfer the equipment, destroy the van they'd been driving since before they'd reached Gaucho, and they'd be ready to roll.

He glanced at the clock. Still plenty of time.

CHAPTER TWENTY

Friday, May 20
Santa Rosa, Texas
8:05 p.m. (CDT)

AFTER BURKE HAD RETURNED from Albuquerque, they'd headed east toward Chicago. He insisted he was fit to drive, but Kim could see he was fighting fatigue even before they reached Santa Rosa, Texas. They crossed into the Central Daylight time zone, and the clocks were showing an hour later. The sun had barely set, casting a rosy glow over the landscape.

When she saw a sign for the Hampton Inn, Kim said, "Pull off at the next exit."

"Why?"

"I'm hungry. You're tired. We won't make Chicago tonight anyway. And we have no idea what to do once we get there," she replied. "Let's get some food and some rest and pick it up again in the morning. By then, Gaspar may have something on Delgado's truck."

"You're the boss." Burke shrugged and flipped on his turn

signal. He never agreed to anything that involved Gaspar. Yet, he didn't argue. He must be even more fatigued than she'd realized.

The hotel was a mile off the expressway. They passed a series of restaurants, but Kim wanted to get checked in and take a shower first. She felt like she was wearing enough dust to plant a begonia.

Burke pulled in and parked under the canopy. "I'll wait here while you check on rooms."

"Okay," Kim replied.

She unlatched her seatbelt and stepped outside. Gaspar's burner phone vibrated in her pocket. She fished it out on her way to register.

"Finally located the truck," he said, without preamble.

"Okay."

"It's in Oklahoma. Can you get there tonight?"

"Probably not. Oklahoma's a long way from Texas."

The desk clerk was waiting expectantly. "Can I help you?"

"Let me call you back," Kim said to Gaspar, disconnected, and stepped up to the counter.

The registration process took longer than it should have. The clerk was a trainee and not sure about things like discounts for government employees and the like. But thirty minutes later, they were inside their rooms.

She'd tossed three phones onto the bed. One burner for Gaspar. One burner for The Boss. And her personal phone. One was vibrating insistently. She glanced toward the bed, unable to identify the culprit from the bathroom.

How important could it be?

"I'll call back," she murmured as she stepped over the bathtub and tilted her face to the shower spray.

Twenty minutes later, she was showered and dressed and scooped up the phones. She picked up the voicemail on her way to meet Burke for dinner.

"Agent Otto, Sheriff Carpenter here. I thought you'd want to know. No murder weapon yet. But we got a positive ID on our victim. DNA matched an army vet. His name was Walter Mayes. I'll send you the details," he said, pausing to clear his throat. "Mayes was honorably discharged about ten years ago. Fell on hard times since then, according to his ex-wife. Said she hadn't seen him for years. Now, all we need to know is who killed him. Anything you can do to help with that, we'd appreciate it."

A deafening roar had filled Kim's ears the moment she'd heard the victim's name.

Reacher wasn't dead.

That was the good news.

Her mission was to find Reacher, who was being considered for a special classified assignment.

To succeed, she needed Reacher alive.

She absolutely refused to fail.

Which meant she'd been on the edge of panic since she'd first seen the brown work boots on that body on the gurney back at the Gaucho Motel. She'd been running on pure adrenaline every moment since then.

Carpenter's message hit her like a blast of oxygen. Shakily, she took her first deep breaths, attempting to steady her nerves.

Kim listened to Carpenter's message again on the way out. She pushed the big glass door open and left the hotel lobby. Burke was waiting under the portico with the SUV's engine running.

She settled into the passenger seat. "The restaurant is about half a mile away, on the right, the desk clerk said."

Burke nodded and rolled onto the street. "You look like you've won the lottery. What's up?"

"Carpenter called," she replied and hit the replay on the voicemail, allowing Burke to hear the message directly.

He gripped the steering wheel tighter and swore. "What the hell? I saw the guy in that hospital bed myself. His face was swollen and bandaged. And the lighting was bad. But it was Reacher. I'm sure of it."

She stared at him. His behavior was bizarre.

It seemed like he *wanted* Reacher to be dead. Which was crazy. Like standing in front of a freight train. If Reacher was dead, Burke's FBI career was dead, too. And hers would be on life support, at the very least.

The Boss had made his position clear from the start. If they failed here, Burke was done.

Whatever had happened to get Burke booted off the FBI's Hostage Rescue Team had been bad. He shouldn't even be here. The hunt for Reacher was his last and only chance to redeem himself.

The mission was clear: Find Reacher.

The mission was not: Find Reacher's dead body.

Kim said none of this, even as her stomach clenched and she felt bile rise into her throat. She reached into her pocket to get an antacid and popped it under her tongue.

Burke found the restaurant and pulled into an empty parking spot not far from the entrance. He shut off the engine and unlatched his seatbelt, still angry or disbelieving or shocked or whatever his issue was.

The antacid had melted and she felt marginally better. "Gaspar called, too. He's found Delgado's truck."

The Boss's burner vibrated with a call. Not surprising. He

monitored everything constantly. He'd no doubt heard their discussion.

Kim put the call on speaker so Burke could participate. "Otto."

"Change of plans," The Boss said. "Reacher's in the wind. Burns, too. Get a meal and some sleep. You'll have new orders in a few hours."

"We're going after Reacher?" Burke asked as if the possibility was akin to a nuclear bomb exploding inside the SUV.

"That's your job. Unless you want to quit now before you screw up again," the Boss replied.

"Are we still thinking Reacher will turn up in Chicago? We could just fly out there," Kim said.

"Possibly. I've got a few more things to check and then I'll decide," The Boss said before he hung up.

Kim slumped back in the seat and waited to see what choice Burke would make. She'd understand if he chose to quit.

He'd acted like he had a lot to prove since he showed up as her new partner back in Memphis. Because he did have a lot to prove.

Much more than his job was at stake. This had become some sort of existential crisis for him.

How much failure and humiliation could one SEAL endure?

Burke stared straight ahead. After a few minutes, he said, "You heard the man. Let's eat and get some sleep. We'll be on the road again soon enough."

Kim nodded. So he'd made his choice. Now, she'd need to make hers. Did she want him to stay on her team or not?

Was she better off with Burke or without him?

And if she asked to have him replaced, where would such a request lead?

CHAPTER TWENTY-ONE

Friday, May 20
Near Fort Meade, MD
10:30 p.m. (EDT)

HUGH SULLIVAN'S CURRENT PERSONAL center of
shadow operations had been built as the headquarters for a
government contractor a few years back. It was within walking
distance of his office at Fort Meade, but the place he somewhat
whimsically called "the snow den" could just as easily have been
on the other side of the globe.

The snow den's moniker was a private joke, inspired by
Edward Snowden, the notorious NSA contractor who had leaked
classified intel and brought the whole weight of the US
government down on his sorry ass.

"Damned traitor," Sullivan said, as he always did whenever
Edward Snowden's name came to mind, which happened way
too frequently, even though Snowden's theft had happened years
before.

Sullivan's snow den was substantially more reliable at

protecting classified intel than the man who inspired its name, which reminded him to watch his back and trust no one.

The brick building was located in a warehouse district. It had no windows and a single door, which could only be opened with Sullivan's biometrics. Three touchpoints were required, presented in a specific order.

First, Sullivan's ten fingerprints and palm print were read simultaneously, right hand first. Followed by two retina scans, left then right. And finally, both ear prints, right and then left.

He had used every ounce of skill he'd ever learned from the NSA to build out the snow den. It was equipped with the precise tech he needed to conduct his business without detection.

No one else had ever entered the building. Which meant the snow den's location was as secret as any facility could possibly be.

In short, Sullivan was more secure in the snow den than anywhere else in the world. He'd stocked up on food and supplies, fresh clothes, and everything he needed for the duration. He wouldn't leave the building until Tuesday.

He'd dubbed the sprawling weekend operation "Wicked Spider."

Five units reported to him as the sole commander.

During the design phases, he'd briefly considered six units, but the logistics became too complicated. Statistics and human nature being what they were, every added team increased risks exponentially.

In the end, he'd settled on five to start.

Each of the five units was intended to be staffed with four members, all ex-military. That plan ran into trouble. Three of the units had ended up with non-military personnel. Sullivan didn't like it. But he'd had no choice.

Each unit consisted of one leader and three qualified specialists.

Unit leaders had once been officers. They understood complex operations, chain of command, need-to-know communications, and essential results.

Sullivan alone had recruited and communicated with the leaders. He used the code name "Patton," one of the most successful generals the US Army had ever produced. Some said Patton had been a tactical genius. No one called him a failure. Ever.

Unknown to the units, each was assigned a secret handler who reported directly to Sullivan. They were well-qualified mercenaries, supremely prepared, eager, and trained to execute orders.

Sullivan brewed a fresh pot of coffee and waited for the aroma to fill the situation room.

The big lighted screen on the wall across from the coffee pot showed five maps with five glowing red dots near the center of each map.

Each unit leader carried five encrypted satellite burner phones. Each phone contained a dedicated GPS tracking device, which fed locations back to the snow den around the clock.

Tomorrow, the handlers would be in position to stream live video from the targets, allowing Sullivan to observe in real-time. But these first five targets were too remote for access to reliable signals.

Tonight's targets were located in five states, Wyoming, Texas, Oklahoma, Colorado, and Nebraska. Small towns with populations under 10,000. Too remote for reliable wireless communications. Large enough to have a community bank with a working ATM fully loaded with sufficient cash.

The community banks were essential for the initial trial.

Recon showed these ATMs were not connected to regional, national, or international banks. Alarms, reporting, and personnel were limited in both expertise and number. Local law enforcement agencies were stretched and not likely to learn of the robberies until after the weekend.

All of which meant that unforeseen errors could not critically damage Operation Wicked Spider's ultimate mission two nights hence.

Sullivan had contingency plans in place for all potential issues that might arise.

Wicked Spider would proceed as scheduled.

The coffee finished brewing. Sullivan poured half the pot into an insulated steel mug. He screwed the top securely to hold the heat for at least an hour. He was well beyond the point in life where he was willing to drink stale or cold coffee.

He poured a smaller mug full and blew on its surface to cool it as he watched the blinking GPS signals on the map.

The five units were on the move, scheduled to be in position not later than midnight. He expected all units to arrive timely at their starting points. Flaws in personnel and tactical planning would become apparent soon enough.

The collection window was slated for one hour, between 1:15 and 2:15 a.m., local time. Residents and law enforcement should be tucked in for the night. Less chance of encountering witnesses or other trouble. The timing would also stagger the operations nicely, given the five geographical locations.

First up were Alpha Unit in Texas, Bravo Unit in Nebraska, and Charlie Unit in Oklahoma. All three were operating on Central Time.

Followed an hour later by Delta Unit in Colorado and Echo Unit in Wyoming, both on Mountain Time.

When each unit was in position, the unit leader sent a thumbs-up text. Snags or issues of any kind were communicated with a thumbs-down text.

Five handlers were watching and standing by.

Sullivan glanced down at the five burner phones on the desk, aligned A–E. All five were ready and waiting.

"Which one of you will fail first?" Sullivan murmured, cocking his head as if he could see the future.

All five units were strong enough to meet minimum standards. Unanticipated mishaps and how they handled them would separate the losers from those who would advance to the second round.

Satisfied with the setup, he had time to eat a bite before the action started. He walked into the kitchen in search of the refrigerator where he'd stashed reheatable meals. He popped frozen lasagna into the microwave and pushed the start button.

As he waited for his meal to heat, his mind turned to Reacher.

He'd had little time to appreciate the impact of Reacher's death, but he was very pleased with the progress so far.

When Operation Wicked Spider was completed, and his war chest replenished, he would turn his attention to Charles Cooper's thwarted plans for Reacher.

CHAPTER TWENTY-TWO

Saturday, May 21
Stockton, Oklahoma
12:11 a.m. (CDT)

ON THE WAY BACK, Doug and Moe drove through a burger joint and picked up bags of burgers and fries. The van smelled like a grease pit, but it couldn't be helped. They needed food and they were running late.

This was where the rubber met the road.

The one-hour window to complete the job was ironclad. Doug's team simply could not fail. He'd worked too hard and too long for this chance. He'd do the job alone if he had to.

Doug had texted Ray and Petey with instructions. At this point, they were both dispensable. They should have the sense to know as much.

The windows on both floors of the motel were dark. If anyone were still awake watching late-night television or something, they weren't looking out at the parking lot.

Moe squelched the headlights as he turned into the driveway

and parked at the end of the row of motel rooms in the same spot as before.

Ray and Petey hustled outside and hurried along the sidewalk. They carried everything the four had taken into their rooms, along with plastic trash bags.

Petey opened the back of the cargo hold and entered first. He tossed two backpacks and a trash bag aside and bent at the waist to clear the low ceiling as he moved to the front. He plopped down on a hard wooden box behind Moe.

There were no windows in the back of the van. Petey wouldn't be able to see out the front window because he was seated too low. The box was hard and uncomfortable, too.

But he'd better not complain. It was his own fault that they didn't have the van with the comfortable chairs. He could damned well suck it up. One more bit of trouble from Petey Burns and he was done.

"You left nothing behind in there, right?" Doug said. "Cleaned up all four rooms like I said?"

"Right," Petey replied, passing two food bags to Doug and Moe. He kept one and placed the fourth near the box behind Doug. "We even brought the trash with us."

Doug nodded. With two men dead already, they were forced to work out of this crap van, and they hadn't even made it to Stockton. He was struggling to contain his anger.

Killing Reacher back in Gaucho because of Petey was okay.

Patton seemed okay with it. So Doug was okay with it.

Reacher was nobody, had nobody.

There would be no blowback on Doug.

But Patton would have been livid about the pizza kid.

If he'd known about the pizza kid.

Which he didn't.

With luck, he'd never know.

The pizza kid was one thousand percent Petey's fault. Doug couldn't deal with that now, but he wouldn't forget about it, either.

After the weekend, Doug would have plenty of time to deal with Petey Burns.

Ray jumped into the van, pulled the back door closed, locked it, and made his way to the box behind Doug's seat. Moe drove out to the road and traveled about a mile in the darkness before turning on the headlights.

"Where's the other van?" Ray asked minutes later.

"We had to make a change," Doug replied as Moe drove out of the motel lot.

"Why? The plan was to keep that van until we got to Missouri." Ray paused with his food bag half open. He was already annoyed and short-tempered and just generally disagreeable.

It seemed to be his natural state since Petey Burns had joined the unit.

Doug was tired of Ray's attitude. He wiped a palm across his face. "Just do your job, Ray. Let me worry about everything else."

Ray shot a glare toward Petey as if he knew the unexpected changes had something to do with Burns. Which they did.

But Doug wouldn't discuss any of that. The less Ray and Moe knew about the dead pizza kid, the better.

"Isn't the genius car thief here supposed to be driving?" Ray snarled, jerking his thumb in Petey's direction as he drew air from the bottom of the empty soda cup through a straw. The noise was unnaturally loud in the quiet darkness.

"Give it a rest, will you, Ray?" Petey leaned his head back

against the cold steel and closed his eyes. "We've got more important things to think about."

Moe drove along the side streets until he reached the county road and turned north toward Stockton. The town was thirty miles northeast along the two-lane road. Without street lights or the moon shining through the clouds tonight, the van's high beam headlights shot straight ahead into the dark, flat distance.

Petey said, "Watch out for wildlife. Night like this, they're likely to be on the road."

Ray sneered. "You're worried about roadkill now?"

"I'm worried about damage to the van that could keep us from finishing the job," Petey said wearily.

"Let's go over this one more time." Doug's patience with both of them was exhausted.

Whatever Ray's problem with Petey was, he had no time to deal with it. He'd worked too long to get to this point. He wouldn't allow either of them to screw things up now.

The always reliable Moe said, "We drive into Stockton. The bank is downtown, at the corner of First and Main. We've all seen the maps and the photos and the videos. We know where we're going, right?"

"Yeah," Petey said.

"Got it," Ray said.

"We have a one-hour window to hit the ATM. The code has been programmed to release the money between one-fifteen and two-fifteen a.m. Before or after that, we're screwed," Doug said.

"Got it," Ray said again, this time for all three of them.

"The big thing is not to be seen. Get in, get the money, get out, and move on. We don't want to deal with any witnesses.

Ideally, no one will notice the theft until Monday morning, after it's all done." Doug nodded, although they couldn't see him in the dark cabin.

"Understood," Moe said.

Ray said, "At this hour, Stockton's downtown should be buttoned up for the night. These people are farmers. They should all be off the streets."

"But we're wearing our black ski masks and surgical gloves anyway. Even you, Petey," Moe said. "No reason to take any unnecessary chances. Somebody sees something, last thing we want is to get picked out of a lineup."

A long silence allowed them to absorb everything he'd said so far before Doug continued to review the plan. "Petey will be behind the wheel. We'll hop out with our duffel at the corner of Second and Main."

"And we'll have our weapons. Don't shoot unless you have absolutely no choice," Doug reminded them all, but his comments were aimed at Ray, who was inclined to shoot first and talk later. "We kill somebody here, and the situation will get way too hot. We'll be pulled off the Missouri job tomorrow night and the Chicago job on Sunday. Nobody wants that."

A few moments of silence was all the confirmation anyone needed.

"After Petey drops us off," Moe said, "we'll head over to the ATM. When we get there, Ray and Doug will stay out of sight while I deal with the security cameras. Then I'll move out, and Doug will enter the code on the keypad, precisely within our time window."

"And the money will spit itself out. All we have to do is catch it," Ray said, amusement in his voice. "Two hundred thousand dollars in twenties. Ten thousand single bills, stacking up in the tray, waiting to be picked up. Easy as sweeping crumbs off a table."

"After we secure the cash in the duffels, we get out of there," Doug said. "And make sure you don't drop anything, not even a gum wrapper. Forensics are way too sophisticated these days. That's how those money mules got caught in Taiwan. One of the guys dropped a bank card and they traced the whole unit from that."

Petey said. "I'll drive the van around the block and pick you up right on time. I'll be at the corner of Third and Main."

"That's exactly right." Doug nodded again. "Remember, this is a practice run. It'll be the easiest of the three jobs we're doing over the weekend. The whole thing sounds simple. And it should be. But keep alert. Something could always go wrong."

"When you guys get back in the van, we head for Missouri. I've got the route memorized," Petey said.

They rode a few more miles in silence.

Doug finished his food and crumpled the bag. The wrappers were crawling with his DNA, so he couldn't toss anything out the window. He dropped the bag on the floor instead.

"The idea is to keep this thing under the radar. What about the other ATMs getting hit tonight?" Ray asked.

"Five units. Five states. Five small towns. Five different banks. Five ATMs," Doug said, although they knew the answers already. Repetition and reinforcement. "Makes it less likely that anybody will figure out the jobs are connected before Monday morning."

He'd endured plenty of training over the years. It seemed like his time in the army was nothing but drills and exercises. He had a healthy respect for repetition and reinforcement. Practice, ingrained muscle memory, and rote responses could save their asses if something unexpected occurred.

Which it would. Something always went wrong.

This mission had already zigged sideways too many times to suit Doug.

Ten miles from Stockton, Doug pointed two fingers toward a stand of trees ahead on the right. Moe suppressed the headlights, slowed, and pulled the van over on the shoulder of the road, coming to rest under cover of the leaf canopy.

The night was black as pitch. They'd passed no light poles for miles. Nor had they encountered any vehicle traffic since they left the motel.

None of which was a coincidence or luck. Patton had planned the operation down to minute details. Scheduling the robberies over the weekend under a dark sky was only one element of his careful planning.

"Petey, you're up," Moe said as he slid the transmission into park, opened the door, and stepped out onto the shoulder to take a leak.

Petey crabbed between the seats, winced at the pain in his ribs, and slipped nervously into the driver's position. He fidgeted with the mirrors and the seat and fastened and adjusted his seatbelt.

Doug's internal warning system lit up. What the hell was wrong with this guy?

Moe climbed into the back of the van and settled on the box behind Petey, who pulled onto the road and continued toward downtown Stockton.

Immediately, the vibe inside the van changed. Petey had both hands on the wheel, thumbs pounding out some sort of rhythm in his head or something. His left leg was bouncing like a jackhammer.

"Knock it off!" Doug yelled. Petey had more annoying habits than his last mother-in-law.

"Sorry," Petey replied. He shut down the percussion show and focused intently on the driving.

A few minutes later, an oversized road sign on the right welcomed them to Stockton, Oklahoma. All-American City 1978. Home of the Wildcats. Population 8,487.

Doug checked his watch against the digital clock on his phone. He relaxed slightly when he saw they were running on schedule.

Petey slowed for the intersection ahead. The county road and Main Street, a four-way stop with a blinking light.

Petey had the red light, which meant he should stop before turning right onto Main Street. But there was no traffic, so he rolled through the intersection.

He accelerated to the speed limit, rounded the first bend, and immediately lifted his foot off the accelerator.

Doug stared straight ahead, unwilling to believe his own eyes.

CHAPTER TWENTY-THREE

Saturday, May 21
Stockton, Oklahoma
12:51 a.m. (CDT)

"WHAT THE HELL?" DOUG exclaimed.

The first thing he noticed were the barricades blocking the road a hundred yards ahead. The second thing were the blinding lights set back off the shoulders illuminating the gaping hole in the road like it was high noon.

He peered through the van's dirty windshield. From this point all the way toward downtown Stockton, the road was closed.

Heavy construction equipment and workers dressed in reflective gear, wearing helmets, surrounded the repaving job on all sides. They looked like brightly attired beetles, buzzing to and fro.

Doug had worked road construction from time to time. He was very familiar with the seven-step process for asphalt pavement installation. Looked like these Okies were doing all seven steps at once, playing beat the clock by working at night, too.

It made sense they wouldn't want the only road into town out of commission any longer than necessary.

Bobcats and forklifts, front loaders, and dump trucks, were handling the demolition and removal of the old blacktop. Graders were preparing the surface and working on the subbase.

Dump trucks with steaming loads of blacktop and roller trucks were working the areas where the subbase was already in place. The surface would be compacted and smoothed. When the whole process was completed, the folks of Stockton would have jet black asphalt with a smooth and shiny finish that should last for years.

But Doug figured they wouldn't be finished for at least another two weeks. Maybe longer.

"Looks like a damned ant colony," Petey Burns murmured under his breath as he slowed the van. "Now what do we do?"

"Hell of a time to be doing road construction," Moe said from the box behind the driver's seat. "Why didn't somebody tell us this was happening?"

Ray swore from his box behind Doug's seat. "This job's been going south ever since we picked you up, Burns. Things were great before. You're some kind of bad luck curse, ain't you?"

"Let me think!" Doug yelled and pounded his fist on the dashboard. He couldn't catch a break. Was the whole damned job gonna be like this? One problem after another?

A worker wearing a reflective vest and helmet glanced up and noticed the van. He held up a flat palm.

Before he could head toward the van, Doug climbed into the back, assuming the guy couldn't see him with the van's headlights shining in his eyes.

Doug tapped Moe and Ray and gestured them to move

farther back into the dark interior. He said, "Petey, act like you're alone in the van. Just find out how you can detour around the construction. Be friendly. You don't want any trouble. And don't waste time. No chitchat."

Petey stared at the approaching worker, waiting with the engine idling.

Doug asked, "Can you handle that?"

"Yeah. 'Course," Petey said, flashing that goofy grin toward Doug in the rearview mirror. The one that Ray said made him want to punch Petey in the face. Doug was beginning to understand the urge.

"Just get the directions and go," Doug said again as he ducked further into the darkness. He crouched low, attached the silencer to his pistol, and waited.

The construction worker approached the driver's side. Petey lowered the window.

"Sorry, buddy. The road's closed. Can't get through. You'll need to go around," the guy said, shouting to be heard over the construction equipment.

"I'm headed to Missouri. Is there another way to get through Stockton traveling east?" Petey asked.

"There's an unpaved road about two miles back. Unmarked, too. Mostly used by the locals. Easy to miss in the dark. It runs parallel to this one," the guy said.

He was probably gesturing, but Doug couldn't see him well from the back of the van.

The man kept talking. "Turn around here, go back the way you came. Look for an old barn on the left and the road is about fifty yards beyond it."

Petey nodded. "I think I saw that barn. Set back from the road quite a bit, right?"

"Yeah. Slow down when you see it. Travel about five miles and you'll come to another paved road. Turn left again. That'll put you just outside Stockton, where you can turn right to pick up Main Street again and head east," the man shouted the instructions while Petey nodded.

"Sounds simple enough. Thanks," Petey said.

"No problem," the guy said, turning to walk back to the construction site.

Petey raised the window, pulled forward onto the shoulder, and turned the van around, traveling back toward Middletown Village.

Doug crabbed his way up front and plopped into the passenger seat. Moe and Ray returned to their boxes.

"The springs on this piece of junk wore out years ago," Ray complained.

Moe said nothing.

Petey flipped on the high beams and Doug watched for the old barn. The headlights cast a cone of light across the road onto both shoulders, but beyond that he saw nothing but darkness.

Doug glanced at the clock. They were cutting it close. Too close. Sweat popped out on his forehead and trickled down from his armpits. "How far have we come from the construction?"

"About a mile, give or take. Shouldn't be long now," Petey replied, both hands gripping the steering wheel as he peered out, watching for the barn. He hadn't really seen it on the way in. He'd just said that to keep the construction dude from droning on.

Doug pointed. "There it is. Slow down. We don't want to miss the turn."

Petey slowed. The headlights shone steadily ahead toward the trees and tall grass on either side of the county road.

"On the left, like he said. Looks like a break in the undergrowth," Doug said.

"I see it," Petey replied.

He slowed even more, peering ahead until he was almost right on top of the unmarked path. He turned left, wincing as the van bounced over deep ruts that might have been a trail to market once upon a time. Now, it was little more than a wide tunnel between a dark canopy of trees.

Petey gripped the steering wheel with both hands, struggling to keep the van in the ruts and out of the ditches as they crawled ahead.

"Speed it up," Doug said. "We don't have time to mess around."

Petey tightened his seat belt and accelerated.

The bouncing van made faster progress, but Doug's insides were jumbled. Every muscle in his body would ache tomorrow. For Moe and Ray, sitting on the hard boxes in the back, it would be even worse.

After much too long, they reached the paved road. Petey turned left. The van's worn old tires had survived, but Doug wasn't too sure about his internal organs.

They passed another small sign on the right welcoming them to Stockton again. Which meant they were on the right road, at least.

Doug looked at the clock again. Time was definitely of the essence here. "Speed it up. We've got twenty minutes to get into position."

Petey pushed the accelerator and covered the final two miles to Main Street in record time. He turned right, heading east.

"Moe, Ray, get ready. Approaching the drop-off point," Doug said. "ETA less than five minutes."

"Got it," Moe replied for both of them.

Downtown Stockton consisted of three blocks along Main Street. On either side of the town, according to the maps and satellite images they'd studied, the place blended into the farmland surrounding it.

The first thing Doug saw as they approached was a few wood-framed houses with neat front lawns lining the street on either side. They were set back off the sidewalk, which had started at the intersection and probably ended on the opposite side of the town. The houses were dark, the citizens of Stockton already in bed. As expected.

The shops were closed up tight, too. Weak streetlights lined the sidewalks at wide intervals. No one was hanging around anywhere that Doug could see. The entire town had indeed closed up for the night.

There was a blinking traffic light at the cross street ahead. And then one more block of Stockton before exiting the town.

"Turn right at the light. Then pull over. That'll be where we get out," Doug said, pointing. "The Stockton Bank ATM is in the middle of the block. Pick us up at the next corner, as planned."

Petey drove as instructed.

When he pulled over, Moe and Ray slid the black knit ski masks down over their faces, donned surgical gloves, grabbed their gear, and jumped out the back of the van.

Doug did the same and stepped out on the passenger side.

When the doors were closed again, Petey pulled away from the drop site.

Doug watched the van roll away for a moment before he followed Ray and Moe in the shadows along Main Street toward the ATM.

So far, so good.

CHAPTER TWENTY-FOUR

Saturday, May 21
Stockton, Oklahoma
1:32 a.m. (CDT)

RAY WAS THE LOOKOUT. He watched to be sure no witnesses or dogs or other activities interfered with the operation. He approached the Stockton Bank ATM first, staying in the shadows, ensuring the area was clear, and keeping it that way.

Moe went next to disable the video surveillance. Avoiding detection or a service call for the machine or the camera before the bank opened on Monday, was essential. Which meant he couldn't simply destroy the surveillance.

The intel Patton had provided identified two types of cameras for this particular location. Stockton Bank's ATM was selected for this test run because it employed both types.

Moe confirmed the exact location of the cameras and avoided having his image captured until he disabled them.

One camera was a standard CCTV mounted on the brick wall at the top left of the ATM. Temporarily interfering with image collection and delivery was a simple matter of standing to one side out of range of the camera's wide-angle and slathering the lens with water soluble grape jelly.

The camera would record dark, muddled, blurry images of no use to law enforcement or private security when the theft was discovered on Monday.

The second unit was an Internet Protocol video feed. The IP camera was mounted on the ATM itself. It was wirelessly connected to the internet.

IP cameras collected and transmitted better resolution images without cables, which meant reduced installation costs and headaches for the bank. They were newer technology, and businesses had become enamored with them.

The easiest way to interfere with the Stockton Bank model was to deploy the specific signal jamming device Patton had supplied.

Doug hung back until Ray was in place and Moe's work was completed. At which point, he would carry the duffel and hustle toward the ATM. He would stay in the shadows, dressed from crown to toes in black, almost invisible.

Of course, Doug was the one who knew the codes.

When Moe flashed the signal, Doug approached the ATM.

He tossed one of the duffels to Moe and hit the 6-2 keys on the keypad.

The ATM began to spit out cash. Rapidly.

The bills collected in a tray near the bottom of the ATM. Doug collected the bills and stuffed them into the duffel.

When the first duffel was full, Moe took it and handed the second duffel to Doug, who continued the process.

Ray slid up toward them, took the full duffel from Moe, and kept walking.

Moe whispered, "Across the street. Three o'clock position. We've got a guy leaning against the building. He's looking this way."

Doug glanced over briefly. He needed to focus on the money. It was spitting out faster than he could collect it and stuff it into the bag.

"I'll deal with him when we're done here," he replied.

Doug filled the second duffel and handed it off to Moe, who provided the third empty duffel.

Moe glanced around and then followed Ray toward the meeting point, where Petey would be waiting with the van.

Doug finished collecting the bills and stuffing them into the third duffel. When the ATM stopped dispensing cash, Doug zipped the duffel closed and turned toward the street.

Which was when he had a chance to deal with the witness.

But the man was no longer there.

Doug crossed the street and peered into the shadows, looking for the guy.

For a moment, Doug considered a quick manhunt. The guy couldn't have gone far.

He glanced at his watch. Emptying the ATM had taken three minutes longer than expected. He was running late and Patton wouldn't like it.

Even if the witness had seen anything, by the time he had a chance to make trouble, they could be long gone.

Doug wasted another few seconds of indecision.

Moving on to Missouri and Chicago was more important than dealing with the guy now. Besides, what would he do if he found him? Haul his ass along to the van and dump the body somewhere along the road?

All of that would take time and carried risks Doug didn't want to shoulder.

In the end, he simply hustled along the sidewalk toward the meeting point.

When Doug reached the van, he opened the passenger door and stepped inside. "Go."

Petey followed orders. The van began to put distance behind them.

"Everybody okay?" Doug asked.

"No problems on my end," Petey said.

"Good here," Ray replied from the box behind the passenger seat.

"Fine as wine," Moe said from the box behind the driver. He didn't mention the witness.

Doug pulled the ski mask off his head and peeled the gloves from his hands. He tossed the third duffel between the seats into the back of the van, grinning widely.

"Mission accomplished," he said, watching downtown Stockton recede in the side mirror as Petey put more miles between them. "On to Missouri."

Doug rummaged under the seat for one of the three specialized satellite burner phones and tore it open. He fired it up and waited for it to connect to the satellite it had been pre-programmed to sync up to.

Barely within the required time window, he sent a text to Patton containing the prearranged symbol at precisely 2:10 a.m. The text whooshed into cyberspace and flashed a "sent" message on the screen.

Doug fell back against the seat and wiped perspiration from his forehead with his sleeve. One down, two to go.

He forced concerns about the potential witness from his mind.

CHAPTER TWENTY-FIVE

Saturday, May 21
Near Fort Meade, MD
4:30 a.m. (EDT)

HUGH SULLIVAN LEANED BACK with his feet on the desk, ankles crossed, staring at the five maps on the big screen. One hand rested across his flat belly. The other held a glass of scotch whiskey, no ice, which he sipped slowly.

Four GPS signals blinked rhythmically as four units moved eastward from their first targets toward the second. They traveled back roads and avoided bigger towns.

Within the next few hours, each unit would arrive at its second preliminary destination, deliver the money collected from the first set of targets, change vehicles, and locate suitable beds to catch some rest and a meal.

Saturday night, all units would repeat the process and then move on to Chicago. Four units, four states, four targets.

Sullivan nodded, sipped, and said aloud, "Four units are making appropriate progress."

He frowned and shook his head. "Echo Unit, on the other hand…"

For more than an hour, Echo Unit's GPS signal from rural Wyoming had glowed steadily at the same location, ten miles south of the first target.

The signal alone might not have raised Sullivan's concern. The GPS could have a problem. Equipment malfunctioned from time to time, after all. It was an undeniable fact of modern life.

Unfortunately, there were other indications that it was not the GPS tech but Echo Unit itself that had failed. Sullivan shook his head. He'd planned for attrition, of course. But he'd hoped all five units would pass the first simple test.

Echo Unit did not.

The collection window had closed fifteen minutes ago.

The unit leader had sent no thumbs up or down text while the collection window was open or afterward.

Echo Unit might have aborted the mission. Or the unit could have been thwarted by unexpected interference. One could imagine multiple possibilities.

Sullivan's equipment showed that the special code he'd supplied to Echo Unit's leader had been entered on the ATM keypad at the Coyote Den Community Bank, right on time.

The unit leader had collected the $200,000 payday.

The blinking GPS signal was ten miles away from the target.

Which meant someone had the money now. Who was in possession of Sullivan's property?

What happened to Echo Unit's personnel? Were they lost? Injured? Arrested?

The only acceptable answer was that they were all dead.

Sullivan would accept a fast and tragic vehicle crash. An unanticipated explosion. Hell, even a Ninja Turtle attack would have been some kind of excuse. Something had thwarted completion of the mission.

"Too easy. No such luck," Sullivan said, sipping the whiskey and shaking his head. "Only one possible answer exists."

Echo Unit's leader was Sergeant Mick Jones. A reliable soldier, from all accounts. Until now, Jones had not been bothersome in the least. Just the opposite. Jones had been all business and all about achieving results, all the time.

Sullivan had even toyed with the idea of keeping Jones under his command after Operation Wicked Spider was completed. He'd appreciated Jones that much.

So what happened? Where was Jones? Where were his men? Where was his money?

More importantly, what the hell did they think they were doing?

Not that it mattered.

The only piece of intel that mattered immediately was Echo Unit's certain failure and how to respond to it.

Sullivan glanced at the digital clock and back to the map of Wyoming on the screen. Echo Unit's GPS signal still had not moved. No text or call came into the burner phone.

He sipped again, swished the last of the warm whiskey around in his mouth, and swallowed. He set the empty glass softly on the desk.

Each unit was assigned a handler. A capable mercenary, Echo Unit's handler was ready and waiting for Sullivan's orders.

He reached for another encrypted burner and pressed the speed dial.

A deep, gruff, raspy voice answered. "Yeah."

"You got eyes on them?" Sullivan asked.

"Yeah."

"Where are they?"

"Fifteen miles east of the target, as expected."

Sullivan inhaled deeply through his nose. Jones or one of the other three members of Echo Unit had ditched the tracker GPS unit. Perhaps they had unsuccessfully attempted to destroy it.

He shook his head.

"They've gone rogue," Sullivan said curtly. "Collect the money and destroy all evidence."

There was a long pause across more than a thousand miles of air between Wyoming and Maryland. Sullivan paused for his orders to be received and absorbed.

"To be clear," the raspy-voiced handler said, "destroy *and dispose* of Echo Unit and all equipment. What about the cash?"

Sullivan was well aware that honor, love of God, and service to the Country went only so far to motivate some men. "Send me proof before sunrise, and the money is yours. Consider it a bonus."

"The money's not traceable?" he asked, sounding slightly surprised.

"It is not," Sullivan said wearily. "When Echo Unit is gone, your part of the mission is completed. Head back to Canada and I'll send transport later. Text me when you arrive so I won't worry about you."

"Copy that. And thanks," he replied and waited for Sullivan to disconnect first.

Sullivan studied the four GPS units a while longer. Each traveled as expected. Each handler would follow his unit to the collection point. He wasn't worried about them. He'd used them all several times before.

Sullivan considered another dram of the scotch, took one last glance at the four advancing GPS signals on the big screen and left the room in search of sleep.

"Another big night tomorrow, and only four units advancing to phase two," he murmured as he settled onto the cot near the kitchen in the back.

He placed the handler's burner on his pillow where he'd be sure to hear the confirmation text when it came through.

"Which of the four units will fail next?" he wondered as he drifted off to sleep.

CHAPTER TWENTY-SIX

Saturday, May 21
Near Chicago, IL
12:15 p.m. (CDT)

KIM CLOSED HER EYES and said a quick prayer of gratitude when her plane landed at O'Hare without mishap, which was never a sure thing. She collected her bags, deplaned, and waited for Burke, who'd been seated a few rows back.

At least a dozen passengers exited the jetway before she saw him behind a woman with a toddler and an infant and shoulder bags on both shoulders. Like a slow-moving pack mule, she held up the entire queue of impatient deplaning passengers.

Kim shook her head. TSA rules governing passengers being what they were these days, no family or friends would have been allowed through security to meet the little family at the gate. Necessary travel was more peril than pleasure for everyone.

When the harried mom came into view, one of the gate agents hurried forward to assist. The mom smiled her apologies toward Burke and the other passengers, impatiently waiting behind her. After a few moments of shifting bags and kids, the agent and the mother moved out of the way. The bottle-necked jetway spewed frustrated passengers, disbursing like ants.

The entire tableau was troubling on several levels. Last night, on a call with The Boss, Burke had insisted that he was fit for work. Kim had chosen to believe him. She might have made the wrong decision.

Burke should have helped the young mom. Maybe he tried and she'd waved him off initially, but he should have insisted.

If he couldn't or wouldn't carry a toddler or extra bags fifty feet along a jetway, how reliable could he be when Kim needed him for backup?

Gaspar had warned her that Burke wasn't the partner she asked for. She'd put Gaspar's concerns down to overprotectiveness. She might have been wrong.

Absently, Kim nodded approval when she heard the gate agent on the radio calling for a golf cart to give the mom and kids a ride. They'd have had a long walk to baggage claim at O'Hare. The mom might never have made it.

As soon as he had the chance, Burke hustled through the jetway door, hurried around the little family, and took long strides toward Kim.

"Let's go," he barked, frustration oozing from his pores as he kept moving.

What the hell was he so annoyed about?

He'd tangled with Reacher and lost a few nights ago, which was not Kim's fault. If he'd stayed with her instead of running ahead to engage Reacher, he'd be fine right now.

Kim refused to trot along behind him while he stomped out his issues. "I'm detouring to the restroom. I'll meet you outside."

Burke didn't even pause. She watched his retreating back

until he blended in with the crowd on the way to baggage claim.

Ten minutes later, Kim had picked up two bottles of water and cookies. She'd have preferred black coffee, too, but she had too much to juggle already.

By the time she made her way to the lower level and outdoors, Burke had had time to collect the SUV.

She stood on the sidewalk, looking for him. Her phone vibrated several times in her pocket before she could retrieve it and pick up the call.

"I'm coming around to baggage claim to pick you up," Burke said. "Silver Toyota 4-Runner."

Less than five minutes later, she saw him. Traffic at the curb was stacked up, so she weaved between vehicles and made her way to the third travel lane where he waited.

He popped the hatch. Quickly, she stowed her bags into the cargo area and hustled around to the front passenger door, opened it, stepped onto the running board, and climbed inside.

Traffic behind the 4-Runner blasted impatient horns, urging the 4-Runner to get going.

"Keep your panties on," Burke said, eyes on the rearview mirror as he lifted his foot off the brake.

The SUV moved slowly forward while she closed the door.

"Any idea where we're going?" Burke asked as the traffic inched slowly toward the exit.

"South. Nine miles to Oak Park." Kim punched the address into the GPS and set the route guidance to start. "Estimated travel time is twenty-seven minutes. But let's find a drive-thru for coffee on the way."

"Mitchell is expecting us and the flight was late," Burke reminded her as if she didn't already know.

"So the sooner we get the coffee, the faster we'll get there."

He frowned in reply.

Burke turned right onto Illinois state highway 171 headed south, and accelerated to blend in with the slow-moving traffic.

Two miles from the airport, she pointed to a fast-food joint on the right. Burke turned in and took a spot at the end of the line without comment.

Ten minutes later, they were back on the road, two large cups of hot coffee resting in the cupholders.

"You've been an FBI field agent longer than I have," Burke said. "What do you know about Andrew Mitchell? Anything helpful?"

Kim munched on one of the cookies and sipped the coffee. "You read the same dossier I did. Andrew Mitchell was formerly assigned to counterterrorism in Kansas City. He distinguished himself there to the point where he was promoted to SAC of some specialized task force headquartered in the Chicago Field Office."

"What did he do that was so impressive?" Burke asked.

"Good question. The files are heavily redacted. Need-to-know and all that," Kim said, watching the sea of red tail lights slowing ahead. "Whatever he did, it seems to have happened in Missouri, although even that's a bit muddled."

"Missouri? I thought the only thing that ever happened in Missouri was Harry Truman," Burke joked, but a cloud had settled on his features when she mentioned the place.

"Apparently, it was seven years ago, and Reacher was involved somehow," Kim replied. The sea of tail lights slowed to a standstill. Traffic was snarled both ahead and behind them. Northbound traffic was just as stacked up.

"Cooper didn't tell you anything more specific?" Burke reached for his coffee and relaxed a bit behind the wheel.

The SUV was effectively parked at the moment.

Kim shook her head. "That's not how this works. The Boss wants us to go in with fresh eyes. He never reveals much of anything in advance. He says he doesn't want to limit the scope of our work or give us any preconceived direction."

"If you ask me, that's a crazy way to investigate anything." Burke stretched and swiped his palm over his face. "It can't be as productive as going in fully briefed."

"You'd be surprised," Kim replied. "Hunting Reacher is not a normal manhunt. You must have realized that by now."

The line of vehicles ahead had begun to move, almost imperceptibly. The GPS announced the original estimated twenty-six-minute trip was revised to forty-five minutes.

Burke said, "We'll definitely be late. Should we give Mitchell a call?"

"No need." Kim shook her head. She finished both the cookie and the coffee. "Mitchell lives here. He knows what traffic from O'Hare is like. Only once in all the years I've taken this trip have I ever made it into the city without delays. And that one time, I was on the train."

Burke scowled. "Now you tell me."

The traffic was picking up speed. He lifted his foot from the brake and the SUV moved slowly forward. The brown UPS truck three vehicles ahead turned off and Kim could finally see what had been impeding traffic.

A flock of Canada Geese waddled across the road, bringing everyone to a standstill as passengers craned their necks to see the show.

The geese had finally made it across to the opposite side of the pavement, where they stopped to peck at the grass.

"Oh, for the love of…" Burke said, exasperated. "Law

enforcement everywhere should hire geese to create roadblocks. They're a lot cheaper to operate and damned good at stopping traffic."

"Could have been worse. They might have flown into the engine of a plane," she said, suppressing the shudder that traveled through her. The catastrophe could have happened to her flight. Much smaller birds had brought down planes before.

As each vehicle passed the flock of geese, it picked up speed and beyond the bottleneck, traffic returned to normal.

The computerized female voice from the GPS advised, "Fifty-six minutes to your destination."

Burke shook his head and cleared his throat. "Back to the Missouri issue. Where, exactly, did Mitchell's star performance take place?"

Kim glanced across the console. Burke's lips were set in a hard line and he held a white-knuckled grip on the steering wheel, belying his casual tone.

He had been acting like a teenaged athlete who'd failed to score the winning touchdown. She'd let his attitude slide, but she needed him to be operating at full capacity, not pouting over past failures.

"Look, just move on. Stop obsessing about losing to Reacher. You've seen his army file. You know he was military police," Kim said. "He was also decorated six times. Silver Star, Defense Superior Service Medal, Legion of Merit, Soldier's Medal, Bronze Star, and Purple Heart."

"I've got my own distinguished military record. And I'm younger than he is, too." Burke shot a quick frown across the console. "What's your point?"

"Reacher had some of the best training in the world. He knows how to handle himself. He's not a street thug or some army washout who couldn't cut it." She paused for a deep breath and a long exhale. "So keep your wits about you at all times. Stay out of reach. Don't expect to fight the guy alone and win. It won't happen. You'll just get yourself killed."

Burke shrugged and returned his attention to the road ahead. "Let's get back to Mitchell. You asked Gaspar for intel, I'm sure. What does Mitchell know that we need to find out?"

CHAPTER TWENTY-SEVEN

Saturday, May 21
Oak Park, IL
2:20 p.m. (CDT)

KIM HEARD THE ANNOYANCE in his tone, but she didn't bother to deny that she'd asked Gaspar about Andrew Mitchell and the Missouri operation. The Boss wouldn't like her actions, either, and was listening to everything they said inside the 4-Runner.

No matter. She'd accepted his routine eavesdropping when he wasn't likely to learn anything she didn't want him to know. The Boss probably knew everything Gaspar had told her anyway.

But The Boss also expected her to uncover the evidence, not simply collect it from Gaspar. He'd made that plain more than once.

Tough.

Gaspar was the only person on this job that she trusted implicitly at the moment.

"We believe Andrew Mitchell was the Kansas City handler

for an undercover agent running an operation aimed at a white paramilitary group," Kim said. "The group was operating in the Midwest. Primarily Kansas and Missouri, but also Oklahoma, Nebraska, and Iowa."

"Do we know the undercover agent's name?"

"No," Kim replied. "We don't know the name of the target organization, either."

"Do we know anything at all?" Burke sneered.

"Not as much as I'd like, for sure." She shook her head. "The mission was accomplished, I guess. The terrorists were thwarted. Mitchell's undercover agent survived. Other people died. Reacher was involved. That's the gist of it."

Burke said nothing for a while. Then he asked, "Can we identify the dead?"

"Gaspar couldn't find a confirmed list," Kim replied, shaking her head, wondering why he'd asked. "You know how it is. When the government eliminates civilians in anti-terrorist operations, we don't like to brag about it."

"Yeah." Burke swiped a palm over his head and around the back of his neck. "Don't I know it."

Kim looked straight ahead, ignoring the coffee churning her stomach. Burke was way too curious about Mitchell's mission. Unless the ancillary facts were related to Reacher's location now, and she didn't believe they were, the whole thing was irrelevant to their assignment.

But not to Burke.

Why?

The GPS said, "One mile ahead, slight left onto Thatcher Avenue."

They traveled in silence until Burke made the turn, and Kim quipped, "So you *can* follow directions after all."

He rewarded her with another scowl. "Yeah, yeah, yeah. You nag like my ex-wife."

Kim widened her eyes. "I didn't know you had an ex-wife."

"It's in the records. You should have asked Gaspar to do a better background check on me, then," Burke said sourly.

"Guess I should have." It really bugged him that she kept Gaspar in the loop. Kim didn't know why, exactly. But she made a mental note of it.

Burke said, "My marital history isn't exactly a secret. Two wives, two divorces. No kids. You?"

"If this were a competition, you'd win. I only have one ex," she quipped in an effort to lighten his mood.

"What happened?"

She shrugged. "Married too young. Didn't last."

Burke nodded. He didn't ask anything else. He continued to drive until he stopped at a traffic light.

The GPS said, "Turn left onto North Avenue."

Burke followed the route without further conversation the rest of the way into the Village of Oak Park.

Kim had researched Oak Park while Burke was still in the hospital. It was not too far from the FBI's Chicago Field Office.

Oak Park seemed a reasonable place for a family man like Mitchell to locate his wife and two school kids. Crime rates were okay and Mitchell was, after all, a cop. He knew how to handle himself and protect his loved ones, should the need arise.

Burke turned onto the upscale residential street and parked at the curb in front of Agent Mitchell's American Foursquare style home. "Impressive neighborhood. Nice house, too."

Kim replied, "Mitchell's been with the bureau long enough to be at the top of the pay scale."

"Yeah, but his wife must have a good job, too, if they can

afford this place," Burke said. "And didn't you say they have kids in private school? That's pricey."

"Get that idea right out of your head." Kim unlatched her seatbelt and opened the door and slid her foot down to the curb. "We have absolutely no indication that Mitchell is anything other than a hardworking public servant."

"I didn't say he wasn't," Burke replied as he stepped out on the street side, casting a wide glance along the manicured lawns, landscaped gardens with stylish pavers, and ribbons of concrete sidewalks without a single crack unmarred by chalk art or graffiti.

Burke's pointed gaze seemed to say *See? I told you so. He's bent.*

Kim closed the passenger door and walked toward the front entrance. The house was painted a modern shade of gray and trimmed out in bright white. What had originally been a large front porch was now an enclosed sunroom.

Everything about the house and the neighborhood screamed upscale. After all, Oak Park had had more than its share of famous residents over the years, including the architect Frank Lloyd Wright and the writer Ernest Hemingway.

She waited for Burke to catch up and they walked to the main entrance, which was on the east side of the home. Kim waited on the sidewalk while Burke climbed seven brick steps to the covered doorway and rang the bell.

Andrew Mitchell opened the door and, standing aside, said, "Agent Burke, Agent Otto, come in. I've been expecting you."

He was dressed in khakis and a pink golf shirt. The shirt sported a polo pony, with a rider atop swinging a mallet, embroidered on the left breast where a pocket could have been.

Mitchell accurately reflected his official FBI headshot. He

had well-trimmed fair hair and a red face. Maybe he'd played nine holes of golf this morning without his sunscreen.

He looked his age, which the bureau file said was fifty-two. Not too tall. A little paunchy. Like a guy with a desk job who long ago surrendered his gym membership.

He led them across highly polished oak floors toward the back of the house. The décor was mission style. The color scheme relied heavily on woods of various finishes, rich neutral paint, and bright white accents.

"Lovely home you have, Agent Mitchell," Kim said.

"Thank you. All my wife's doing. She's a genius at homemaking. I don't know where she finds the time. She's a busy surgeon. Works long hours. But she says homemaking is a relaxing hobby," he replied as if he realized they'd been wondering about his financial status and wanted to eliminate all suspicion. "She'll be back with the kids soon. If you're still here, she'll tell you all about it. She's worse than Martha Stewart sometimes."

Kim shot a look toward Burke that said, *See? Not bent. Just better at spouse selection than either of us.*

An abundance of windows allowed the sunshine in on all four sides of the home. Most of the interior walls had been removed, creating a spacious, open floorplan but left a few walls for art or even family photographs.

When they reached the kitchen, Mitchell opened the back door and led them out to the patio. The backyard was fenced and as pleasantly appointed as the rest of the home.

"It's a warm day. We can sit out here." He gestured toward seats at a round patio table.

When they'd settled in, he said, "How can I help you?"

CHAPTER TWENTY-EIGHT

Saturday, May 21
Oak Park, IL
2:45 p.m. (CDT)

KIM TOOK THE LEAD with Mitchell. "We're with the FBI Special Personnel Task Force. We've been assigned to complete a background check on a former army officer who is being considered for a special classified assignment."

Mitchell nodded, leaned forward, and folded his hands on the table. "Yeah, my boss told me that when he set up this interview. Jack Reacher is your candidate. I doubt that I know anything that will help you."

"You met him, talked to him. You're a qualified, experienced federal agent. We want your impressions. We need to know whether Reacher's qualified for the job." Burke said, spewing the approved blather they'd been authorized to reveal.

"I have no idea what Reacher's qualifications are. I never interviewed the guy. What kind of job does the bureau want him for?" Mitchell replied, frowning as if he didn't like Burke's questions for some reason.

Kim dialed back to a level more likely to get cooperation. "We have very little information. We understand you've met Reacher and worked with him. Seven years ago. When you were posted to the Kansas City Field Office."

Mitchell narrowed his eyes and pouched his lips before he replied. "That operation happened a long time ago. It's not something I can talk about, even if I wanted to."

Kim nodded. She'd run up against this kind of stone-walling before. "The job Reacher's being considered for is, uh, delicate. We need to determine his fitness, on a variety of levels. He's been out of the army fifteen years now. We're filling in the blanks, making sure we're not hiring the wrong guy."

Mitchell pulled a cigar from a box on the table. He offered the box to Burke and Kim. They both declined. He lit the cigar and puffed on it a bit, mulling something over in his head.

Finally, he nodded. "It wasn't my operation. My role was ancillary. Reacher was a civilian and the operation was delicate. The team wanted Reacher out of the way. I drove him to a safehouse and left him there. That's all I know."

Burke said, "And you haven't seen him since?"

"Nope."

"You have no idea where he might be?" Kim asked.

Mitchell shook his head.

"Or who might know where he is?" Burke asked.

Mitchell sat back and puffed and shook his head again.

"What was that old operation about? Terrorist threats, we were told," Kim said.

Mitchell's eyes widened. "My role was to support the other

agents. Like I said, I didn't really see any action. I'm not sure what was going on or how it all got resolved."

Burke narrowed his eyes and studied Mitchell for a couple of moments before he shook his head. "That's bullshit."

"What?" Mitchell said, holding the smoke in his cheeks.

"You got promoted to this SAC job based on what happened back then. Terrorists were thwarted, sure. But people died. Good people. Then the FBI buried the whole thing and kicked you upstairs." Burke stabbed his index finger toward Mitchell with every accusatory word. "You absolutely know what the operation was about. You were involved in it up to your eyeballs. Stop jerking us around."

"Sounds like you know plenty about it already." Mitchell seemed unmoved. He puffed out a few perfectly formed smoke rings while he thought about it. "Suppose you tell me why you're asking, Burke. The truth this time. Not that crap you already tried to feed me. Why do you care so much, huh?"

Burke gave him a pugnacious stare and Mitchell returned it in equal measure. Neither one backed down.

"Okay, look. We're all on the same side here." Kim had grown tired of the contest.

But Mitchell's question was a good one. She filed it away with all the other unanswered questions she had about Burke. Questions she intended to get answered as soon as she had the chance.

"Nobody's trying to jam anybody up. We're looking for intel on Reacher," Kim continued. "You say you don't have any. Our boss believes otherwise. We can't leave here until we get whatever you know."

Nobody blinked.

She tried another, more formal approach. "Agent Mitchell,

you said you took Reacher to a safe house and left him there. Where was this safe house?"

"It was a secure location. That's all I can say."

"Is it still there?"

"Probably. I'm not sure. I haven't worked out there in the field for seven years. Ask the locals."

"We will, and we'll tell them you sent us. One way or another, we'll find the truth." Burke said angrily.

Kim shook her head. "And you're saying now that you deposited Reacher and never saw him or heard anything about him again."

Mitchell said nothing.

"Here's the thing. I've been on this Reacher assignment for seven months. Every single time I've been sent to interview a witness like you, the witness knows way more than they admit," Kim said. "Why should I believe you're telling us the whole truth?"

Mitchell shrugged. "Always a first time for everything."

A few moments passed, but he didn't volunteer anything else.

"This is a nice house, Mitchell. Nice neighborhood. We're told you've got a nice family to go with it all," Burke said, shaking his head. "What I don't get is why you want to jeopardize all of this by lying to us about Reacher."

"Yeah, well, when you figure it out, let me know," Mitchell replied.

"We'll put your responses into our report. Don't be surprised if someone else comes around to follow up." Kim pushed her chair back. "We're wasting our time here, Burke. Let's go."

Mitchell said, "There is one thing you might try while you're here if you're seriously looking for intel on Reacher."

"Yeah? What's that?" Burke said, still hostile.

"After the Midwest operation concluded, I was curious about Reacher. I pulled up his files and made a few calls," Mitchell said.

"And what did you learn that might be useful to us?" Kim asked.

"Reacher had a sergeant he particularly liked back when he was running the Army's 110th Special Operations Unit. Her name was Frances Neagley," Mitchell said as if they might not know the basic information even a newbie would have sussed out if given a chance.

He should have assumed that Reacher's army files had been provided and thoroughly reviewed.

"You're wasting our time." Kim stood, prepared to leave.

"Here's the thing," Mitchell continued. "Neagley lives and works in Chicago. Her office is downtown. Her home is out in Lake Forest. She'd be able to tell you a lot more about Reacher than I can."

"Now you think we don't know how to do our jobs or read," Kim said, shaking her head. "I'll mention that in my report, too."

She left the patio and stalked along the side drive to the street. Burke hung back and then followed a few moments later. She was getting tired of Burke's macho posturing.

When they were seated in the 4-Runner again, Kim said, "You want to tell me what your actions back there were about?"

Burke fastened his seatbelt and started the engine. "That guy's a liar. I told him we knew he was lying, and the bosses wouldn't be happy about his non-cooperation."

"I suppose you wanted to put him under the lights and hit him with a rubber hose?" Kim replied with a cheeky grin.

"Sounds like a good start," Burke snarled as he pulled the

SUV away from the curb. "Some people require stronger motivation than others."

"Why do you care so much about Mitchell all of a sudden?" Kim asked. "Everybody lies. Especially where Reacher is concerned. Mitchell was more forthcoming than most of the witnesses I've interviewed on this case. He did offer up Neagley as a substitute."

"He's supposed to be on our side. Yet, he only confirmed what we already knew. He didn't give us one lead or fill in any of the blanks. We all know he could have been a lot more forthcoming." Burke gave her a dark scowl. "Now what?"

"If Reacher is in Chicago, and The Boss believes he is, then Mitchell's right that Frances Neagley might know where to find him." Reluctantly, Kim paused before she added, "We'll go ask her."

"Who the hell is Frances Neagley?" Burke said. "Former girlfriend?"

"So Mitchell was right about you, at least. You didn't read Reacher's army files, did you?"

Burke gave her a frown in response. "Cooper didn't give me Reacher's army files. I didn't get much of any files at all."

"And you didn't ask," Kim said.

"When, exactly, would I have had the time?" Burke shot back.

Kim shook her head, wondering how much background investigation Burke had completed and why he hadn't done more.

Maybe Gaspar was right about him. Maybe he wasn't the right partner for her. Full intel was absolutely essential here. Burke didn't even try to dig deeper to educate himself. Ignorance of all things Reacher was a dangerous way to proceed.

"Neagley was definitely not Reacher's girlfriend. Back then or now. Reasonable guess. But no," Kim said, taking a deep breath. "Not in the normal sense, anyway."

"I'm starting to get that nothing is ever normal with Reacher," Burke replied wearily. "So where do we find her?"

Kim smirked. "Finding Neagley isn't the problem. The trick is to get her to help us and survive the effort. Neagley is seriously scary. Even Reacher is a little afraid of her."

"Reacher? Afraid of a woman? Have you ever seen the guy? You can't be serious." Burke threw back his head and roared.

When he finally stopped laughing, Kim said flatly, "I'm serious as a heart attack."

CHAPTER TWENTY-NINE

Saturday, May 21
Chicago, IL
3:45 p.m. (CDT)

BURKE GAVE HER A side-eye and a grin. "So you've tangled with Frances Neagley before. Sounds like it didn't go well."

"Give that man a cigar," Kim replied sourly.

Her encounters with Neagley had started bad, moved to catastrophic levels more than twice, and ended up somewhere that might be described as an uneasy truce.

In short, Kim would have been just fine staying out of Neagley's way indefinitely.

She believed Neagley felt the same.

Sticking her head back into that particular lion's mouth was not something Kim was keen to repeat.

Yet, Mitchell was right, too. If Reacher was in Chicago, Neagley could know where to find him.

Or at least, she could know *how* to find him. Which might be even better.

Kim would prefer to find Reacher on her own terms instead of slamming up against him without warning. Neagley could help with that.

The question was whether she wanted to do it or not. Because there was no forcing Neagley to do anything.

Burke interrupted her thoughts. "It's still Saturday afternoon. Where do we find Neagley on the weekend? Home?"

"She probably works pretty much around the clock," Kim said, slipping her sunglasses on to block the late afternoon glare and Burke's pointed gaze. "Let's try her office first. She's probably there if she's not traveling on business. And her office is closer."

"She's got no family? No hobbies? Nothing but work to keep her occupied?" Burke asked from behind his own dark glasses.

Kim nodded. "Last I heard, anyway."

She pulled out her phone and found Neagley's office address and punched it into the GPS. "Looks like a twenty-seven-minute drive along Interstate 280. Depending on traffic."

Burke followed the route guidance through Oak Park to I-280 and took the southbound entrance ramp. Traffic was moving along about forty miles an hour, which was slow but tolerable. He moved into the center lane, sliding into a spot between two SUVs similar in size to the 4-Runner.

"So tell me about Neagley," Burke said, once he was comfortable with their position of travel. "And how'd you get her personnel file, anyway?"

"I'm resourceful," Kim replied.

Burke nodded and didn't press the issue. "How long was she in the army? Couldn't have been too long, given she never advanced beyond the rank of sergeant."

"Actually, she refused Officer Candidate School. Four times."

Burke's eyebrows shot up above his sunglass frames. "That's weird. My experience is that most soldiers want command. It's one of the only ways to get paid a living wage in that job. She doesn't like money?"

"Ask me that after you see where she lives," Kim replied easily. "More relevant to us is that ten of her years were spent in close proximity to Reacher."

"Which means she probably knows him better than his own mother," Burke mused. "Has he had any other relationship that lasted ten years?"

"He was in the army for thirteen. But I guess you're asking about personal relationships," Kim cocked her head, trying to think of one. "He left home at eighteen for West Point. His older brother left home first. His dad was a Marine, deployed a lot, not home much. So I guess he had more than thirteen years with his brother and eighteen with his mother."

Burke grinned. "Which means Neagley is the longest personal *adult* relationship Reacher's ever had."

"I'd say that's a safe bet," Kim replied. "Although he's been out of the army for fifteen years, so it's possible there's been someone else. But we haven't found any evidence of that."

"You said Neagley wasn't his girlfriend. So she was like a sister or a pal?"

"Something like that. They were definitely friends. They served together in the same department as military cops. He was a mentor to her. She was a worthy partner," Kim said, thinking about her close business relationship with the Boss. "Those bonds can be stronger than blood or romance."

Charles Cooper had recruited Kim to the FBI and nurtured

her career for a long time. He'd been a mentor and, she'd thought, a friend. When he gave her the Reacher assignment, she'd been flattered. The job was a stretch for her, and they both knew it.

The assignment carried the potential for a leap up the career ladder, too. She'd thought she was being groomed for promotion.

Not until much later did she realize she was actually cannon fodder. Totally expendable. It also turned out, the relationship with Cooper she'd cherished had been a figment of her imagination. Complete fiction.

Whenever she thought about Cooper now, she felt stupid. And angry. So she tried not to dwell on him at all. Which was harder than it should have been.

"So why did Neagley leave the army?" Burke asked, interrupting her thoughts.

"Good question. There's no real answer to that in the files," Kim replied. "I suspect it's because Reacher left, so she didn't find the army worthy of her talents anymore. If you get the chance, you can ask her."

The traffic ahead slowed as they approached downtown. Burke cocked his head. "Okay. I'll bite. Why did Reacher leave the army after thirteen years? Seems like an odd time to muster out. At that point, most guys would have stayed for the full twenty. There's a story there."

"Reacher was honorably discharged, but you're right. There was something hinky about the situation," Kim replied, watching the crawling traffic. "The subtext I read between the lines?"

"Yeah, let's have that."

"He was asked to leave. Promised a carrot if he left. Threatened with severe discipline if he refused."

Burke snorted. "Why does that not surprise me."

Kim clamped her jaw to hold back the retort she wanted to make. She'd almost said, "Takes one to know one."

Burke had his own bad job history to worry about. Gaspar had dug up and shared the truth. She'd kept quiet because she didn't see any reason to humiliate her partner.

At some point, Burke would realize she knew about the sexual harassment and assault complaints that had forced him from the Hostage Rescue Team and almost got him fired.

That conversation would be beyond uncomfortable. She wasn't looking forward to the moment.

"Neagley was an attractive young woman. She had more than her share of guys trying to hit on her. She made it clear the attention was unwanted," Kim said, hoping he'd catch the warning in her tone. "Several of those guys lived to regret their bad behavior."

Burke glanced quickly toward her and then returned his eyes to the road. He cleared his throat. "What did she do to warn them off? I mean, maybe they thought she was receptive to their advances, you know?"

"Several men filed excessive force complaints against her when they ended up with busted bones and painful bruises. She was never reprimanded," Kim replied.

"Whoa," Burke said followed by a low whistle. "Her reactions to flattery and flirting sound pretty extreme."

"Effective, though. Word got around, and men stopped touching her," Kim shrugged. "So don't touch her or try to, and you might be okay."

"What do you mean?"

Kim took a deep breath before she replied. "Neagley's files are littered with reports of excessive violence. She's got lighting fast reflexes. When she fights, she wins. You'll want to keep that in mind."

"Sounds like you've had some personal experience," Burke said.

Kim didn't respond.

Burke flipped the turn indicator and took the exit that led toward Neagley's State Street office.

"Good to know she's still alive and we can find her, at least," he said.

A beat passed. Two.

Kim replied, "Is it?"

CHAPTER THIRTY

Saturday, May 21
Chicago, IL
4:45 p.m. (CDT)

AN ODD SENSE OF déjà vu engulfed Kim as Burke drove along State Street. Not many people were wandering around late on a Saturday afternoon. This section of State Street consisted mainly of offices occupied by weekly workers. Few would be working now.

An SUV was pulling away from a spot along the curb in front of a coffee shop, which was closed for the weekend.

"This is a good place to park," Kim pointed.

Back in November, she and Gaspar had used a window table inside that coffee shop to stake out the entrance to Neagley's historic office building.

Kim shivered as jumbled visceral memories of that day flooded her body.

The bone-chilling cold, shots fired, Neagley's hostility, the cold cement stairwell floor where she and Gaspar lay, drugged and unconscious. Everything came rushing back all at once.

Burke pulled into the parking spot and shut down the engine. "You really think we're likely to find Neagley here now?"

"She might not be in the office. But she's a notorious workaholic. Easy enough to check," Kim said, stepping out onto the sidewalk.

She walked around to join Burke and placed a warning hand on his forearm. "Stay alert. Neagley's clientele leans toward volatile and violent. Last time we were dodging bullets."

Burke nodded, looking straight ahead. "Understood."

Kim said no more, although she was fairly certain that he understood exactly nothing about Frances Neagley.

Security was tighter than the Pentagon in Neagley's suite of offices on the tenth floor, which was built like a fortress. The entire suite was an impenetrable Faraday cage. No electronic eavesdropping of any kind was possible. It was also heavily soundproofed.

The last time Kim was here, gunshots inside Neagley's lobby were so completely muffled that she and Gaspar didn't hear them from the corridor.

Visceral memories sent a total body shiver from her toes to her hair.

They jaywalked across State Street to the entrance. The revolving door was locked. Kim pulled the heavy side door open and stepped inside the lobby.

The experience was like stepping back to the early days of the last century.

The information desk across from the entrance was manned by a bored part-timer who didn't bother to look up as they came inside and walked past him.

Only one elevator car was operating. It rested on the twelfth floor. Kim pushed the call button and waited while the car descended so slowly it seemed to defy the earth's gravitational pull.

With heavy sarcasm, Burke tapped his toe impatiently and said, "Historic restoration of ancient equipment is a wonderful thing, isn't it?"

"What's the rush?" she replied, reaching into her pocket for an antacid to settle her queasy stomach.

The elevator car arrived before the end of the decade, and the doors slowly parted.

Kim stepped inside and Burke followed. The doors closed with glacial speed and the car jerked as its motors and pulleys tried to lift the heavy old box to the tenth floor.

Just for fun, Kim checked her watch against the rate of ascent.

Kim had read that elevators in a skyscraper in China could travel forty-seven miles an hour straight up.

The Freedom Tower in New York's elevator traveled only twenty-three miles an hour, but it was optimized for the view and not the speed to reach its destination.

Neagley's elevator felt like it was traveling at the blazing fast speed of three feet per week, but it was probably ascending faster.

Kim felt sure she could win a foot race to Neagley's floor, even if she ran up ten flights of stairs in spiked heels.

"I'm gonna be five years older by the time we get where we're going," Burke complained over the noisy mechanical equipment.

Eventually, the old car reached the tenth floor and bounced a few times before it finally stopped moving.

Seconds passed before the doors began a leisurely opening slide.

When a two-foot gap was eventually achieved, Burke turned sideways and slid through. Kim followed.

They emerged twenty feet left and across the corridor from the highly polished mahogany entrance door to Neagley's offices. Once again, Kim was struck by the absolute silence in the corridor.

For Kim's ears only, Burke muttered, "Who the hell is that?"

An armed guard stood formally at his post on one side of the door. Not the same guy who'd been covering that position in November. That one had been retired Secret Service. Big, competent, controlled, confident. Not to be messed with, even though he'd had a clever, snarky sense of humor.

This one looked similar in all the ways that mattered. Neagley's choices exhibited a clear preference for the type.

Today's sentinel probably had played basketball or football in college. After that, some kind of government service where he'd been trained hard and well.

He was a foot and a half taller and outweighed her by 150 pounds at least. Brown hair, brown eyes, clean-shaven. He wore a dark suit, a starched white dress shirt, no tie, and shoes so highly polished they reflected the light.

He stood solidly at ease, hands folded in front, not acknowledging them as they approached, like a guard at Buckingham Palace or a human statue in Central Park.

Kim had guessed his age a little too young. Up close, she saw the crow's feet around his eyes and deep nasolabial folds suggesting he was closer to forty than thirty. Which meant he'd developed judgment and maturity to complement his size and training.

In short, the man was terrifying.

Burke stepped past him and reached to open the door. No

luck. The door was locked as well as guarded.

"We'd like to see Frances Neagley," Kim said to the guardian at the gate.

"Do you have an appointment?"

"We don't," Burke said reasonably. "Purely a spur-of-the-moment thing. We were in town. Wanted to stop by."

"She doesn't take walk-ins."

"She and I are old friends," Kim replied. "I'm sure she'll want to see me."

It wasn't exactly a lie. Wasn't exactly the truth, either.

"Make an appointment," he said pleasantly. "Meanwhile, give me your card. When I see her, I'll tell her you were here."

Burke pulled out his badge wallet. "FBI Special Agent William Burke. This is Special Agent Kim Otto."

He nodded but didn't offer his own name in response. The other guy had behaved the same way. Which meant Neagley had ordered her sentinels not to reveal their names.

"If she's not here, why are you manning your post?" Burke asked, slipping his badge back into his pocket.

"Just in case."

"In case of what?"

"In case things come up."

"What kind of things?" Burke asked.

"Sometimes old friends stop by without an appointment." He smirked. "You know. The usual things."

Kim said, "Just tell me whether she's here or not. So I don't waste my time driving to Lake Forest."

"Sorry."

He didn't sound at all sorry.

Burke looked like he wanted to start a fight, but Kim had been down this road before with the previous security guard.

Which was how she knew all efforts to use brute force to get past this guy would be a waste of time.

"Let's go." Kim tapped Buke on the arm to get his mind off his fomenting rage. She nodded at the guard. "Thanks for your help. I'll be sure to tell Ms. Neagley how much I appreciated your cooperation."

He gave her a real smile and a quick wink in response but said nothing more.

She walked back the way she'd come and pressed the button to wait for the ancient elevator.

She was in luck. No one had called the car since they'd first arrived.

The elevator dinged and the old doors began to separate as fast as a speeding sloth.

When the opening was wide enough, Kim realized Burke hadn't followed.

The elevator doors continued the slow slide to the fully open position, where they paused and then began to close. Burke still had plenty of time to show up before the elevator car started down.

She heard raised voices. Burke and the guard had moved from trading sarcastic jabs and quiet insults to shouts and curses. Over the noise of the wheezing and whining of the old car's hydraulics, Kim could only make out a few words.

Burke demanded to see Neagley.

The guard refused.

The argument got more heated.

"What the hell?" she murmured as she hurried back to Neagley's door.

As she rounded the corner, Burke shoved the sentinel and the guy pushed back, knocking Burke against the wall.

Burke charged forward and threw a solid punch to the guard's jaw.

The guy yelled and retaliated with a hard-fisted jab to Burke's left shoulder.

Kim dashed to break up the fight, but before she could reach them, Burke pulled a knife and slashed the guard's face.

Horrified, she knocked Burke aside and grabbed the knife before he realized her intention. Her interference derailed his rage. He looked at her after the fog of anger lifted.

"What the hell is wrong with you?" she said to Burke as she hurried over to help the guard. Blood was gushing from the cut on his forehead.

He slapped his big paw across the cut to staunch the bleeding. "I'm okay."

"Are you sure?" Kim said. "Can I call an ambulance? Take you to a doctor?"

"No. I'll be fine. We've got a first aid kit in the office," the guard replied, still wiping blood from his face. "Get him out of here before things get worse. I don't need Chicago PD here. Neagley wouldn't like that either."

Kim stood a moment longer, fighting indecision. The guard was still bleeding. But the wound was superficial. "Burke, call the elevator. I'll be right there."

Still breathing hard, Burke nodded and walked around the corner toward the elevator.

"If you change your mind, give me a call." Kim pulled out a business card and handed it to the guard. "We'll file a full report. Burke will be reprimanded, at the very least."

He took the card and slid it into his pocket. "I won't change my mind. But thanks."

She nodded. "I'll explain what happened to Neagley."

"I'd rather you didn't mention it to her, either. Just let this go," the guard replied. "But keep that guy away from here. He's a loose cannon. And watch your back."

"Thanks," she said, following behind Burke. When she reached the elevator, the doors were two feet apart.

Burke lurched and fell sideways into the car.

"What the hell?" she exclaimed.

"I asked him to open the door and let me into Neagley's office. He refused. And he was a jerk about it," Burke replied as if his behavior had been totally justified. "Things turned sour from there."

He jabbed a button to close the door half a dozen times as if it might make the old equipment move faster.

A few moments later, the doors abutted tightly and the elevator car began its slow descent.

Burke didn't look damaged. Neagley's guard took the brunt of the dispute, for sure.

"Give me back my knife," he said.

She handed it over without discussion. Neagley probably had the elevator car under surveillance. The least she could do was keep the guard's confidence. If he wanted to advise Neagley, he would.

Burke pulled his shirttail out of his belt to wipe the knife blade. He folded the knife and slipped it into his pocket.

He smoothed his hair and straightened his clothes. He didn't say more and Kim didn't press him because she already had a fairly clear picture of what had happened.

The elevator bounced and stopped on the first floor and the doors opened.

Burke stepped out and hurried around the corner, past the part-timer at the desk, and through the heavy glass door to the sidewalk.

Kim quickly followed him across the street. Burke pushed the key fob to unlock the doors on the 4-Runner.

They climbed in, belted, and he pulled away from the curb.

"How do we get to the Interstate from here?" Burke asked. "We've got to put some miles between us and those guys."

"Guys?" Kim asked. "How many?"

"No clue. And I don't want to find out. Do you?" Burke kept driving north.

"Neagley is a solid lead here, Burke. We need her to help us. So you slice up her staff? You think that's likely to motivate her? What the hell is wrong with you?" Kim asked again.

Burke picked up speed, timing the traffic lights to avoid stopping for any reason as if he thought she might jump out.

Kim fumed. But she didn't have any better ideas at the moment. Neagley was always a prickly problem with a wicked temper and a short fuse. Pissing her off was never a good plan.

While Kim wrestled with the situation, Burke continued to follow the signs to I-294 North.

In a matter of minutes, they were on the ramp, merging with northbound traffic headed out of the city toward Lake Forest, an hour's drive along the west side of Lake Michigan.

CHAPTER THIRTY-ONE

Saturday, May 21
Near Fort Meade, MD
6:30 p.m. (EDT)

HUGH SULLIVAN HAD SPENT the day revising and reworking, and rehearsing tactical plans. Planning was one thing. Execution was another. Failed attempts to eliminate Reacher had proven the old axiom.

Reacher was an exceptionally worthy adversary, which was why Cooper wanted him. And also why Sullivan couldn't allow Cooper to find Reacher alive.

Operation Wicked Spider, on the other hand, had unfolded within the margin of error.

Execution of the Friday night ATM thefts had produced a twenty-percent failure rate. As predicted.

The problem was always the same. Inadequate personnel. More specifically in this case, greedy thieves who could not be trusted.

"Human capital is inherently unreliable. Which is why you

factored in attrition," he said aloud to the empty room. "Everything within your control performed perfectly."

The first phase malware he'd installed via spear-phishing email to each of the five different community banks had functioned as expected. Once the malware was activated, the ATMs spit out the cash precisely as planned.

"Hard to believe that bank employees still fall for those phony emails, but they do," he said, shaking his head. "Humans are flawed."

Tonight's second test added another layer of complexity to the malware.

The second group of test targets was two branches of two regional banks in two new states.

Again, he confirmed that the malware was in place. On simulators, it was operating as required. Technology was far from perfect, but it was much more reliable than people.

Setting the timer to dispense the cash at ATMs outside of two branches of the same bank simultaneously required a higher level of precision.

Add to that, the electronic funds transfer, which increased the risks another two hundred percent.

Tonight's plan was to test the transfer of funds from the home office for each regional bank. The electronic transfer would take place during the collection window when the ATMs at the branches were spitting out cash.

The simultaneous transfers from two systems produced another level of complexity.

The hacker he'd paid to copy and improve upon the Carbanak software had done his job well.

The malware had developed and expanded as expected. No reason to worry.

But Sullivan was a belt and suspenders kind of guy. He liked rehearsals and redundancies.

"Who will fail tonight?" he asked, glancing up.

He fully expected to lose another unit tonight. Only three units were slated for the Chicago plan. If by some quirk of chance all four units performed well tonight, the weakest unit would be eliminated anyway.

Sullivan pulled a fifty-dollar bill from his pocket, which he would use to place his bet.

One of the computer screens on the left of his keyboard held five rows of headshots. Each row was dedicated to a single operations unit.

A total of twenty-five photos.

He'd organized the units weeks ago in order of skill and expertise while he'd identified, reviewed their backgrounds, and recruited each one.

All were men. Age ranges between thirty-five and forty-five.

No fathers or spouses or siblings or living parents. None with serious emotional ties to a significant other.

"Loose lips sink ships," he'd reminded himself over and over as he rejected better candidates who had close ties with whom they might have shared too much.

Or those who had people who cared about them. Because after Monday, only the five handlers would remain above ground. The last thing Sullivan wanted was an outraged spouse or kid making a nuisance of themselves after the dust settled.

He scanned the photos again. They were arranged in order of value to the operation.

The top row of photos displayed the members of the Alpha Unit. The first position was the handler, who was known only to Sullivan and was the most essential to the unit.

Second position was the unit leader, a military vet, who was capable of performing all unit operations. Third was the unit tech expert. Fourth was the unit security man. Fifth was the driver.

The second row depicted those positions for Bravo Unit. Third row was Charlie Unit. Delta Unit fourth. Echo fifth.

Photos for each member of Echo Unit were covered by the International No Symbol. A red circle with a diagonal line slashed across it from upper left to lower right. All five had been removed from play. Four dead and the handler released.

Which meant twenty percent of mission personnel were currently off the board.

"That's a good start," Sullivan said.

He spent the next hour checking in with the remaining four handlers, who ran surveillance for each unit in real-time. No negatives were reported from Alpha, Bravo, Charlie, or Delta units.

The replacement van for Charlie Unit had been located. The handler would deliver it to Charlie Unit and collect the first night's cash tonight.

Sullivan's motto was, Go Forward. Retreat and surrender were never on the table. Each of the handlers and unit leaders was aware of Sullivan's views on the matter.

Mistakes and failures would be eliminated during tonight's trial run. The final and much more sophisticated operation was on schedule for Chicago on Sunday night.

All systems go.

Which led his mind back to Reacher. He couldn't be allowed to screw up Operation Wicked Spider, either. Again, Sullivan wondered whether Doug had been the right man for the job.

Sullivan placed his fifty-dollar bet on the unit he expected to eliminate tonight. Of course, he'd win the bet and collect the fifty dollars regardless of which unit lost. Still, he liked to test his instincts about people, although he was rarely wrong.

He stood to stretch the kinks out of his body. He'd been sitting too long.

He glanced at the clock. "Time for dinner."

He walked into the kitchen and stuck another reheatable meal into the microwave, thinking about all the good he'd do in the world when all that money hit his bank accounts. The buying power he'd have was staggering.

He imagined the giant slot machine he'd seen in Vegas at the Four Queens Casino. It was ten feet tall and nine feet wide. He'd watched a guy win once. The payout was only fifty thousand dollars.

Way, way less than Sullivan would collect by electronic transfer from Chicago tomorrow night.

The microwave dinged. His meal was ready.

Sullivan smiled. "Winner, winner, chicken dinner."

CHAPTER THIRTY-TWO

Saturday, May 21
Lake Forest, IL
7:05 p.m. (CDT)

THE SUN WAS NEAR the horizon as Burke pulled up in front of Neagley's Lake Forest home. Kim had said very little since they'd left downtown. He'd been unusually quiet, too.

The Boss was well aware of Burke's actions. He would confirm the status of Neagley's injured security staff. Kim wanted him to do it soon. An hour ago would have been even better.

Burke turned left onto Neagley's street. Her address was two blocks ahead.

The neighborhood hadn't noticeably changed since Kim was here in November. This time, no police cruisers blocked the street and no pedestrians gawked from the sidewalks.

Huge houses were set back from the road and surrounded by at least an acre of green space. Lots of doors and roofs and huge windows and giant garages. The brick pavers alone would've cost Kim a year's pay.

230 | Diane Capri

Burke rolled the SUV to a stop alongside the curb out front of Neagley's home. He slid the transmission into PARK. He whistled. "Wow. Neagley's business must be a lot more prosperous than I thought."

The house itself was a mansion roomy enough for at least three families to reside in comfortably. It had been constructed to suit the whims of a wealthy railroad baron early in the last century.

"You wait here," Kim said, unbuckling her seat belt. "Call The Boss. Find out what happened at Neagley's office after we left. Confirm the status of the wounded."

"You'll need backup," Burke said, ignoring her orders and releasing his seat belt.

"She's probably not even home yet."

"And if she is?"

"Neagley knows me," Kim replied, without explaining the circumstances, which he had no need to know. "She won't be pleased that you attacked her security team."

"I didn't attack anyone. It was self-defense." Burke insisted, running a hand over his head in frustration.

"I doubt Neagley will see it that way," Kim replied as she opened the door and slid down to the pavement. "She's more likely to be candid if I'm alone. Call when you have intel from the Boss. Until then, wait here. Don't wander around the neighborhood. These people have armed security and surveillance everywhere."

"Yes, Boss," Burke said snidely. "Whatever you say."

Kim didn't bother with a snappy retort. No point. She *was* the boss, and she was still furious with his behavior back in Neagley's office.

He didn't have to like her orders, but he was required to follow them. He'd been a SEAL. He understood the chain of command, even if he didn't often follow the rules.

She had already started thinking about how to replace him. She wanted to give Burke a fair chance, but he was rapidly wearing out his honeymoon period.

Kim closed the door and walked to the treelined sidewalk leading to Neagley's front entrance.

Light snow was forecast for the early morning hours. She shivered when a cold breeze blew across from Lake Michigan and sliced through her clothes.

"Spring in the Midwest. Hot and cold and constantly changing," she murmured, remembering the unpredictable weather of her childhood all too well. She moved close to the front door, out of the wind, and pressed the bell. Sonorous tones sounded from inside.

The first time she'd seen Neagley's house, she'd been overwhelmed with everything about it, including the spacious open floor plan and pricey interior décor. Artwork she recognized filled the rooms, and the sheer volume of high-end stuff everywhere had seemed so unlike the practical Neagley.

Once she met Neagley, Kim suspected she had bought the house completely furnished and had simply never changed anything.

After a few moments of waiting in the cold wind, Kim pressed the bell again and wrapped her arms around her body for warmth.

When she'd waited at least five minutes, Kim returned to the SUV. Seeking warmth, she hurried inside and closed the door. She flipped the heat on and held her chilled fingers close to the vents.

"Any word from the Boss?" she asked, rubbing her hands together for the warmth of friction.

Burke shook his head. "My call went straight to voicemail. Wouldn't Neagley let you inside her house, either?"

"She's not here. Let's get some dinner," Kim said. She searched the internet for local restaurants and selected the address for a classy-looking diner nearby on McKinley.

Burke followed the GPS, parked the SUV in the restaurant lot, and headed toward the entrance. "You coming?"

"Find a quiet table where we can talk. I'll be right there."

Kim took a few minutes to move things around in the cargo compartment and retrieve her laptop bag. She checked the contents to be sure she had everything she needed before she zipped up the compartments and then followed Burke inside.

The table he'd selected was in a corner near the back. No one else was seated nearby. A waiter stood unloading a tray laden with coffee cups, water glasses, flatware, and menus.

Burke was finishing up on a phone call. By the time Kim reached the table, Burke had disconnected and the waiter had withdrawn.

"He'll be back after we've had a chance to look at the menu," Burke said as she settled into the seat facing the door.

"Great." She sipped the coffee while she set up her laptop and her secure hotspot. Within minutes, she was online, exchanging texts in a private chat with Gaspar.

"What are you doing?" Burke asked with a scowl.

"Asking Gaspar to check on Neagley's security guy," Kim said. "I want to know he's okay before I interview Neagley."

Burke scowled. "Cooper's already working on that."

"Is he?" she replied distractedly. "I thought you hadn't talked with him."

"I haven't. But we know he is. He'll check the status. That's his job."

"Okay," she said, still chatting with Gaspar online.

"What does that mean?" Burke demanded.

"It means that you sliced that guy almost two hours ago. The Boss should have already acquired the intel and shared it with us. But he hasn't," Kim said. "It's kind of clueless behavior that you still believe he will do the right thing here."

"Why wouldn't he?"

"Great question. When you figure that one out, you can enlighten me," she replied, focused on typing.

She'd outlined the issue to Gaspar briefly, including relevant data points.

Gaspar typed back that he'd begin working on Neagley's CCTV immediately. "But you know Neagley's security is tighter than the Kremlin. It may take me a while."

"I'll wait," she replied, just as the waiter walked back to take their orders.

Kim absently ordered a burger and fries without checking the menu. She paid no attention as Burke placed his order and the waiter strode off toward the kitchen.

She kept one eye on the laptop's screen, waiting for a response from Gaspar as she asked Burke. "Who were you talking to when I walked in?"

"What?"

"You were finishing a call when I came inside. Not The Boss, you said. So who was it?"

CHAPTER THIRTY-THREE

Saturday, May 21
Lake Forest, IL
8:35 p.m. (CDT)

BURKE PAUSED A SECOND too long to come up with the lie. "I called my mother. It's her birthday."

Kim nodded. "So you weren't reporting to Cooper behind my back?"

"Why would I do that? He's made it abundantly clear that he doesn't want to hear from me," Burke scowled and gulped the coffee, which was way too hot to gulp.

His eyes widened as the hot liquid burned his mouth. He grabbed the ice water and swallowed half the glass to squelch the heat.

"Tell me why you attacked Neagley's security man," she said after he'd solved his hot coffee problem.

"I told you. Repeatedly," Burke insisted, his gaze steady on hers. "I didn't attack him. He came at me. I hit him and he doubled down. I was trying to slow him down so I could get out of his way. That's it. End of story."

"And when Gaspar comes up with the security footage, the video will back you up?"

Burke frowned. "I guess we'll see."

"And you're sure he made the first move?" Kim asked, cocking her head.

Burke dropped his gaze to the coffee and raised the water glass instead. He was stalling.

Kim said, "Because I've gotta tell you, I've never met that guy before today. But he didn't seem like the sort who would attack you for no reason."

Burke's chin jutted forward and his eyes blazed. "And I do seem like that kind of guy, is that what you're saying?"

Kim shook her head slowly. "Not exactly."

"Well, what are you saying? *Exactly.*" Burke demanded as if she might fold under the weight of his anger.

"You're quick to take offense. Too quick. And it leads you down paths that are not effective. Sometimes even destructive. To the mission," Kim replied, watching him carefully.

She needed to get a solid understanding of Burke's reliability. Her work required a strong partner—ideally, one with both physical and mental strength, as well as loyalty and trustworthiness.

Burke had repeatedly fallen short on the measures she prized most.

Was he loyal to her? Could she trust him? He said he wasn't reporting to Cooper behind her back, but she'd caught him on a private phone call twice now.

Which didn't necessarily mean anything.

Unless it did.

He stared at her but said nothing.

"Let's be clear," Kim said. "This is not a combat mission.

We're not trying to seek and destroy an enemy. I've read your file. You're great at that sort of deployment."

"Well, gee, thanks," he replied with heavy sarcasm.

Kim was undeterred. "But this is not that."

"No? Seems like there's been plenty of both offense and defense needed since I came on board. You disagree?" Burke shot back as if they were fencing where the basic tools were thrust and parry. He seemed incapable of finesse on any level.

The waiter returned with their food, interrupting the conversation.

She glanced at the laptop screen. Gaspar had not replied. She closed the lid and set the laptop aside to make room for her plate. The waiter refilled the coffee and the water, took his tray, and left.

"Let's try this again." Kim stared across the table, not touching her food. "Tell me what happened with Neagley's security man. Keep in mind that I know Neagley. And I know what kind of personnel she employs."

"So what?"

"So no bullshit this time."

"Don't overcomplicate it. I told him I was going inside the office. I reached for the doorknob. He didn't try to stop me. He probably thought the door was locked like it had been when you were there. I think we were both surprised that the knob turned." Burke said as if he'd relived the sequence of events in his head several times since the incident happened. He probably had. "I pushed the door open."

Kim nodded, listening closely.

"That's when the guy stepped in to block me. He gave me a hard push with his forearm, attempting to shove me away from the entrance." Burke paused, maybe trying to settle the action in his mind. "I threw a punch to his jaw, and he barely flinched. No way I could have bested him in close quarters combat. He had fifty pounds on me, even if I were in top condition. Which I'm not, as we both know. Thanks to Reacher."

"Go on," Kim said, nodding.

"He hit me back. A hard jab to my shoulder. It knocked me back a couple steps. My instincts and training kicked in." Burke took a deep breath. "I grabbed my knife, reached up, and slashed him laterally across the forehead, about an inch above his eyebrows. A sheet of blood gushed down, blinding him for long enough to let me get out of his reach."

"An odd choice under the circumstances," Kim said, head cocked. "They don't teach us that move at Quantico because it only stops the guy for a few seconds at best."

"Yes, it's an old knife fighting trick. Unnecessary. Flamboyant, even. Won't kill him or even maim him much. The blood temporarily blinds him. That's all. But it buys time," Burke took a breath. "I intended to use the time to slip into Neagley's office, since I had the door open."

Kim nodded, cocked her head, thinking about it. The situation could have happened that way. Possibly.

He looked at her like she should have agreed with him already, and he was none too happy that she hadn't.

Burke said snidely, "You heard the part where I had my hands full? Knife in my hand, fighting off a guy twice my size and way healthier than me? While my partner was standing around twiddling her thumbs, I might add?"

Kim ignored the snark as she dipped a french fry in mustard and munched on it. She took a bite of the burger and chewed it thoughtfully as if he'd asked her a real question.

Burke fell on his food like a hungry wolf.

They ate in silence until Kim's laptop dinged.

Gaspar. She wiped the mustard off her fingers with the paper napkin, lifted the laptop from the chair, and opened it. His message was cheeky.

"No record of casualties at Neagley's office today at area hospitals or local PD. Security tighter than ever. Called her to get a copy of the footage. Response was terse. Told me where I could go." He'd included a winking face emoji at the end to show he was joking. "I'll write again from my new digs in hell."

Kim grinned and shook her head. She typed back, "Did she share anything useful?"

He replied. "She invited you to her home for coffee tomorrow morning. She'll show you the video of Burke's fight with the guard. In exchange for which she wants ten minutes alone in a room with Burke."

Gaspar was kidding. Probably. In ten minutes, Neagley could do more damage to Burke than her goons could do in a week. Kim shuddered.

She typed, "Meanwhile, any intel on Petey Burns?"

"Sent you a file. Located the van leaving Delgado's Bar. Traced to Oklahoma. Van was unoccupied, sanitized, and abandoned," Gaspar said. "Locals still working."

She replied, "Reacher?"

"Delgado's truck sighted. Heading east through Oklahoma and toward Chicago. Still checking."

Kim closed the laptop and returned her attention to the food. The french fries were almost cold. She loved fries, but only if they were fresh and hot. Her stomach growled and she considered placing another order.

Burke had finished his meal. He pushed the plate aside. "What's the plan now? Go back to Neagley's place?"

"Find a place to sleep. Appointment with Neagley tomorrow morning," Kim replied.

Burke grabbed the bill from the table as they walked toward the cashier at the exit.

Kim carried her laptop bag out to the SUV and tossed it into the cargo hold while Burke started the engine and turned on the heat.

CHAPTER THIRTY-FOUR

Saturday, May 21
Matilda, MO
9:45 p.m. (CDT)

A SHARP RAP ON the motel room door jarred Doug XYZ from exhausted slumber. He stretched, opened his eyes, and took a quick, reassuring look at his sleeping partner.

He'd put the three duffels full of cash on the king-sized bed for safekeeping. They were still resting exactly where he'd placed them.

"Are you in there?" Moe's voice called from the other side of the door as he rapped again.

The best thing Doug could say about the drive from Oklahoma to Missouri along the back roads was that the old van had completed the trip. Moe did the best he could with the driving, but Doug's body felt like it had been tossed into a cement mixer with several bags of rocks pounding him on all sides for eight hours.

The trip had been even less pleasant for Petey and Ray, sitting on those wooden boxes in the back. Petey didn't have the balls to complain. Ray, on the other hand, did nothing but gripe the whole time.

Under different circumstances, Doug would have thrown Ray out of the van along the way. As it was, they needed Ray for muscle on the next two jobs. The only choice was to put up with him. For now.

They'd arrived at the motel on the outskirts of Matilda, Missouri, mid-afternoon. They'd stopped three times along the way for gas and food and to give their bones a rest from the jarring ride.

At each stop, they mingled with locals, listening for gossip about the five ATM robberies last night. They heard nothing at all, which eased tensions a bit.

The witness, if he'd seen anything, had not come forward to report the theft. Or, if he had, the report didn't make it through the grapevine.

Moe rapped on the door again, louder this time. Rumbling thunder in the distance amplified Moe's efforts.

Doug tossed back the covers and slid his feet to the floor. He was a cautious man. He grabbed his gun off the bedside table, walked to the door, and took a quick look through the peephole.

Moe was standing close, probably thinking the shadows would conceal him from casual witnesses.

Doug unlocked the door. Moe came inside quickly and closed it behind him. Thunder sounded again. A storm was headed this way.

"Let me get a quick shower. Ten minutes, tops, and we'll go," Doug said on his way to the bathroom.

"Okay." Moe plopped onto the bedside chair and waited. He

turned on the television and ran through the channels, pausing only for local news.

While Doug got dressed, he said, "Anything worrisome?"

Moe pressed the off button. "The usual. Foreign wars, domestic violence. Yada yada yada."

Fifteen minutes after Moe's first knock on Doug's door, they were leaving the parking lot with Moe behind the wheel of the decrepit old van and the three duffels full of cash riding in the back.

"Ten miles to US 65 and head south," Doug said, swigging from a bottle of water he'd snagged from the minibar in his room.

Moe found the turn and drove along the meandering country road. They'd driven on roads exactly like this one all damned day. The pavement never really deviated and never stayed straight. Farmland on both sides stretched farther than they could see in the dark.

"We're looking for a Texaco gas station, a Lacey's food store, and a McDonald's, grouped loosely together," Doug said, repeating what Patton had told him. "Our new ride will be waiting for us in the McDonald's lot, behind the building."

"It's so damned dark out here. No light pollution at all. Electric lights from a gas station, a food store, and a fast-food joint should light up the sky from a long way off," Moe replied, swiveling his head to look through all corners of the windshield and both side windows.

Doug saw nothing but black sky and occasional lighting to the west. Last night's dark moon had evolved into a slight crescent that was almost as invisible. The storm rolling in from the west, pushing heavy clouds overhead, blocked whatever celestial glow might have otherwise existed.

Ten miles down the road, Moe stomped on the brake, throwing Doug forward. He caught the dashboard with both hands to protect his head from slamming into the windshield.

"What the hell, Moe?" Doug yelled. "You trying to give me a concussion?"

"Sorry. Spotted it too late. We passed it. They're closed up for the night," Moe said, sliding the transmission into reverse. He used the side mirrors to back up along the pavement about a hundred feet.

Doug watched as the van's headlights revealed the buildings, invisible in the dark night.

No wonder they'd missed all three. They'd been looking for the familiar lights, but there were none.

The gas station was a tangle of strange dark shapes rising up out of the ground. The grocery store was huge and angular and blended into the landscape like a hill.

With its yellow and red neon fluorescent arches turned off, the McDonald's silhouette looked like any other low rent A-frame building.

Moe found the driveway and turned into the parking lot, dodging big potholes.

"Drive around behind the building," Doug said again.

Moe, as usual, did as he was told.

When they rounded the corner, the van's headlights illuminated a large dumpster. Beyond that were two vehicles, not one.

The replacement van, which they were expecting. And a silver SUV, which was an unwelcome surprise.

What the hell?

Moe braked slowly to a stop. "Friends or enemies?"

"Dunno. Leave the transmission in gear. Get your weapon

ready." Doug grabbed his gun from the floor and settled it comfortably in his right hand. "Kill the headlights."

With his palm, Moe flattened the knob flush with the dash. The headlights went off. The old van and its occupants became just another shape in the darkness.

Doug opened the passenger door about three inches.

The blinding bright dome light turned on in the cabin, illuminating both driver and passenger. When Doug figured any friendly observer should have had enough time to see and identify them, he closed the door again.

The world shrank around them, instantly dark blue and misty once more.

Doug waited a full minute. No one approached the van. Nothing happened at all.

"Guess that SUV could belong to one of the employees. Maybe he got a ride home after work or something," Moe said, barely loud enough to be heard over the idling engine, still holding his weapon.

"Stay here. Keep the engine running. Keep quiet. Keep your gun ready," Doug said. "If anything goes wrong, don't be a hero. Get the hell out of here and just keep going. Take the money and run."

"What about Ray and Petey?" Moe said. "Should I go back and pick them up?"

Doug said, "They can take care of themselves."

Moe exhaled slowly. "Okay." He rested his gun comfortably, ready to fire.

Doug reached up and turned the dome light switch off so it wouldn't automatically illuminate a second time. He grabbed a heavy flashlight from the console. Then he opened the door again, wider this time, and stepped out into the darkness.

The wind had whipped up and a few drops of rain began to fall. Rumbling thunder and intermittent lightning in the distance warned of the approaching storm. As quietly as possible, he pushed the door and heard the latch click softly closed.

The distance from the van to the two vehicles parked bedside the dumpster was not more than fifty feet across the empty parking lot.

There was nothing between here and there he could use to cover his approach. No parked vehicles or anything else to shield him from view. The darkness alone would have to suffice until he reached the SUV on the other side of the dumpster.

Doug waited a few moments for his eyes to adjust. He remembered the night vision headsets stored with the gear in the back of the van. Too late now.

Heart pounding, blood rushing in his ears, he slipped into the darker shadows and approached the SUV first. Moe couldn't see him on this side of the dumpster.

Doug lifted the gun in his right hand and the heavy flashlight in his left. When he was positioned properly, he turned the blinding light on and shined the beam directly into the SUV's cabin.

Both front seats were unoccupied.

He kept the flashlight's full power beam shining into the SUV's cabin, moving it around to flash on the backseat and the cargo compartment. He saw no one.

To be absolutely certain, he stepped closer and checked again.

Doug turned off the flashlight and moved deeper into the darkness, behind the two vehicles.

"Anybody out here?" Doug asked, loud enough to be heard.

A sharp, hard jab to his right kidney, possibly from the butt of a rifle, knocked him off-balance and pushed him forward.

Doug doubled over, sucked in pain, twisted fast in the direction of the attack. He raised the heavy flashlight and the gun at the same time, prepared to shoot.

His assailant had slid away.

Doug couldn't see what or who had hit him.

Adrenaline raced through his body, dulling the pain while sharpening all his senses. Hearing, smell, vision. All acutely alert. None revealed the nimble fighter's location.

Without warning, a strong kick from a hard-soled boot landed behind Doug's right knee and knocked him forward to the graveled pavement.

He landed flat on his belly. He turned his head fast and the side of his face hit the ground instead of full face down. Which saved him from a severely busted nose.

His right kneecap hit the pavement with all of his weight half a moment later.

The fall knocked all air from his lungs. He struggled to breathe.

The attacker knelt on his back and grabbed both hands. He jerked the gun and the flashlight away and slipped a heavy plastic twist tie around both wrists. He snugged the wrist restraint tight, cutting painfully into Doug's flesh.

After Doug was immobilized, the attacker held Doug's head against the pavement with a strong gloved palm.

"Stay down," a gruff voice demanded. "Patton sent me for the money. Where is it?"

"Three duffels in the van," Doug said, his response muffled by his position on the pavement and continuing shortness of breath.

"Okay. Leave the money. Load up the new van with all your

gear and get the hell out of here," the voice instructed. "I'll handle the rest. You've got work to do."

"Copy that," Doug mumbled.

"No more crap from your unit. Last warning. Follow the plan. I'll be watching." The attacker gave Doug's face another strong shove into the gravel. "One more screw up and you're done. Got that?"

"Got it."

"Count to ten before you get up," he said before he rose, backed away, and blended into the darkness.

Doug waited a couple of minutes to think, allowing the adrenaline rush to subside and his breathing and heartbeat to slow again.

And to give his attacker time to slide into the shadows.

Patton wouldn't like it if Doug took the guy out tonight.

But this wasn't over. Not even close.

Doug stood and limped back to the van, hands still bound behind him.

"Moe, don't turn on the lights," Doug said, loud enough to be heard through the side glass. "I need you to cut me loose. Let's get the transfer done and get the hell out of here."

As always, Moe did as he was told.

Less than twenty minutes later, the transfer was complete and the storm had moved closer. Moe questioned nothing.

Doug, seething, replayed the entire incident in his head on the way back to the motel. He wondered whether his attacker was the same man Moe and Ray had seen last night, across from their ATM target. The witness who had simply disappeared.

It could have been the same guy. Or not. Hard to say since Doug never saw him at all.

He burned the man's voice and his size and his methods into an indelible memory.

When the Chicago job was finished, he'd find that guy again. And make him pay.

Whether Patton liked it or not.

CHAPTER THIRTY-FIVE

Saturday, May 21
Matilda, MO
11:25 p.m. (CDT)

DOUG XYZ TOOK A final walk around his motel room to be
sure he'd left nothing behind. He'd showered off the parking lot
grime and wrapped his knee, which was the best he could do for
now.

He tossed the room key on the dresser and when he left, the
door locked automatically.

Petey was behind the wheel of the replacement van with the
engine already idling smoothly. The wipers slapped slowly,
scraping intermittent rain off the windshield.

The storm was forecast to strengthen, which was okay.
Fewer potential witnesses were likely to be wandering around in
inclement weather. Should make tonight's job somewhat less
tense.

Moe and Ray were seated in the captain's chairs in the back.

All the gear had been stowed in the cargo compartment.

The van was as dark and anonymous as a nondescript vehicle could possibly get. It was also stolen, as were the front and rear Missouri license plates.

Doug had found two stolen Illinois plates in the back when he and Moe had changed vans. Orders were to switch out the plates when they crossed the state line into Illinois.

All of this meant that from now until after the Chicago job tomorrow night, transportation was sorted.

Doug opened the passenger door. He leaned heavily on his left leg as he climbed into the front passenger seat. From inside, he glanced once more around the exterior of the motel.

Was the watchdog Patton had sent to monitor his operation blended into the shadows? If so, he was better than good. Doug didn't even catch a hint of him out there.

"Everybody good to go?" Doug asked.

A chorus of affirmative words from the crew was mumbled in response.

"We're forty minutes from the target, which is on the north side of Matilda," Petey said as he reversed out of the parking space and turned toward the exit.

Doug noticed the motel rooms were dark, heavy curtains closed. The guests had turned in for the night. Only the lights from the office still emitted a soft glow.

Petey looked in the rearview mirror as if he was trying to make eye contact with Ray. "This van drives a thousand times better than the old one. Everybody should have a better ride."

If Ray was moved to forgiveness by the apology in Petey's tone, he didn't say so.

Doug shook his head. The relationship between Ray and Petey had been a problem from the start and was getting worse. Doug didn't know why and he didn't care to find out.

All they had to do was be civil to each other long enough to finish two more jobs. Afterward, the two never needed to lay eyes on each other again.

"You know where we're going, Petey?" Moe asked from the back seat.

"Yeah. I studied the maps. Go straight up US 65 and then east. Looks easy enough," Petey replied. "No traffic. Other than this storm, I don't expect any problems."

Moe was the peacemaker in the group. Doug had known and appreciated Moe for a long time. He was older, wiser, calmer. More experienced and competent. More patient, too.

Ray and Petey were the newcomers. Doug admitted to himself that he'd made two bad choices when he'd brought them on.

He wouldn't be working with them again. Not individually and definitely not together. He had zero interest in acting as a referee.

Ray's bad attitude lingered. Belligerently, he said, "Where's our money? You had the duffels in your room. Tell me you didn't leave them back there."

"We get paid at the end of the job, Ray. All or nothing. That was the deal from the start," Doug said wearily. His knee throbbed like a bastard and sharpened his retort. "The incentive for us is to do all three jobs successfully. One down, two to go."

"I know the deal," Ray replied. "What I'm asking is what happened to the money."

"We handed it over, as planned," Moe said. "When we dropped the old van and picked up this one."

"And why do we trust this guy you gave the money to?" Ray demanded.

"Just keep your eye on the prize, Ray." Doug shook his head

and sighed. He didn't intend to discuss the watchdog with Ray or anyone else. "Steady on, man. Less than twenty-four hours, we'll be done, and we'll all get paid."

"You better hope so," Ray growled. "I didn't take this job for giggles."

"Or you can walk away empty-handed now. Your choice," Doug replied evenly.

Petey swiped another glance in the rearview, but he didn't say anything, which was the smart way to go here.

They drove for a while in silence. The rain intensified, landing in thick sheets everywhere. Watching the road was like looking through an opaque plastic curtain.

Petey turned up the speed on the wiper blades to the maximum. They slapped hard back and forth, barely clearing the view with each swipe.

There was very little traffic on the road at this time of night, making the driving easier than it otherwise could have been in the storm.

Moe began to talk in an even tone, as if to soothe frayed nerves.

"Matilda, Missouri, is a bigger town than Stockton, Oklahoma, where we hit the ATM last night," Moe said. "Tonight's bank is bigger, too. A regional bank this time, not a local community one."

"Yeah. So what?" Ray challenged.

"Bigger bank, better security," Moe said reasonably. "Bigger town, greater chance that something can go off the rails."

"We're aware of the situation, Moe," Ray snarled. "How many times we gotta go over it? Petey's not all that smart, but he's just the driver. The rest of us know what the hell we're doing."

STRAIGHT JACK | 255

"Of course, we do," Moe replied evenly. "But it doesn't hurt to rehearse. If something goes wrong tonight, training and instinct will save our bacon."

Ray inhaled deeply and rapid-fired the plan in a monotone, all in one breath. "Petey drops us off and meets us at the pickup point when we're done. We approach the ATM. Moe disables the cameras and punches in the code. Doug moves into place. The machine spits out the money. Doug collects it in the duffel. Moe takes the first duffel to the van. I take the second duffel full of cash. Doug finishes up and brings the third duffel. Petey drives us off. We're done."

As if to punctuate Ray's speech, a loud thunderclap overhead jarred the silence.

Moe waited for the noise to pass. "Pretty much. But the devil's in the details. We had a witness last night and we lost him. He might have been too drunk to understand what was going on. Or he might have reported suspicious activity at the bank. Or a thousand other scenarios. We can't let that happen again."

"What would you have me do this time? Kill the guy?" Ray growled as if he'd like nothing better than to eliminate witnesses. "Or would you rather we took him hostage? Carried him around for a couple of days? Dumped his body in some river somewhere?"

"Okay, okay, okay. Knock it off." Doug rubbed the stress from the back of his neck as if he was holding on to the last of his patience. "We've got five crews hitting branches of two regional banks tonight. The chances of a screw-up somewhere along the line are five times higher than last night. So keep your wits about you. That's the point."

Doug's right kneecap was throbbing like an SOB after he'd

cracked it on the pavement. It was swollen, too. He'd had trouble pulling his jeans past it when he got dressed. He'd had plenty of broken bones in his life. He knew the kneecap was probably fractured.

And his kidney wasn't feeling all that great, either. He already had a bruise the size of a basketball. He'd swallowed a handful of Tylenol. So far, they hadn't made a dent in the pain.

He had no patience for Ray's behavior now.

But Ray wouldn't let anything go. "My job is security, Moe. I'm here to supply the muscle. You let me worry about the witnesses. You do your job. How about that?"

Moe said nothing.

They made the rest of the drive in total silence.

Silence suited Doug just fine.

Petey turned onto the county road that led into Matilda. A mile later, the roadside sign announced they'd reached the town limits.

Doug glanced at the digital clock glowing from the dashboard. As before, the ATM would spit out the cash only during a specific one-hour window. Too early or too late, and they'd get nothing.

Petey had rolled the van into the outskirts of Matilda right on time.

So far, so good.

CHAPTER THIRTY-SIX

Sunday, May 22
Matilda, MO
12:50 a.m. (CDT)

AS THEY ADVANCED, DOUG noticed a few houses spaced widely apart along both sides of the road. Closer to downtown Matilda, they passed a few businesses.

Gas stations. A scattering of fast-food places. Convenience stores.

Everything was closed up for the night, as expected. But a few lights were left burning inside here and there. Probably to deter local kids from breaking in and hanging out or trashing things. Not much excitement for a teenager in a town like Matilda, Missouri, after hours. Idle hands and all that.

The Matilda State Bank branch they wanted was on the north side of Main Street, near the center of downtown. The branch manager routinely refilled the ATM with extra cash on Saturday morning during business hours.

Local residents would have withdrawn some of the money

258 | Diane Capri

already. Intel suggested they'd have taken only about ten percent. The rest should still be there.

Which meant the haul tonight should be more than last night. Like Moe said, bigger town, bigger bank, more money.

Made sense.

"Suit up," Doug said, "Departure point three minutes out."

Moe, Ray, and Doug pulled on their black knit ski masks and latex gloves. Moe stuffed supplies into his deep pockets. Ray settled his weapons and picked up the three empty duffels.

Petey turned left at the first traffic light and then right into the alley, running along the back of the buildings on Main Street. The bank was four blocks down.

Doug said, "Ready."

At the second block, Petey rolled to a quick stop.

Doug reached up to turn off the dome light. He slid out of the passenger door, careful to land on his left leg, and closed the door quietly. He turned his collar up against the driving rain. No one was likely to be wandering around town on a night like this.

Ray and Moe exited the van from the side door.

When they were outside, Petey slow-rolled the van into a left turn and kept moving. He'd wait at the meeting point on the other side of the bank, four blocks from here. With luck and no further problems, Doug would be able to hobble that far with his fractured knee.

Moe moved ahead, careful to stay in the shadows. The rain-slicked pavement slowed his progress, but he moved steadily in the right direction.

Doug grabbed the first empty duffel from Ray, tucked it under his arm, and followed a few paces behind Moe, careful to keep his feet planted so he would not to end up on his ass.

Ray shoved his weapon into his pocket to keep it dry. He

scanned the area looking for trouble. He waited a full minute before Doug heard him moving along behind.

At the next corner, Moe stopped. Doug and Ray caught up. They hugged the shadows, flattened against the brick building under the overhang, and waited for any signs of activity.

After two minutes, Doug said quietly, "Good to go."

Moe crept across the street and ducked into the dark alley on the other side.

Doug followed.

Ray brought up the rear.

At the next corner, they stopped again to look and listen for problems. Doug heard nothing aside from the gusting rain slapping the windows. Neither Ray nor Moe raised a flag of any kind.

The Matilda State Bank's ATM was located in the middle of the next block. Doug gave the signal to move ahead.

Moe crossed the street and turned onto the sidewalk. Doug followed a few feet behind. Ray brought up the rear.

If anything went wrong, this was where it would happen.

Doug stayed in the shadows and kept alert.

The shops along Main Street were closed and there were no bars around here that might be open late on a Saturday night.

Recon intel reports said no CCTV was aimed at the sidewalk in front of the four storefronts on either side of the bank or across the street.

Traffic cams had not been installed on Main Street, either.

This was a small town in the middle of farm country where everyone knew everyone else. The violent crime rate was so low that nothing other than bar fights had been reported since one of the normally level-headed farmers went crazy and killed his neighbor's cows half a dozen years back.

All of which meant the town counsel spent the budget on snow plows and schools and parades, not cameras and cops and jail cells.

And even if the intel were wrong, the rain would interfere with cameras. Images clear enough to allow positive identification were unlikely.

Doug nodded. He didn't normally believe in divine intervention, but the weather had improved his luck tonight.

Moe crept forward to the alcove around the bank's front entrance. He quickly disabled the ATM cameras, stepped aside, and waved Doug forward.

Doug craned his neck to scan the area. He saw nothing concerning. The rain obscured everything anyway.

He slid along the side of the building and ducked into the ATM alcove, a haven from the pouring rain.

He'd memorized the code. One wrong keystroke would abort the entire operation. He repeated the sequence silently to himself and visualized pushing each button in the precise order required until he was satisfied.

Doug checked his watch again to confirm the timing. He prepared the first duffel. Not a moment too soon nor a moment too late, he punched in the code.

The ATM came to life. The machinery made several noises that went unnoticed during normal operating hours and were muffled tonight by the storm. Even if anyone were around to hear the mechanics of the operation. Which they weren't.

The ATM began to dispense crisp bills continuously into the collection tray.

Doug grabbed the cash as soon as the tray filled and stuffed the money quickly into the first duffel. Soon, the first bag was filled to capacity.

He signaled Moe, who grabbed the full bag, zipped it closed, handed Doug an empty one, and slipped away toward the pickup point with the loaded bag of cash.

Doug continued to collect the money. This ATM dispensed much faster than the older machine the night before. He could barely keep up. The second duffel was filling up quicker than expected.

If he didn't grab the bills as the collection tray filled, what would happen? Would the machine jam? Stop dispensing? Sound an alarm?

Doug forced his mind to focus on the tray and the bills and the duffel, which was getting too heavy to hold with one hand while leaning all his weight onto his left leg.

His right knee continued to throb with pain. But he'd be done here soon.

He could finish here and make it to the van unless his knee collapsed. He refused to consider falling as a real possibility.

He needed that third bag, and he needed it now.

Where the hell was Ray?

CHAPTER THIRTY-SEVEN

Sunday, May 22
Matilda, MO
1:55 a.m. (CDT)

DOUG STEPPED OUTSIDE THE alcove briefly and craned his neck in all directions. The rain and the clouds and the shadows combined to conceal everything out there.

He peered into the gloom, but nothing seemed to be moving.

A brilliant flash of lightning high above the buildings illuminated Main Street briefly but didn't reveal Ray's position.

The thunderclap that followed a few moments later sounded loud enough to wake the dead. Doug used the distraction to move onto the sidewalk briefly for a better look.

Nothing.

Ray must have found a covered recess nearby to keep out of the weather. He was angry about Petey, but he was a pro. He'd do his job. Doug could count on that much, at least.

Ray would be along shortly.

Meanwhile, Doug returned to dealing with the money.

The second duffel was filled to overflowing, and the ATM was still dispensing bills.

Doug set the duffel down by his feet, grabbed the cash from the tray, and shoved it into his pockets. He unzipped his jacket and stuffed more bills inside. Soon, he'd be forced to set the bills on the ground and take his chances with the wind and the rain.

"Come on, Ray. Where the hell are you?" Doug murmured.

"I'm here," Ray said breathlessly as he came into view and tossed the empty duffel toward Doug with one hand.

"About damned time," Doug said in reply, glancing quickly toward Ray to grab the duffel.

That was when he saw that Ray's left arm was tight around the neck of a uniformed police officer.

The ATM continued to dispense cash.

The cop was struggling to break free, and Ray tightened his grip. He could kill the guy with that choke hold. Killing a cop was a one-way ticket to a lethal injection.

Kill a cop in the course of a bank heist, and the feds would be all over Ray's ass. Moe, Petey, and Doug's, too.

"What the hell?" Doug asked, grabbing the duffel and opening it wide enough to start shoving the money inside.

Hurriedly, he emptied his pockets and his jacket and continued collecting the bills as the ATM fanned them into the tray.

Ray growled, somewhat breathlessly as he struggled with the guy, who carried about twenty extra pounds around his midsection. "Rent-a-cop, I think. Too nosey. He was shining his flashlight into every nook and cranny. Headed this way. Couldn't leave him out there."

Doug pressed his lips into a thin, hard line. "Okay," he said because there was no other possible response at the moment.

"Meet you at the van," Ray said, dragging the squirming cop along the sidewalk away from the bank, leaving the second full duffel with Doug instead of hauling it, too.

Doug had no time to deal with Ray or the cop or anything else while the cash kept spitting out of the ATM.

The window of time allotted to collect the money was closing. He had to stay focused until 2:15 when the cash flow would stop. Unless the machine ran empty and it stopped earlier.

He'd be relieved if it did.

But it didn't.

Already worrying about whether he could carry both bags on his bad knee, Doug quickly zipped the second duffel and continued filling the third.

At 2:15 a.m. precisely, the last bill landed in the collection tray. The ATM stopped making noises. The bills stopped fanning out. The collection window slammed shut.

Doug zipped the third duffel, picked up a bag in each hand, and moved along toward the meeting point in the alley two blocks away.

The wind had picked up and the driving rain pelted his body. The duffel slowed his progress. The money was heavy. The sidewalk was slick. His knee throbbed and his right kidney ached. He couldn't hurry any faster.

When he reached the end of the block, he turned left onto the side street. The downpour was shielded by the buildings and felt slightly less intense as he moved north.

His arms burned with the weight of the bags. His fractured kneecap burned with every step. The bruise on his kidney made every movement torture.

He wanted to scream with agony, but he didn't dare risk the noise. He clamped his jaw and pushed on.

At the next corner, Doug turned into the alley. Petey was there. He almost fainted with relief. Engine running, lights off, the van was parked in the shadows ahead, precisely where it should have been.

Adrenaline and anger fueled him now.

He couldn't see clearly. The sopping ski mask clung to every inch of his head and face and interfered with his ragged breathing. Cold water ran into his collar and down his back and chest.

Twenty feet before he reached the van, he heard Ray's and Moe's stifled voices. Most of the words were curses, but the substance of the argument was about the cop, crumpled on the ground.

He plodded forward until he reached his crew.

With one deep breath and the last of his strength, Doug tossed both duffel into the open side door of the van.

"Let's go," Doug said, opening the passenger door. "Now."

"Bring him or leave him?" Ray asked, pointing to the cop.

"Is he dead?" Doug asked as he struggled to step up into the cabin.

"Not yet," Ray replied.

"Get him in here, then. Fast. We're burning too much time." Doug didn't mention that Patton's spy had warned against screwups. He'd said he'd be watching. He might arrive at any moment.

Doug closed the door and slumped back in the seat.

Moe climbed into the van and heaved the duffels out of the way, leaving Ray to deal with the cop alone.

Ray stuck his head inside and commanded gruffly, "Burns. Get your ass out here and give me a hand."

Petey seemed to realize that this was not the time to complain. He put the transmission in park and scurried to assist.

Ray and Petey struggled with the unconscious man, who was dead weight at best, and brain dead from asphyxia at worst.

Moe sat quietly in his seat.

Doug ignored whatever the hell argument was going on between Ray and Moe. He'd sort it out later when they were way the hell down the road.

The last thing they needed today was Patton's man reporting this debacle back to his boss.

CHAPTER THIRTY-EIGHT

Sunday, May 22
Near Fort Meade, MD
2:55 a.m. (EDT)

JUST LIKE HE'D DONE the night before, Sullivan leaned back in his chair, feet on the desk, a glass of whiskey in his hand. He watched the second night's action on the screens as it unfolded in real-time, captured on a live video feed this time by each of the handlers.

Delta Unit had arrived late and missed half of the collection window. Gross incompetence at a regional bank in nowhere Iowa. Delta Unit had proven unreliable for the higher stakes presented by the international targets in Chicago. Sullivan had given the order to terminate all members of Delta Unit.

"It's done," the handler said when he called back to report.

Sullivan shook his head as he watched the streaming video. Four sets of dead eyes stared at the camera. "Dispose of the bodies. Take the cash with you. I'll wire your fee to the account in the Caymans tomorrow."

270 | Diane Capri

"If you need me again, you know where to find me," the handler replied before he disconnected.

Another sip of the whiskey warmed the chill from Sullivan's body as he pocketed the fifty-dollar bill. He took pleasure in being right once more.

He nodded toward two of the three remaining video feeds. He watched as Alpha Unit in Iowa and Bravo Unit in Missouri completed the thefts with skill and speed. They had worked together as smoothly as any Olympic relay team.

He murmured, "Nicely done."

The two units had provided the distraction Sullivan needed to trigger the electronic transfers. He'd moved one million dollars from each bank to separate offshore accounts. The untraceable deposits were hidden inside several layers of impenetrable corporate cover, which he'd set up before.

"All's well that ends well enough." Sullivan sipped again, nodding his head as he confirmed receipt of the test funds. Tonight's dry run had ended well enough.

Alpha Unit and Beta Unit were tonight's stars, as expected.

Two issues were still open.

Reacher remained at large.

And Charlie Unit's status was uncertain.

Sullivan rewound the feed and watched the video again, shaking his head as Charlie Unit's actions unfolded once more.

A storm had raged through the area, increasing in intensity as the evening progressed. The wind, rain, thunder, and lightning had provided natural cover. Which was uncommonly good luck.

All systems ran smoothly as the unit arrived and deployed to the various stations.

Petey positioned the departure vehicle expertly, away from streetlights, snugged into the shadows, ready to go.

Moe disabled the cameras without error and moved aside. Doug filled the first duffel easily. Moe collected the bag and hustled to the waiting van without incident.

While Doug was in the alcove with the ATM filling the second duffel, Ray waited for his signal, tucked into the alcove of a clothing shop three doors down.

Which was when the operation went off the rails.

A uniformed police officer approached along the sidewalk, emerging as a vague silhouette from the cover of the driving rain, barely visible on the video.

He approached each shop and checked the doors, confirming each was securely locked. He shined his flashlight into the windows, perhaps checking for intruders. Presumably finding none.

The cop scalloped from door to door, rain at his back, the wind pushing him forward. He moved silently, relentlessly closer to the bank. At the current pace, Doug would not finish collecting the cash before the cop discovered the theft in progress.

Perhaps Ray should have rushed toward the danger.

He didn't.

He waited.

The cop approached, his head tilted down against the driving rain. He must have seen Ray's shoes. He lifted his head as if he'd been startled.

His flashlight swept up to shine its full beam onto Ray's black ski mask.

The cop seemed stunned into stillness.

Ray acted quickly, seizing his advantage.

He stepped forward and slipped his arm around the cop's neck and squeezed. Not too hard, but hard enough.

The cop went limp against Ray's body but remained upright.

Ray reached around and lifted the cop's gun from his holster.

He said something into the cop's ear that Sullivan couldn't make out on the video.

Ray half walked and half dragged the hapless cop toward the bank. He tossed the third empty duffel toward Doug and marched the cop farther along the sidewalk's shadows to the waiting van.

When he arrived at the meeting point, Ray and Moe argued. Again, the storm covered the conversation. The video didn't capture their words.

After too long, Doug rounded the last corner and struggled to the van, carrying two duffels heavy with cash.

They pushed the cop into the van's cargo hold. They climbed into the van, Petey revved up, and headed off.

The burner phone rang. Sullivan picked up the call from Charlie Unit's handler. "Yeah."

"Orders?" his gruff voice replied.

"State your recommendation," Sullivan demanded.

A moment of silence traveled across the miles as if the handler was thinking about the options.

Which, of course, he wasn't.

Only two options existed.

Not much time was required to consider them.

He said, "Could go either way. They've got a long drive ahead. The final decision can wait an hour or so."

"Call me in an hour with your recommendation." Sullivan disconnected.

He watched the video again, shaking his head slowly, considering the alternatives.

He craved order and discipline because his world was too

often defined by chaos and anarchy. Humans were unreliable and untrustworthy by nature. *Flawed*, as human resources departments everywhere were wont to say.

Sullivan accepted that reality.

It was why he'd built redundancies and contingencies into every plan.

Losing Echo Unit the night before had not been a significant blow. Losing Delta Unit tonight was also okay. He'd assumed from the outset that he'd lose up to two of the five units due to various causes before they reached Chicago.

He'd been right.

But now he had a third unit on the bubble.

Alpha and Bravo Units were solid. Dependable.

Two reliable units in Chicago tomorrow night could be okay.

But three would be better. Especially if Reacher showed up.

Charlie Unit might still pull this off. Sullivan could keep them in the rotation.

Depending on what they did next.

As far as Charlie Unit knew, Sullivan remained unaware of the unit's current status. Every moment the unit delayed reporting mission status was a reliability problem, at best.

Once the cop was neutralized and removed from the scene, Ray should have killed him. Keeping a cop alive was a risk. A sign of weakness.

Which meant the team had a bigger problem that affected the entire mission.

How the unit responded to that threat would determine whether they advanced to Chicago or terminated in Missouri.

Were they cop killers?

Which would mean Charlie Unit would advance as planned.

Or were they not?

At this point, Reacher's status remained unknown.

And Charlie Unit's situation could go either way.

The odds were the odds.

Sullivan had no emotional attachment to the result. He pulled the fifty out of his pocket again and placed his bet.

He drummed his fingers on the desk and waited for the handler to call.

CHAPTER THIRTY-NINE

Sunday, May 22
Missouri
3:55 a.m. (EDT)

AN HOUR NORTHEAST OF Matilda, Missouri, Doug glanced at the clock on the van's dashboard. The drive to Chicago allowed plenty of time to find a place to eat, sleep, and deal with the unconscious cop in the back.

He simply had to wrap his head around the problem and figure out what to do.

Then, as the old television commercial said, just do it.

Doug's knee cap continued to shoot sharp pains up and down his leg without warning. His torso throbbed with every move. Nothing he could do would fix any of it until after Chicago. He'd reached the level of mental toughness sufficient to suppress the agony, for now.

Petey had driven out of the worst of the storm. It was still raining, and the windshield wipers slapped double time. But the thunder and lightning and the driving wind had subsided.

Whatever was going on between Petey, Moe, and Ray demanded zero tolerance. He simply didn't have the headspace to deal with their issues. Or the cop, who was sniveling on the steel floor in the back.

Conversations inside the van must be kept to a minimum, until he decided whether to kill the cop. Which, now that Doug thought about it, made the decision to kill him seem obvious.

So then it came down to how and when.

"Seven hours' drive time to Chicago, give or take, right?" Doug asked, since he no longer needed to be circumspect about his plans. It's not like the cop would ever tell anyone.

Petey nodded. "On the interstate. We should stay on the back roads, which will mean ten hours. But we're less likely to run into trouble on back roads."

Soon, the sunrise would lighten the sky. Farmers would be waking up to start the day. Businesses would open up, anticipating daily traffic.

Wherever they chose to dump the cop's body, they should do it soon.

"Moe, tell me what you know about Missouri," Doug said, expecting Moe's usual brand of mixed intel with which he frequently won trivia bets in bars.

"Two of Missouri's famous sons were Harry Truman and Mark Twain," Moe replied. "The five most dangerous animals in the state, besides humans, are snakes, black bear, coyotes, black widow spiders, and Lyme-infested ticks. You're more likely to die from a lightning strike in Missouri than about twenty-nine other states."

"What's the most common cause of death?" Ray asked.

"Same as everywhere else. Heart disease," Moe said. "Followed by cancer, lung disease, accidents, stroke, and so on."

"What about suicide?" Doug asked.

"Number ten, if memory serves."

"What kind of accidents?" Petey wanted to know.

"Mostly motor vehicle-related. By a wide margin. But also drug overdose, drowning, bad falls. Some gun crime. All the normal stuff," Moe said. "There's just not a lot of dangerous stuff in Missouri. It's a pretty safe place to live, compared to a lot of others."

"Too bad," Doug murmured. No easy way to make this look like a common traffic accident, really. And nowhere to hide the body either.

They were traveling along a two-lane county road. No oncoming traffic had passed for almost an hour. Nothing but farm land in every direction as far as the naked eye could see.

Around the next bend in the road, Doug spied an opening in the tall weeds ahead on the right. Four trees huddled together in the darkness, twenty feet from the pavement.

"Call of nature." He nudged Petey's arm. "Pull over onto the shoulder up there. That looks like a cow trail of some kind. Drive back to that stand of trees."

Petey slowed the van and rolled onto the soft shoulder. There was no ditch. The road had been built level with the natural ground.

The cow trail on the right, if that's what it was, hadn't been used in a while and was mostly obscured by weeds.

Petey braked to a stop and slid the transmission into park. "Might not be hard enough to drive along that two-track, Doug. After all this rain, we could get stuck in the mud."

Doug lowered his window and focused a flashlight beam for a better view.

"Okay. You and Moe wait here," Doug said.

He collected his gun as he stepped out onto the grassy shoulder. There was nothing but farmland for as far as the eye could see, but sound could travel farther. He grabbed the suppressor, too.

"Ray, bring your cop and come with me."

Moe and Petey said nothing.

To his credit, Ray didn't argue, for once.

Ray walked to the back of the van and pushed the door open. The cop had been sleeping. Ray grabbed him in another chokehold, jerked him off the floor, and dragged him toward the back.

The cop seemed to understand what was happening. He began to kick and flail, grabbing for anything he could reach, trying to slow Ray's progress.

Ray was stronger and had better leverage.

He pulled the cop out the back and onto the ground, keeping him off-balance and barely upright on his feet. When the cop's attempted vocalizing noises got louder, Ray gave his neck an extra squeeze between his forearm and his bicep, cutting off the poor bastard's air supply.

Doug attached the suppressor and held the gun by his side, out of sight.

He set out on the trail, holding the flashlight in front of him. The last thing he needed was to step on one of those snakes Moe mentioned. His knee objected to every uneven footfall, but he kept going.

Ray followed, pulling the desperate cop along behind. It might have been easier to kill him and then dump the body. But keeping him on his feet and helping to move his weight had seemed like a better idea.

When they reached the stand of trees, Doug aimed the

flashlight beam in the center. "Take him over there," he said. "Get him as deep into those trees as you can. If we get lucky, no one will find him for a few days."

The cop continued to struggle. He kicked, flailed, jerked his body, and dragged his heels. But none of it was enough to defeat Ray, who was bigger, stronger, and in control.

"This is about as far as we can go," Ray said from the trees, slightly out of breath from the exertion.

"Okay. Let him go and get out of the way," Doug said.

Ray released the cop and stepped aside.

Doug took aim and fired. The first shot hit Ray full in the chest. He crumpled to the ground. The cop stood open-mouthed, horrified until the second shot dropped him the same way.

Doug struggled along the grass to get a closer look at both bodies. He shined the beam into their eyes. The cop's dead stare was unmistakable. Ray's pupils reacted to the light.

Doug raised the gun and placed one shot into Ray's face. For good measure, he did the same to the cop.

He turned and hobbled along the path until he reached the van again. He waved the flashlight around the pavement to be sure nothing had fallen out in the cop's struggle. Then he closed the back doors and returned to the passenger seat.

"Let's go," he said, returning the gun to the floor near his seat.

"What about Ray?" Petey asked.

"Ray didn't make it," Doug replied.

CHAPTER FORTY

Sunday, May 22
Lake Forest, IL
9:05 a.m. (CDT)

KIM GOT A SOLID night's sleep. After coffee and a shower, she'd spent hours reviewing the files she received from Gaspar. She'd been instructed to come alone to her meeting with Neagley, which gave her a good excuse to leave Burke behind, as she'd intended anyway.

She called a car service for the short trip to Neagley's house and left Burke and the 4-Runner at the motel.

The car dropped her off at the curb and she hurried through the cool morning air to the front entrance. She pressed the doorbell twice.

She wasn't worried about finding Neagley's house empty again. She wouldn't schedule an appointment and then stand Kim up. Neagley would consider that a bush league tactic and her skills were far above standard on every level.

The big front door swung open.

The greeter was a man Kim recognized. She gave him a wide grin. "Morrie. Good to see you're still employed."

"Come in, Otto. It's cold out there." Morrie smiled, stepped aside, and then closed the door behind her. "Of course I'm still here. I'm indispensable and a handy guy to have around. You said so yourself."

She cocked her head and gave him a quizzical look. "Funny, I don't remember saying that."

"If you didn't, you should have." His grin widened.

Kim chuckled. She liked Morrie. She felt better simply standing in his presence. He was, as she'd once said, a handy guy to have around.

Morrie was a formidable mountain of a man who had certainly been indispensable to the joint rescue operation in Mexico last November.

He was a supremely competent former member of the Secret Service. Which meant he was about as good as a bodyguard gets. Neagley was lucky to have him. No doubt, she was fully aware of his skill set.

The security personnel Burke had engaged back at Neagley's office yesterday had probably been handpicked by Morrie.

Which meant Burke could be in bigger trouble than Kim had expected. Burke's behavior had no doubt angered both Neagley and Morrie. Not helpful at all.

Morrie pointed to a large signal-shield box resting on a table near the door, expecting her to know the rules about electronics inside the house. Which was to say, no electronics were allowed under any circumstances.

Neagley maintained that her home was surveillance-proof.

Every inch of the house and grounds was monitored constantly. She claimed no one, not even foreign governments, could hack into the place.

Meaning that Neagley's home was as secure as it was possible to make any physical location.

Which, Kim knew, wasn't the same as saying The Boss or Finlay's equipment couldn't penetrate here. Not everything the government could do was disclosed to outsiders. Other bad actors were similarly prepared to do whatever it took to get wherever they wanted to go.

Neagley had to know all that, too.

"I'm expecting a call from my partner. I left him back at the motel," Kim said, raising a pro forma objection to forking over her lifelines.

"When he can't get a call through, he'll show up and ring the bell. Or he'll wait until you call him," Morrie replied flatly, unpersuaded.

Kim shrugged. She routinely carried three cell phones now. She dropped them inside the signal-shield box.

She half expected him to demand her weapon, but he didn't. She took that as a sign of trust.

Or maybe his supreme confidence that she'd be no threat should she try to use the gun.

Morrie closed the lid with a crisp snap.

"This way," he said, leading her through the mansion to the back of the house.

Kim followed, nerves humming. Her skin felt too tight on her frame.

She and Neagley had parted in Mexico last year on good terms. Something approaching genuine friendship had sprouted between them, Kim had thought at the time.

At the very least, she had been reasonably sure Neagley wouldn't try to kill her.

But that was before Burke had engaged and injured Neagley's security personnel. At this point, Neagley's potential for violence pushed Kim's internal threat level all the way to red and held the needle there.

When Kim walked through the archway, Neagley was seated at the kitchen table with a big mug full of black coffee. She was as sleek and fit as ever, but she also looked a little tired and worn down, Kim noticed.

Her brother's death seven months ago had hit Neagley hard, although she would never say so. She held herself responsible for her brother's safety, and she had failed. Failure was not acceptable to Neagley. Never had been, never would be.

She had dealt with the killers swiftly and finally, but her vengeance did not bring her brother back to life.

"I've been expecting you," Neagley said, lips parting in what passed for a smile. She gestured to a chair and a waiting mug.

Kim sat across from her and inhaled deeply. "Coffee smells great."

"I buy it in bulk from the same source the army uses," Neagley replied with a nod. "Reacher swallowed a million gallons of the stuff while we were active duty."

"No wonder." Kim nodded, sipping the black coffee appreciatively. When she set the mug down again, she said, "Speaking of Reacher. Is he here?"

"You know I wouldn't tell you if he were." Neagley lifted the corner of her mouth, which was not quite a smile. "But as it happens, he's not here."

"Sounds like you meant to say he's not here *now*. You've

seen him recently, though. Haven't you?" Kim asked and sipped appreciatively.

The coffee really was some of the best she'd tasted. She loved black coffee and drank it by the gallon some days. Which probably didn't help her queasy stomach much.

Neagley's gaze held steady. "Tell me about your new partner. Will Burke, right?"

Kim nodded. "That's right. He was a SEAL. Navy, not army like you."

"Seems like I've heard the name before, but I can't place where or when," Neagley replied. "It'll come to me."

Kim said, "Meanwhile, back to my question. Where's Reacher?"

"Why do you ask?" Neagley shook her head slowly. "Lucky for Burke that he wasn't at my office today. My doorman was not as effective as Reacher would have been. Good news for Burke. This time."

"He'll be glad to hear that," Kim said, more relieved than she'd let on in front of Neagley. Later, she'd need to think about why.

Neagley replied, "You don't have to worry. He won't be looking for payback against Burke. Unlike Cooper, I don't recruit from NSA."

Kim cocked her head. Who was recruiting from NSA? What the hell was Neagley talking about?

Neagley glanced toward Morrie and nodded. Morrie left the room.

Then Neagley changed the subject. "I'm hearing Reacher did a favor for a vet back in New Mexico. The man was down on his luck. Needed a shower and a bed for the night. A guy tried to get Reacher and killed the vet instead."

Enough people had been involved with the shooting in Gaucho. If her curiosity was piqued, Neagley could have learned about the victim and the shooter with a few well-placed questions.

But the bit about Reacher doing the vet a favor and Reacher being the shooter's intended target could only have come from one source.

"Reacher feels bad about it. He wants the shooter to pay. So he's been following the guy. They call him Doug XYZ," Neagley said, pausing to drink from her coffee mug. "Thought you might be interested because that escaped convict you're looking for from the prison break? He and two others have teamed up with this shooter."

"I'm not involved in the manhunt for Petey Burns." Kim cocked her head. "But I'm surprised he has reoffended like that."

"Seems consistent with his criminal record, doesn't it?"

"Not really. Petey Burns is a repeat offender, for sure. But his convictions are all about grand theft auto. Non-violent crimes," Kim said, not mentioning her recent encounter with Burns in Las Vegas. "Reacher was hitchhiking somewhere, and Burns picked him up. It's the kind of thing they both would do. Burns has proven himself to be a good car thief, not a killer."

"Well, it seems like he's moving up the crime ladder." Neagley nodded as if she was processing something. "Brings me to the interesting thing I wanted to discuss with you. Looks like he's branching out from cars to banks. These four may be involved in ATM theft now."

"ATM crime usually comes in two basic varieties. They try to steal the actual machine. Or they rob users to steal the money already withdrawn from the machines, which is a whole different level of crime," Kim said, thinking about the ATM armed robbery she'd thwarted on Thursday.

"I've been looking into it and I'm still putting the pieces together." Neagley left the table to refill her coffee. She brought the pot back to top off Kim's mug. When she replaced the flask on the burner, she said, "Come with me. I'll show you what I know so far."

CHAPTER FORTY-ONE

Sunday, May 22
Lake Forest, IL
11:15 a.m. (CDT)

KIM FOLLOWED NEAGLEY DOWN a long corridor to another wing of the house. She stopped in front of what appeared to be a solid, wood-paneled wall and moved a painting aside, revealing a keypad.

Neagley entered a seven-digit code and the faux wall slid open to reveal a high-tech security office. She used the room as a secure base of operations.

Kim had been here before. She half expected to find Reacher waiting. But he wasn't there. She didn't sense that he'd been there recently.

Multiple screens were mounted along one wall with remote controls to operate them. Neagley punched a few buttons on one of the remotes and the largest screen in the center of the wall sprang to life.

Quickly, ten fixed images populated the screen. Each

showed an ATM mounted near a door of a business. Like those posters Kim had seen depicting residential front doors with titles like "The Doors of Dublin" or "The Doors of Boston."

These ATM fronts were similar but not the same.

"What am I looking at here?" Kim asked.

"That's the question, isn't it?" Neagley said, sipping the coffee and staring at the screens as if the images might reveal their secrets when she focused correctly.

Kim scanned the photos, which had a few common elements.

All were taken at night. Lighting was weak, diffused, and shadowed.

The object in the center of each image was an automatic teller machine, with all the familiar touch screens, buttons, and slots for depositing and dispensing.

None of the machines were freestanding, like the kind found in gas stations and shopping malls and movie theaters. Instead, they were built into and flush with the walls. Which suggested access to maintain the machines was located inside each building.

Neagley waited expectantly, allowing Kim time to evaluate the photos. But she needed more than time to make sense of the display.

"I don't see enough to make a solid guess about anything. These ATMs could be located anywhere. They don't seem the least bit unusual in and of themselves. I've probably seen a hundred or more of these over the years. You probably have, too." Kim shook her head, continuing to peer at the images while she drank the coffee.

"Okay. For what it's worth, I agree. I was hoping you'd see something I missed."

"Sorry," Kim replied. "None of these look familiar to me in

any way. How confident are you that these machines are relevant to Burns and his group?"

"Hard to say for sure. I just started working on this a few hours ago, so I don't have much to share yet. I've isolated these nine locations based on a lot of data sifting," Neagley replied, pointing toward the screen with the remote. "Ten machines. The first group has five different banks in five different states. The second group has two banks, two branches per bank, located in two states."

"Have you confirmed that money was stolen from all of them?" Kim asked.

"We've checked with the banks. They have confirmed that all the cash stocked in each machine was dispensed. None can say exactly how that happened," Neagley replied.

Kim nodded. "Which suggests Petey Burns is working as part of a larger crew. At least five groups, all stealing money from ATMs."

"I think so," Neagley replied. "The first five ATMs were hit in the early morning hours, Saturday. But something happened because they only hit four banks the second night. The four on the bottom row."

"The machines appear to be undamaged. So they didn't try to steal the machines themselves or bust into them. How'd they get the money?"

Neagley said, "They could have used fake ATM cards to get the cash dispensed. Which is not robbery, but theft or fraud, legally speaking."

"Seems like a lot of work for relatively little money. Doesn't it? Small banks, small towns, five crews of four people each. Means twenty greedy palms to share smallish sums of cash," Kim said. "Petey Burns steals cars worth a hundred grand or more. This feels like chump change for him."

"Except we're not dealing with small sums. For various reasons, these machines had more cash on hand than you'd expect. They got one to two hundred thousand from each ATM. So we're looking at a million dollars just on the first night," Neagley shook her head. "Who knows how many times they've done this? Millions have been stolen using fake cards in other scams around the world. But this situation feels different to me."

"Why?" Kim asked, leaning back against a chair, coffee mug in hand, relaxing her focus as if she might divine whatever secrets were contained in the photos from a fuzzier picture.

Too bad she couldn't read Neagley's mind.

"Lots of reasons it feels different. But mainly because the second night, the thefts were much larger," Neagley said, taking a seat and propping her heels on the table. "While the ATM thefts were happening, in all four physical locations, malware was activated remotely to transfer a cool million from each of the two banks."

"Simultaneously? Six thefts, all at once?" Kim asked.

"Exactly."

"Which means there's a mastermind behind all this." Kim nodded slowly. "It's not Petey Burns and his pals stealing walking around money."

"Right. There's way more going on here than meets the eye," Neagley said.

"Which is probably why Doug XYZ tried to kill Reacher. He was traveling with Burns and Doug wanted him out of the way." Kim sat down at the table, too. She propped her elbows on the chair arms and leaned back.

"That's half of it," Neagley said as if Kim were a particularly apt pupil.

"What's the other half?"

"Come on. Think about it. You know the players." Neagley paused for emphasis. "Why hasn't Reacher already evened the score? He could have dealt with Doug XYZ long before now. Why didn't he?"

"Because Reacher wants to know who's behind it all. Who's pulling the strings," Kim said slowly. "And why."

"He says they're planning another operation in Chicago tonight. A bigger one." Neagley paused. "And he thinks you're involved."

"What?" Kim arched her eyebrows. "Why does he think this has anything to do with me?"

"Oh, come on, Otto. Don't play the innocent. It doesn't suit you," Neagley replied.

"I told you. I'm not involved in the manhunt for Burns. None of this business was even on my radar until you told me," Kim said. "I'm looking for Reacher. I thought he was with you."

"You let Burns slip through your fingers in South Dakota. You found Burns again in Denver and Vegas. Burns drives to a town that's not even on the map in New Mexico, where Doug XYZ tries to punch Reacher's ticket. He fails by a stroke of luck. And you show up a few hours later," Neagley paused for a breath and a pointed stare. "Burns is on his way to Chicago, and now you're here. Reacher thinks it's all a little too convenient. So do I. Can't say we're wrong, can you?"

Kim nodded. Neagley's summation was a thorough and accurate report of Kim's movements the past few days, which wasn't at all surprising.

She *was* following Reacher, after all. Both Neagley and

Reacher knew as much. She hadn't found him yet, but she'd come close.

Neagley's litany of accusations suggested that Reacher was keeping tabs on Kim.

Something she'd suspected but had no hard evidence to prove. Until now.

And Neagley was a woman of many talents. She might have been helping Reacher watch Kim all this time. The idea was not preposterous.

"So do you know where Reacher is right now or not?" Kim asked, offering no rebuttal or excuse.

Neagley shook her head.

"Where is this big job happening tonight in Chicago?" Kim asked.

"Wish I knew," Neagley shrugged. "We're running short on time. I thought you might be able to help with that."

Kim understood what she wanted. Neagley thought The Boss was behind all of this.

And maybe he was.

But if this whole situation was some elaborate trap Cooper had concocted to catch Reacher, he hadn't shared any of those plans with her. Yet.

Still, whether Cooper was orchestrating the whole thing or not, the plan seemed to be working.

Reacher was here in Chicago. Neagley didn't deny it.

Kim could find him. Chicago was a big city, but until now, she'd been searching the whole country. Which made Chicago seem doable. In theory.

All she had to do was figure out where Reacher was likely to be tonight and wait for him to show up. Simple as that.

What she knew now that she hadn't known two hours ago

was that Reacher was following Doug XYZ. Which meant Reacher would find him.

When Reacher succeeded, Kim would be ready.

"I've got work to do," Kim said, rising from her chair. "I'll be in touch."

"I'll keep digging, too. We'll get further if we work together," Neagley said. "Keep in mind time is of the essence here."

"It always is," Kim replied.

She walked back to the front door on her own. Neither Neagley nor Morrie tried to stop her. She paused at the signal-shield box to collect her cell phones and let herself out.

Standing on the sidewalk after the big door closed and locked behind her, she remembered that she'd left the SUV with Burke at the motel.

She called the car service first. Then she fished Gaspar's cell phone from her pocket and walked toward the sidewalk at the end of the driveway while she waited for him to answer.

"What's up, Sunshine?" Gaspar said in a worried tone with full focused attention.

"I'm leaving Neagley's house now. I need help. How much time do you have?"

A black Crown Vic pulled up to the curb and the driver lowered his window.

"All the time in the world for you, Suzy Wong," Gaspar replied from the driver's seat.

CHAPTER FORTY-TWO

Sunday, May 22
Lake Forest, IL
1:15 p.m. (CDT)

KIM GRINNED, DROPPED THE phone into her pocket, hurried around the front, opened the door, and climbed into the passenger seat.

She settled into the Crown Vic's seat, pulled out the alligator clamp she kept in her pocket and anchored it firmly to the shoulder harness at the retractor to keep it from cutting her head off.

"I see you're still trying to kill me with this monstrous sedan," she joked.

He gave her a smirk.

She had lost every debate and given up arguing about transportation with Gaspar after the first day they worked together.

He was persuaded that no vehicle on the planet was suitable for their purposes except the Crown Vic Police Interceptor. He

298 | DIANE CAPRI

liked the powerful V-8 engine and tough, body-on-frame construction. Rear-wheel drive was better for rough driving over curbs and potholes and other urban road hazards. Reduced spin-outs, too, he claimed.

The problem was, Ford had stopped production in 2012 and the big tanks were a challenge to procure.

Gaspar's new employer possessed the breadth and scope of influence that allowed him to acquire vehicles and a lot of other things that were unavailable to mere mortal FBI agents.

As he pulled away from the curb, she said, "Don't get me wrong. I'm thrilled to see you, Chico. But what are you doing here?"

"I've always got time for you, Suzy Wong. You know that."

"Of course. Right back atcha." She gave him a smirk. "But really."

He shrugged. "Seemed like you needed the help. I wanted to send Flint, but he was unavailable."

He meant his colleague Michael Flint, a former clandestine operative and top-end investigator who boasted that he could find anyone, anytime, anywhere.

"Too bad," she replied with a grin.

Kim had worked with Flint before and found him to be a solid partner. She had the feeling that Flint's particular skill set could be useful before this night was over. Assuming they could figure out exactly what was going on with Petey Burns.

"And I wanted to meet Burke. Size him up for myself," Gaspar said reasonably, which Kim figured was the real reason he came. "Where is he, anyway?"

"Back at the motel. I left my gear there, too. Let's head over there." Kim found her cell phone and called Burke.

He didn't pick up.

She left a quick message and frowned as she disconnected. "That's strange."

"No answer? That guy's AWOL too much when you need him, if you ask me," Gaspar said, frowning above his aviators.

Kim didn't argue the point. Gaspar wasn't wrong. Facts were facts. "How long can you stay?"

"Just a few hours. I've got a flight this afternoon that I can't miss," he replied. "So let's get to it. What have you learned lately?"

She spent the rest of the short drive time bringing Gaspar up to speed on Neagley's intel since he wouldn't have heard the exchange inside Neagley's situation room.

He nodded and made a series of noises suggesting he understood. Which he probably did.

When they reached the motel, Gaspar parked the big old boat and unloaded two bags from the trunk. She offered to take one. Predictably, he refused.

He was barely limping today. Which could mean his right leg was hurting him less than usual or that he'd been mainlining Tylenol since he left Miami.

When they reached her room, he opened the bags and set up several laptops and secure hotspots. In short order, he was remotely connected to his office at Scarlett Investigations in Houston and banging away on the keyboards.

Kim left him to work while she went in search of coffee and pastries. Gaspar downed sweets like a drug addict. He'd want a shot of sugar soon.

When she came back carrying a bag of donuts and two large coffees, he took a break to scoff down the sweets and bring her up to speed.

"I've been looking at those ATM thefts Neagley told you

about," he said while chewing a donut hole that had dusted his chin with powdered sugar. He quickly repeated the same commonalities between them that Neagley had discovered.

"Did you find anything that might predict where they plan to hit next?" Kim asked, sipping the hot coffee.

"Yeah. Hang on." He dusted the sugar off his hands and leaned back, crossing his feet at the ankles, hands folded and resting on his flat stomach, which was his favorite sitting position. "What do you know about the Carbanak cases?"

"Carbanak? Not a lot. As I recall, it was a theft ring operating inside the US and globally. Some called it the biggest digital heist in history," Kim replied, kicking off her shoes and settling on the bed in the lotus position. She stretched tension from her muscles.

Gaspar nodded. "There were several elements to the various thefts involved, but they all relied on a type of malware that Carbanak installed at banks and financial institutions."

"How was the malware delivered? Spear-phishing?"

"Yep. Specific emails were sent to specific people, so they looked legit. But they weren't. And when the recipients opened them, the malware was downloaded and installed," Gaspar said, popping another donut hole into his mouth. "The thieves used the malware in various ways. One method was to cause ATMs to spit out cash automatically at a specific time. Money mules, as they called them, would be in place to collect the cash and haul it away."

"How much cash are we talking about?"

"More than you'd think, in the aggregate. On one weekend alone, the Carbanak gang hit forty-one ATMs at twenty-two branches of one bank. When the dust cleared, they'd collected almost three million dollars," Gaspar said.

"And you think that's what's happening here? Same as the Carbanak cases?" Kim asked, thinking about Neagley's photos this morning. "Neagley said so far they'd hit nine ATMs in different locations, spitting out cash. Money mules collected the bills."

Gaspar swallowed and swigged coffee to push the sweets down. "It's a big operation. A lot of mouths to feed from the proceeds."

"Right."

"But as you said, that's not enough money to make this whole enterprise worthwhile." He paused. "Like Neagley said, last night, in addition to the ATM thefts, the banks involved were simultaneously relieved of a million dollars each in an electronic wire transfer theft."

"And where did the money go?" Kim asked. "Neagley either didn't know or didn't say."

Gaspar said, "Transferred to offshore banks at precisely the same time as the ATMs were disgorging cash."

Kim nodded. "So you think the ATM thefts Neagley uncovered were a diversion. Meant to distract attention from the larger electronic wire transfers."

"Once a thief pulls off something like the Carbanak heists, there are bound to be copycats."

"And if that's true, then tonight in Chicago," Kim said, thinking things through aloud, "we'll see ATM thefts simultaneously timed to wire transfers from the same bank."

Gaspar nodded and licked the sugar off his fingers, popping one at a time into his mouth like a five-year-old.

"Very mature, Chico," Kim grinned. "Did you learn that from your kids?"

Gaspar nodded, and when he'd finished licking, he said,

"Only I think the transfers tonight will be a lot larger."

"Because the other towns and banks were small. Those thefts were dry runs for a bigger operation in Chicago," Kim said flatly.

"Makes sense, doesn't it?" Gaspar said, giving up on his childlike grooming and heading to the sink to wash the stickiness from his hands before returning to the keyboards. "All we need to do is figure out which bank is the target. And which ATMs they plan to hit. And when. And get there before they do."

"So easy even a child could do it," Kim replied sarcastically, running the logistics through in her head.

"I think I can help with that," Gaspar said from the sink in the bathroom.

Hard knuckles rapped on the door. "Otto? Are you in there?"

Gaspar said, "Burke?"

"Ready for your closeup?" Kim climbed off the bed to open the door.

CHAPTER FORTY-THREE

Sunday, May 22
Lake Forest, IL
4:15 p.m. (CDT)

BURKE MARCHED THROUGH THE open door like he owned the place, demanding, "Where have you been?"

"Please do come in, Burke. It's so good to see you," Kim replied tersely.

Burke's tirade stopped abruptly when he looked around the room. Gaspar's donut bag and empty coffee cup were still on the desk. His laptops were open, screens still alight.

The toilet flushed and water ran in the sink. Kim suspected Gaspar was simply announcing his presence before he opened the door and walked into the suite.

"Hello, Burke," Gaspar said.

Burke scowled. "What the hell are you doing here?"

"Seems like the question is why you weren't here, doesn't it?" Gaspar replied easily.

"Take a breath. You two can do pistols at twenty paces later.

Right now, we've got work to do. Grab a seat," Kim said as she climbed onto the bed and sat cross-legged in the middle.

Using his all-purpose gesture, Gaspar shrugged and returned to the desk. Burke plopped into one of the guest chairs.

Kim looked at Burke. "When I tried to reach you, my call went to voicemail. What's wrong with your phone?"

He had the grace to look sheepish, at least. "Forgot to charge it. Didn't realize it until I hadn't heard from you. Sorry."

Kim cocked her head and narrowed her gaze, but she accepted his excuse. For now. "Gaspar flew in for a few hours to help us out."

Burke nodded. "Sorry I missed the briefing. Catch me up."

She was tempted to ignore him and get back to business. But the stakes were too high for that kind of nonsense at the moment. Dealing with Burke would have to wait.

She said, "Have you talked to the Boss?"

Burke shook his head. "I tried a couple of times. No luck."

"Some things never change," Gaspar said without rancor.

Kim shot a glare his way before she gave Burke a quick rundown.

When she finished, his mouth hung open. "So you think there's at least eleven guys, maybe more, plus Reacher. And the three of us should try to take them all down and capture Reacher tonight on our own? Are you crazy?"

"Two of you," Gaspar grinned.

Burke shot an annoyed glance Gaspar's way. "What?"

"There's two of you. You said 'three of us.' Unfortunately, I can't stay," Gaspar explained like he was talking to one of his kids. "So there's two of you. Against at least eleven of them. Plus Reacher. As far as we know. Could be more."

"Two of us." Burke's chin jutted forward as he turned his

gaze back to Kim. "Exactly how are we supposed to handle those numbers?"

"We were just about to figure that out," Kim replied evenly. "Obviously, you'll need to show us you can play better with others than you've demonstrated so far."

"She means you'll need Neagley. Morrie, too." Gaspar grinned. "And I gather neither one of them is particularly fond of you at the moment."

Burke ran a hand over his head in frustration. "Yeah, well, the feeling's mutual."

"Suck it up, buttercup," Gaspar said and laughed heartily when Burke delivered a dark scowl in response.

Kim hid her amusement by feigning a yawn, but the situation was far from funny.

"This is a job for Cooper, isn't it? He's the one who wants Reacher so damned bad. Have him send in the Marines, or the National Guard, or some damned thing," Burke suggested, not kidding.

"Exactly how are you planning to make that happen?" Gaspar had finally lost his patience. "Cooper doesn't seem all that interested in talking to you at the moment."

Burke glared at him, and Gaspar yawned.

The insolence was too much. The last straw.

Burke shot out of the chair, advancing as if he might pummel Gaspar right on the spot.

Gaspar didn't move. Not so much as an eyelash. Calm as a scorpion before a fatal strike.

Which caused Burke to pause briefly.

"Burke!" Kim yelled. "Enough!"

He snapped his head around toward her voice. His eyes were wild. His chest heaved.

Gaspar's words had pushed the right buttons to trigger Burke's enraged response. Was it because he'd said Cooper wasn't supporting Burke? Which was true. And nothing new. But still, Burke's reaction was extreme.

"Take your seat. We have work to do. Enough of this crap," she said as sternly as she could speak.

The pause seemed to be enough to deflate Burke's adrenaline rush. He slumped into his chair. But his eyes were still hard and his nostrils flared with every rapid, heavy breath.

Gaspar's gaze met Kim's. He nodded slightly and raised one eyebrow as if to say, "I told you to watch yourself with this guy. He's unstable."

Kim turned her attention to Burke. "We're not taking down whoever is involved in this series of bank heists. The locals can handle that. We're only interested in finding Reacher. That's what we're here for."

"Okay," Burke said, nodding, calmer than before. "So how are we planning to find him?"

"We were just about to figure that out," Kim replied sternly. "We think we know where he'll be tonight, which is more than we've ever known before. We can't lose this chance."

Gaspar turned to one of the laptops and punched a few keys on the keyboard. The screen sprung to life. He brought up a web page. A large image consumed one hundred percent of the real estate on the screen.

It was an unfamiliar logo.

P&K

"Based on the data we have, my best guess for the thieves' target tonight is Pace & Kent International Bank," Gaspar said. "One of the largest banks in the world, with branches throughout Chicago. And one of a limited number of potential targets that meet all of our criteria."

"Just what criteria is that?" Burke demanded.

"Reasonable question," Gaspar nodded. "I've made some assumptions based on the intel we've collected."

"Such as?" Burke asked.

"The most significant is the time when we expect the thefts to be executed." Gaspar held his annoyance in check. "The past two nights, they hit the targets at the same time. Very early in the morning, when they were less likely to be observed."

"Right," Burke said.

"So we're assuming they'll hit at the same time tonight."

"Makes sense," Kim said, nodding.

"The second big assumption is escalation," Gaspar continued. "The first night, they stole two hundred thousand dollars from each machine. Last night, they stole the same amount of cash from each machine, but they added the two wire transfers. The transfers were one million dollars each. We're assuming the thefts and the transfers were dry runs for larger thefts tonight."

"Seems logical," Burke said. "Do we have any reason to believe these thieves are logical?"

"The thieves themselves may not be," Kim replied. "But so far, the data we have suggests that someone has developed this entire enterprise. It's too complex to have been worked out on the back of a napkin at the pool hall over a beer by a bunch of petty criminals. We believe the puppeteer is the logical one."

"And we have no idea who that puppeteer might be," Burke said sourly.

"Since the ATM thefts are limited by the amount of cash in each machine, the most likely way to increase the take is exactly what Carbanak did. Wire transfer more money tonight than last night," Gaspar explained. "Wire transfers like this can be almost any amount. I'm assuming our thieves want as much money as they can get."

"Which means the ATM targets are located in an area likely to be unoccupied late at night and owned by big banks with a lot of assets readily available," Kim summarized, nodding as she followed along.

"That's the most likely scenario," Gaspar agreed. "But that's where we hit a fork in the plan."

"Why?" Burke asked.

"The first night, our thieves hit five banks in five states. The second night, two banks in two states," Gaspar replied. "They could hit two or three banks again tonight. We just don't know. And we can't cover that many locations. As Burke said earlier, we don't have the manpower."

"But you don't think they're going for two or three banks," Kim said slowly.

"You do this work long enough, and you get a feel for criminal behavior patterns," Gaspar replied, shaking his head. "It feels like they've been building to one big bank. There's a lot of reasons why that makes sense."

Burke asked, "Shouldn't we assume it'll be two or three banks, though? Just to cover all bases?"

"If we had the manpower or time to gather more intel, that would be the best plan, sure. But we don't have any of that," Kim said. "We've got you and me. Plus whatever personnel we can persuade Neagley to contribute. And we've got one shot at this. We need to make our best guess and stick with it."

"There's a huge margin of error there, though," Burke objected again. "Can't we at least try to get Cooper to handle the other two banks? Just in case we guess wrong?"

Gaspar gave her a look.

Kim sighed. She'd opened a bottle of water. She took a drink and screwed the cap back on. "Yeah. Sure. That would be great. Why don't you try to contact him again. Give him the facts. See what he says."

Burke nodded. "As soon as we're done here, I'll do that."

"Okay," she said, turning her attention back to Gaspar. "So why did you settle on Pace & Kent?"

"Burke is right. There's a huge margin of error here. The only thing I can do is try to narrow it down," Gaspar said. "Three possible banks that make sense. If I can locate the malware on their systems, then they're still in play. In which case, we've got to find more backup."

"And if the malware isn't installed on those systems?"

"Then that bank should be struck from our list," Gaspar said. "With luck, we'll be able to eliminate two banks and be left with one clear choice. As your mother says, when there's only one choice, that's the right choice, Suzy Wong."

"How long will all that take?" Burke asked. "It's getting late."

Gaspar shook his head. "I don't know. I've been working on it since Neagley first shared her intel with us. We should ask her what she's found out."

"All of this came from Neagley?" Burke asked, eyes wide. "Why the hell would we trust her to be straight with us?"

"Do you have any better ideas? Because if you do, we're all ears." Gaspar said angrily. His patience with Burke was exhausted. "If not, then just shut the hell up."

"Is there any other way we could find out?" Kim said before Burke flared up again. "Anyone I could ask to check out the malware for us?"

"Unfortunately, no. There's no way to find this specific malware other than looking for it on each individual bank's computer. We've got the stuff we need to do that back at my office. I'm already digging into it," Gaspar said definitively, moving on to the next issue. "There are several big banks in Chicago that have a lot of money on hand. At least, according to their security filings and electronic data—"

Burke interrupted again, eyebrows arched. "You've got a warrant to examine secure databases for private banks, I assume."

Gaspar gave him a glare in response. "But only one of those banks has three ATMs located in close proximity in an area of downtown Chicago that is likely to be abandoned in the wee hours of the morning."

"Pace & Kent," Kim said, nodding toward the logo on the laptop screen. "Assuming the malware has been installed there. Which you'll confirm before we move forward."

"Right," Gaspar replied. "Pace & Kent."

"And the location?" Burke asked. "Where is this mythic place that will be abandoned in the country's third-largest city tonight?"

Gaspar paused and took a breath. "Navy Pier."

Burke stared at Gaspar as if he'd completely lost his mind.

Kim searched the internet on her phone for the operating hours for what was, perhaps, Chicago's most popular tourist attraction. "Navy Pier closes at ten o'clock tonight. Can we predict what time the thefts will occur?"

"Not precisely. But the prior thefts have occurred at the same local time for all of the banks. There must be a reason he made that particular choice," Gaspar replied. "My educated guess is that he's got a window of opportunity baked into the malware that requires some kind of code. He can only exploit that malware at exactly the right time in precisely the correct location."

"And when, exactly is that?" Burke asked.

"The window of opportunity most likely runs from 1:15 a.m. to 2:15 a.m." Gaspar replied.

Kim glanced at her watch. "It's seven-fifteen. We've got six hours, give or take. Can we do this?"

"Not unless we get started." Burke stood and approached Gaspar, hand extended. "Sorry I lost it earlier. I didn't realize I was so tense."

"No harm done." Gaspar graciously accepted the olive branch. "Your suggestion makes sense. Call Cooper. Maybe he'll do the right thing."

"On my way," Burke said as he turned and left the room.

Kim waited until the door closed before she asked Gaspar. "Should I get Finlay on board? He's got the resources. He can do things we can't. We've seen it before, Chico."

"Neagley's a better idea. She's right here. She has manpower. She's ready, willing, and able," Gaspar shrugged as he packed up his gear. "Plus, if you don't call her, she'll be pissed as hell. Which is not healthy—for you."

"Burke's not wrong about Neagley, though. She's devoted to Reacher. I'm not confident that she'll stand by and let us capture him," Kim said quietly. "Are you?"

"Honestly? Not at all. You'll have to figure that out when the time comes," Gaspar said. "But calling Finlay is a bad idea. If Cooper learns you've reached out to Finlay, you'll have an even bigger problem on your hands than you've got now."

Kim cocked her head. "Are you sure you're not in favor of my suggestion because you just don't like Finlay?"

"And there's that," Gaspar replied with a grin. "Look, I don't trust the guy."

"No kidding," she replied drily. She didn't mention that she'd talked to Finlay three days ago and hadn't heard from him since.

"But realistically, unless Finlay's somehow got a head start on all this—and why would he?—by the time he can do anything, all of the excitement will be over," Gaspar said, popping the last of the donut holes into his mouth as if the matter was done and dusted.

Kim wasn't so sure. Thing was, Finlay and Cooper were both monitoring her every waking moment.

And Neagley wasn't trustworthy when she had another agenda. Such as protecting Reacher.

Gaspar's opinions *were* colored by previous bad experiences with both Finlay and Cooper.

Nothing Kim could do about any of that. Nothing she could do about her own ambivalence, either.

While Gaspar packed up to leave, one of his laptops pinged. He clacked a few keys on the keyboard.

"What's up?" Kim asked.

"You want the good news or the bad news or the ugly news?"

She gave him a side-eye.

"One of our three possible banks has been eliminated. No malware on their systems," Gaspar said. "The bad news is that we have two banks showing positive. The malware is there, and its operating. Something's in play."

Kim took a deep breath. "What's the ugly news?"

"One of the two possible international bank targets is Racine International, a client of Neagley's," Gaspar replied, frowning at

STRAIGHT JACK | 313

the screen as if he might have read the characters incorrectly. "I can't tell her Racine has malware on its systems or how to find it. And neither can you."

Kim nodded, which wasn't the same as consent. "Does Racine have three ATMs that are solid targets for tonight's thefts?"

"No. Not even close," Gaspar said. "The bank you want is Pace & Kent."

After a few moments of silence, Gaspar shoved the third laptop into his bag. "I really do need to go. I sent the intel to you via your secure server. Share whatever you think is necessary with Neagley, but don't tell her where you got it."

"Why?" But as soon as she asked, his expression told her the answer. Gaspar had the ability to access a lot of classified and confidential intel. Which wasn't the same as having the legal right to look at any of it, let alone use it or share it.

"Just because Burke is an asshole doesn't mean he's always wrong." Gaspar shrugged, zipped his bag and tossed it over his shoulder, and headed out.

At the door, he turned. "Seriously, Kim. Be careful around Burke. He's got a short fuse and a mean temper. I've known a lot of guys like that. You have, too. Don't let him take you down with him."

Kim nodded. After he left, she called Neagley.

CHAPTER FORTY-FOUR

Sunday, May 22
Chicago, IL
7:35 p.m. (CDT)

DOUG XYZ HAULED HIS battered body into the hot shower and stood under the spray for an hour to loosen his muscles. He hurt all over.

His knee was swollen and painful with every step. At some point, he'd get an X-ray and a cast, but that couldn't happen for the next three days, at least.

His kneecap might need to be replaced, judging from the pain. The bastard who had shoved him to the pavement must have weighed two-fifty at least.

The dark purple bruise on his right torso was the size of a basketball. And both shoulders screamed with pain every time he tried to lift more than ten pounds.

His conscience, however, was clear. Ray was a dead man the moment he took that cop hostage. And the cop almost certainly had brain damage from Ray cutting off his air supply with the chokehold. Both of them were better off resting for all eternity in that stand of trees.

When he shut off the water and climbed out of the shower, he heard someone at the door. He wrapped one thin bath towel around his waist and used the other one to dry his hair. He was expecting Moe.

Doug grabbed his gun from the bedside table and looked through the peep hole first, just to be sure his visitor was Moe. Then he threw the deadbolt and opened the door.

"Come on in. I'll be ready to go in five," Doug said, walking back toward the closet to dig through a duffel for clean clothes.

Moe pointed, "What the hell happened to your kidney? And that knee looks twice as big as the other one."

"Patton's guy blindsided me. Roughed me up when we picked up the van. Guess he was pissed off about the extra work or something," Doug replied, pulling on his boxers and sitting on the bed to struggle the jeans past his swollen knee.

The pressure of the denim sleeve along his leg relieved some of the pain. He popped a pair of oxycodone pills to handle the rest. They were already a man down. He couldn't be sidetracked by pain tonight when they had so much riding on the final heist.

"Where's Burns?" Doug asked.

"Left him in his room. You want to bring him along?" Moe asked.

"No." Doug slipped into a clean shirt. "But I don't want to come back for him, either. Too risky. And we'll need him tonight."

"Okay. I'll get him. We'll meet you at the van. When are we gonna ditch him for good?"

"Tonight. Soon as we can. Depends on how it goes."

"Works for me," Moe said on his way out, after a glance

toward the duffels full of cash resting on the bed. "Pick you up out front in ten."

Doug finished dressing, slipped his feet into his shoes, and located the burner phone to call Patton.

He should have called in hours ago. But he didn't know how to play the situation. Ray was dead and gone, and a cop killed. The beatdown from Patton's goon. With so many variables, he still didn't know what to say. But if he didn't call, Patton would replace Charlie Unit before tonight's final heist. Doug definitely didn't want that to happen.

The duffels full of cash he still had were nice. But if he stayed on track, there was a lot more to come at the job's end. After he eliminated Burns and Moe.

Patton's instructions were to leave the duffel bags in a self-storage facility near Navy Pier. A locker at the bus station would have been easier, but everybody was worried about security and unattended bags in big-city transportation buildings these days. Entire businesses were built around temporarily storing luggage for travelers.

Doug took a swig of water, swallowed, and dialed Patton's number. Beads of sweat dampened his upper lip and his hairline. When the voicemail prompt finished, he cleared his throat and left a succinct message without embellishment. "Second package retrieved. Deposit pending. Third package collection on track."

He disconnected the call and shoved the phone into his pocket. He gathered the duffels and his personal bag and headed out to the van.

Petey was behind the wheel. Moe climbed out and tossed the duffels and Doug's bag into the cargo hold. When Moe and Doug were seated, Petey slipped the transmission into gear and rolled toward downtown.

"You sure you can do this, Petey?" Moe asked from the backseat. "You've never driven in Chicago before, have you? It can be confusing."

"We're doing the dry run now so he can get familiar with it," Doug preempted Petey's reply. "Besides which, we have no other options since Ray's gone. Petey will have to park the van. We can't get dropped off and picked up at different locations this time."

Petey continued driving north toward the city until Doug saw the self-storage place and said, "Turn in here. Park at the end of the lot."

Petey followed directions. When he pulled the van into the parking slot, Doug said, "Open the side door. Moe, grab those duffels and come with me. Petey, stay here."

Doug stepped out of the passenger seat and closed the door behind him. Moe climbed into the cargo hold and pulled the duffels. He followed Doug around the corner to a storage unit secured with a combination lock.

Doug bent over the lock and moved the dial clockwise and counterclockwise until the shackle clicked open. He pulled the lock from the loop and flipped the hasp open. He opened the door.

"Toss the duffels in here," he said, gesturing to the empty concrete floor.

For the first time since they'd started the mission, Moe hesitated. "Are you sure? We could keep the money with us. A bird in the hand and all that."

"Toss it in. Come on."

Moe said, "It's a lot of money. We could just quit now. While we're ahead."

"Just do it, please. We have a lot of ground to cover," Doug said wearily.

Moe gave up. He tossed the duffels into the room.

Doug closed the door, replaced the lock, and turned the dial randomly a few times. He tugged on the lock's case to be sure it was fully closed.

"Let's go," he said before he headed back to the van, Moe following behind.

When they were settled again, Petey returned to the main road, headed toward the city.

"Have you been to Navy Pier before?" he asked.

"No," Moe replied.

"No," Doug said. "Head northeast and turn left onto South State Street toward Roosevelt and turn right. Cross the Chicago River and turn right onto Grand Avenue. Watch your speed."

Petey drove carefully enough. Doug had procured four counterfeit driver's licenses for this phase of the mission, but he didn't want to produce them to a cop at a traffic stop.

Traveling along South Lakeshore Drive might have been pleasant under different circumstances. At the moment, Doug wanted to get to the destination and settle the logistics in his mind.

"Moe, watch for a parking place. We need to blend in, but we want to be close enough to the ATM so we can get back quickly afterward," Doug said, watching closely as Petey drove along the city streets.

He had one chance to get this right. Solid reconnaissance was essential.

Based on the videos and still photos he'd seen, Navy Pier was a fortunate location, particularly given his physical limitations.

Even with his bad knee, he could walk Moe and Petey to the water at gunpoint. Which would make the bodies easier to dump.

They would wash ashore eventually, but he'd be long gone by then.

Petey located a secluded place to leave the van in a side alley. "Moe, you want to check for surveillance before we settle in?"

"Yea," Moe said. He donned his ski mask and slipped out the side door.

"Straight up. No bullshit. What do you think our chances are here, Doug?" Petey asked when Moe was out of earshot.

"Hard to say. We've done this twice now, smooth as silk." Doug peered through the windshield and the side window, looking for problems. "Your job is the easiest. All you have to do is be the lookout and make sure to show up precisely on time to collect the second duffel. Any idiot could do that, don't you think?"

Petey seemed nervous. Probably because of what had happened last night with Ray. This was not the time to get spooked.

"Look, we'll leave the van here while the Pier is still open. That way, we'll be inside when they close up," Doug said as if Petey didn't already know the plan. "We find the meet-up location inside the secure perimeter. We come back together. Safety in numbers and all that, like my mother used to say."

"Yeah. Sure. Okay," Petey replied. "I'm not that good with a gun. My specialty is driving and stealing cars."

"You won't need to shoot. And if you do, just point the gun at the center of the guy's body and pull the trigger. Shooting a man's no different than playing a video game. Nothing to it," Doug said. He'd done it plenty of times.

The storms they'd come through in Missouri had followed them to Chicago. The wind had picked up and the rain's drizzle steadily intensified to a heavy downpour. He saw a brilliant thunderbolt in the sky and heard the sharp crack that followed.

The storm was a good thing. Nobody would be out wandering around in weather like this. Doug grinned and kept moving toward the target.

CHAPTER FORTY-FIVE

Monday, May 23
Near Ft. Meade, MD
12:35 a.m. (CDT)

SULLIVAN'S STOMACH FLUTTERED, WHICH he recognized as a manifestation of slight anxiety. He imagined even Olympic athletes felt the same butterflies immediately before the big contest they'd trained and sacrificed hard and long to perform.

Within the next two hours, this mission would succeed or fail. So many lives were hanging in the balance.

He'd done everything he could do to ensure success.

Like the Olympians, he ignored his anxiety and jumped full force into the game.

Charlie Unit's handler had called back, recommending Charlie Unit to move on to Chicago. He'd said Doug XYZ had done the right thing. Killed the cop and Ray as well. Charlie Unit had proven themselves reliable.

Given that Echo Unit and Delta Unit had been terminated and the operation was planned for three units in Chicago, Sullivan agreed. Charlie Unit advanced to the games in Chicago.

Which meant three crews and three handlers, fourteen men in the field, any one of whom could cause the entire mission to collapse.

Sullivan scowled. Fifteen men if he counted Reacher.

Efforts to take Reacher out of the equation had failed. Nothing they could do but work with the cards they'd been dealt.

Reacher against three handlers, Sullivan's seasoned warriors.

Unfortunately, Reacher had proven more difficult to eliminate than expected.

Sullivan blamed Doug XYZ for the Reacher problem. Reacher shouldn't have been a factor in this mission at all.

Reacher came with Burns. Doug had added Burns to Charlie Unit.

The equation was so simple a three-year-old could understand it. No Doug, no Burns, no Reacher.

This was why Sullivan had assigned Charlie Unit to the ATM in the middle of Navy Pier tonight. The most vulnerable position, the most exposed target, the operation most likely to draw attention to itself, the assigned team destined to fail.

With any luck at all, Charlie Unit's failure would take Reacher down, too. Sullivan had instructed the handlers to shoot to kill if they spotted Reacher anywhere, any time.

He felt immense pleasure every time he thought about the whole batch—Doug XYZ, Petey Burns, Moe Smith, and Jack Reacher—flat on their backs and staring at the dark sky with dead eyes.

It would serve them right.

Sullivan glanced at the clock. The collection window would

open in ten minutes. He took a quick trip to the urinal, refilled his whiskey glass, and returned to the desk.

He checked his video feeds.

Tonight's actions would be streamed via live video feeds at the three ATMs. He rechecked the feeds again. All were good to go.

Ten burner phones, lined up on the desk, were fired up and fully charged. Nine were assigned to specific numbers. The tenth was a spare.

Sullivan liked redundancies.

He opened two laptops, each of which had been designed and calibrated to handle one transfer.

Two transfers tonight.

The first, Pace & Kent, was the big prize to which the prior thefts this weekend had been leading.

Sullivan had also successfully installed the malware at another bank target.

The second bank, Racine International, was a fresh challenge and demanded different tactics.

If he could successfully complete an electronic transfer from Racine International tonight, in the future he could eliminate the need to divert any bank's security system to simultaneous ATM thefts.

If he succeeded with the Racine bank transfer, he'd never need to manage a group of ATM thefts. A simple bank transfer using the malware alone would be more efficient and reduce the body count to zero.

Not that he minded eliminating the deadwood. But there were easier ways to do it.

If the Racine bank transfer succeeded, he planned to deploy the streamlined process globally. There were a lot of banks in the world available for the plucking.

Sullivan glanced at the big clock. Both the Pace & Kent and the Racine transfers were scheduled to be completed at precisely 1:28 a.m. Chicago time. He ran quickly through the scenario again.

One billion dollars from each bank, delivered instantly to offshore secrecy jurisdictions, and moved twice more in short order. Hidden so well not even a bloodhound could find them.

Within the hour, the two billion would rest in overseas accounts to which only Sullivan had access.

At precisely 2:28 a.m. Chicago time, both missions would be accomplished.

He leaned back in his chair and propped his feet on the desk to watch the action on his video feeds. Last night's storm had moved into Chicago with a vengeance. Hard rain and thunder clouds darkened the images. He narrowed his eyes to make out the action.

He swished and swallowed a large mouthful of the warm whiskey. He felt the glow from his throat to his toes.

On the first screen, Alpha Unit was in place. The driver stopped and three personnel stepped out, dressed from head to toe in black. They were drenched in a few short minutes, but the first theft was underway.

Screens two and three showed Bravo and Charlie Units in the same positions.

The thefts had been planned for a time and place that should have been abandoned even in good weather. The storm was a lucky break. No tourists or pedestrians would be roaming around in such a downpour.

Sullivan focused on the video streams, watching as the three units approached the three Pace & Kent ATMs, disabled the cameras, and punched the codes into the keypads. After two nights of practice, they performed like a synchronized gymnastics team.

The ATMs began to spit out cash. While the first duffels were being filled at three separate Pace & Kent machines, Sullivan opened the first laptop.

His fingers moved across the keys deliberately, accurately, in the correct sequence.

He hit the space bar and watched the laptop as it entered the digital vault and transferred one billion dollars from Pace & Kent, the first of two international banks.

Then he did the same with the second laptop for Racine, the second bank.

When the transfers finished, he closed the laptops with satisfaction. He spent less than a full second enjoying his newfound wealth.

Celebrations would come later.

Cleanup was required now.

He returned his attention to the ATM thefts.

Each of the three units was transitioning to their second duffels.

CHAPTER FORTY-SIX

Monday, May 23
Chicago, IL
1:45 a.m. (CDT)

SPRING STORMS CONTINUED TO move across the city.
Clouds further blackened the already dark sky and rain had
started an hour ago. Kim heard a sharp crack of thunder just
before the wind whipped up, and the rain began to fall in
torrents.

She'd lived with storms coming in off the Great Lakes all
her life. Mostly hard wind and rain and cold. But they could
spawn dangerous, unpredictable tornadoes. She pulled her rain
hood tighter and zipped her black slicker.

Navy Pier, one of Chicago's premier tourist attractions,
jutted into Lake Michigan. During operating hours, the area was
flooded with civilians, but the pier and all of its attractions were
closed tonight.

The rain was a lucky break for Petey Burns and the others.
Even if a foolish pedestrian might have wandered onto the pier

in better weather, this night was fit for neither tourist nor resident.

The city itself felt too quiet. Muffled by Mother Nature. Only the rage of Lake Michigan churned the waters off Navy Pier.

Burke had parked the SUV on the street. They went the rest of the way on foot, head down against the cold, pelting rain.

They separated at the corner, Burke headed around the block to the south, and Kim focused on the entrance to the Pier.

"Keep an eye out for Reacher. That's all we care about. Neagley will call in the locals. Chicago PD will handle everything else," Kim reminded him.

"Got it," Burke replied, but she had the feeling he wasn't listening to her.

For some reason, Burke's fixation with Reacher had become unnatural. She didn't know what he was thinking.

She'd put it down to the fight he'd had with Reacher back in Vegas. Burke was a proud SEAL. Reacher had bested him.

Kim understood Burke's wounded pride.

But she'd begun to suspect there was more to worry about.

Whatever it was, she'd handle it tomorrow. Tonight required extreme focus on the immediate matter at hand.

Finding Reacher.

The first ATM was halfway down the block on the north. The second ATM was half a block south. The third was on the pier, closer to the water's edge.

The machine located on the pier was the most dangerous of the three. It was open to surveillance in a way that the others were not. Gaspar had promised to keep all three under surveillance.

Neagley had predicted that Doug XYZ's group would be

assigned the ATM on the pier. Kim asked whether Reacher had simply given Neagley the intel. She had denied it.

But Kim wasn't sure. She trusted Neagley in many ways. But she'd learned the hard way that during bad luck and trouble, Neagley's first loyalty was to her own. Always.

"Doug XYZ has already tried to kill Reacher once. He'll try again," Kim said.

"You'll be there if backup is required," Neagley had replied. "How much help do you think Reacher needs?"

"When are the locals coming?" Burke had asked.

"We've been over this," Neagley replied. "I'll call them once we're sure we've got the right ATM targets. We won't know that until you confirm. We don't want to divert law enforcement resources to the pier when they should be on the south side dealing with the homicide epidemic over there."

Burke had said nothing more, but Kim knew he didn't like the setup. She wasn't all that thrilled with the setup either.

When they were alone again, she'd said, "Just keep your eyes on the prize. We want Reacher. None of the rest of this is our problem."

"Until the shooting starts," Burke had mumbled under his breath.

Kim looked around again. The heavy rain interfered with visibility. Blinding rain pelted her face.

She saw nothing suspicious yet.

If the three ATMs were scheduled to be hit at the same time as the previous heists, then the thieves should be in place by now.

How long did it take to collect all of the cash from a full ATM? Gaspar had tried to look that up.

Calculations were complicated. There were a large variety of

ATMs and none were precisely predictable.

But the timeline the thieves had used during the previous heists seemed to permit a one-hour window to arrive, collect the money, and escape.

Kim stayed in the shadows and traveled close to the buildings until the pier ATM was visible ahead. She backed into the trees to wait.

The machine was set back into an alcove, like several others the thieves had hit previously.

From her observation point, she couldn't see whether anyone was standing at the machine yet. She changed her position for a better view of the sidewalk on either side of the alcove.

Which was when she got lucky.

A man hustled along the street toward the ATM. She almost missed him. He blended into the stormy darkness dressed in black with a black ski mask over his head.

Something about the way he carried himself triggered Kim's lizard brain. She'd seen the man before.

Half a moment later, her synapses made the connection. Petey Burns. She'd bet money on it.

His hands rested in his pockets. The right pocket looked weighted, which suggested he could be holding a weapon.

Something flat was tucked under his left arm close to his body.

He approached the alcove and stepped inside where she could no longer see him.

When he came out a few moments later, the flat thing was gone and he carried a full duffel bag in his left hand. The bag looked heavy. He seemed to have difficulty handling it.

Kim crossed the street where she'd have a better viewing angle. She waited to give him a good lead before she followed.

As she passed the alcove, she glanced into the small, dimly lit space. A similarly dressed man was standing, facing the ATM, but she couldn't see what his hands were doing.

A moment's hesitation gripped her. She could thwart the theft, here and now. Capture the thief in the act. He could be arrested and interrogated. His accomplices apprehended.

But any Chicago cop could do that soon enough.

Instead, she followed the man with the heavy duffel.

If the guy was Burns, and if Reacher had joined up with him, now was the time to find Reacher. She was close. She could almost guarantee it.

The man she thought was Burns hurried along the sidewalk to the corner and turned right, headed farther onto Navy Pier.

Kim followed from the shadows.

She heard a gunshot behind her.

What?

She sucked in her breath and waited for another gunshot.

After a moment, she flattened her body against the building and hurried back toward the ATM.

From a distance, through the storm, Kim saw a big man standing in the street in front of the alcove, pointing a handgun.

CHAPTER FORTY-SEVEN

Monday, May 23
Near Ft. Meade, MD
2:05 a.m. (CDT)

"WHAT THE HELL?" SULLIVAN pulled his heels off the desk
and sat upright in his chair, peering into the stormy chaos
reflected on his video feeds.

All of a sudden, out of nowhere, all three units were in
trouble.

He noticed Alpha Unit first. The driver and the man with the
first duffel had already headed back to the van. The leader was
halfway through filling the second duffel when a big man
planted himself close to the alcove.

He held a pistol pointed toward the unit leader collecting
cash from the ATM.

The big man yelled something.

Sullivan's gaze scanned the entire area, zooming out to
broaden the scope of the video. Where was Alpha Unit's
handler?

Was the big man Reacher? All three handlers had been told to shoot to kill.

He was standing there, a huge stationary target. Why didn't Alpha's handler take the big man out of play?

Alpha Unit's security man ran up from his position half a block back.

The big man turned and shot him three times squarely in the chest as he was still running forward.

He dropped to the pavement and stayed down.

Return fire erupted from the unit leader still collecting the cash spewing from the ATM.

The big man turned and fired twice into the alcove.

No fire was returned after that.

The handler never showed up.

The big man ducked into the alcove for a moment. When he emerged, he hurried toward Alpha Unit's getaway van. He did not have the second duffel in his hand.

Sullivan switched his attention to the second screen. Bravo Unit's work was in the same state of play as Alpha Unit's had been.

Driver and first man already at the van. Leader collecting the money and filling the second duffel from the machine.

Security man fifty feet away.

A smaller black-clad figure approached the ATM assigned to Bravo Unit.

Sullivan blinked. The driving rain interfered with the feed. Could that be a woman?

She might have been yelling something, but Sullivan's video feeds did not have audio capability.

Bravo Unit's security man ran toward her. In a furiously fast blur of limbs, she lashed out in all directions at once.

Before Sullivan had a chance to blink, she'd laid the security man out on the concrete. His weapon skidded along the pavement.

Once he was down, she gave him a hard kick to the belly. He didn't move.

Then she ran toward the ATM where Bravo Unit's leader continued to collect cash, stuffing it into the second duffel and looking quickly over his shoulder to keep track of her position.

He was probably planning to run before she got close enough to do him serious damage, but he stayed a moment too long.

She attacked him like a banshee. Her face was contorted as if she were screaming on approach.

He swung the duffel and hit her hard in the torso.

Sullivan said, "Oof!" as the blow landed as if he'd been the one battered by the heavy bag.

She barely flinched and paused briefly.

While she recovered, Bravo Unit's leader dashed toward the waiting van.

He ran no more than three steps when she regained her balance and took off after him.

She jumped into the air and landed both feet in the center of his back, knocking him to the ground.

The heavy duffel went flying as he hit the concrete. His head bounced before his face kissed the pavement and stayed there.

She stood over his prone body for a few seconds before she ran toward Bravo Unit's van. Sullivan assumed she'd make quick work of the driver and Bravo Unit's leader.

But before she reached the van, Bravo Unit's handler stepped into her path.

He was a smaller man than the security guy. He stood like a

block of solid stone. The knife blade in his hand glinted off the streetlight, flashing a jagged edge of lightning against the dark sky surrounding his body.

Sullivan's anxious stomach roiled with excitement. This opponent was fierce and deadly. She'd destroyed half of Bravo Unit in less than two minutes. The man had done the same to Alpha Unit.

Had they also eliminated the complete units and moved on to his handlers?

Sullivan would be fine with these two eliminating Alpha and Bravo Units. But not his handlers.

He'd spent way too many resources on the three handlers to lose them to vigilantes.

Operation Wicked Spider was falling apart at the finish.

Activity on the third screen caught his attention. He zoomed in to get a better view through the violent downpour.

He set his glass down with a loud thump. "What the hell? Where did these killers come from?"

A big man stood on the pavement directly outside the alcove where Doug XYZ was collecting cash from the ATM at Pace & Kent in the middle of the pier.

His shooting arm was raised. He pointed a pistol into the alcove.

Sullivan watched as he squeezed off two shots.

"Dammit! That's enough!" Sullivan roared.

He sent a quick text to each of the three handlers. "Vigilantes on scene. Watch your six."

Then he picked up the correct burner phone and pressed the preset number for Chicago PD.

When the desk sergeant answered the phone, Sullivan put a civilian's breathless, frightened urgency into his voice.

"There's an armed robbery happening right now on Navy Pier. At least twelve men with guns ran up. They're killing each other! Send the SWAT team. Maybe two teams."

The sergeant seemed properly alerted. He requested more details.

Sullivan disconnected.

He busted the burner phone with a hammer and flushed the pieces down the toilet. He did the same to the three burners he'd assigned to each unit leader. He wouldn't be talking to them again.

When Sullivan returned to the desk, Chicago PD squad cars were arriving on the scene. Lights flashing, sirens blaring.

A SWAT weapons truck pulled up closer to the marina.

A police boat was speeding toward the pier.

Pure chaos erupted.

CHAPTER FORTY-EIGHT

Monday, May 23
Chicago, IL
2:05 a.m. (CDT)

WIND BUFFETED KIM FROM all sides, blowing rain along with it. She squinted to see the big man holding the gun pointed into the alcove.

She ran toward the shooter.

She shouted, "Stop! FBI!" but the wind carried her words away into Lake Michigan.

The big man shot into the alcove. Twice. Then he blended into the storm and she couldn't see him anymore.

Burke rushed forward from his surveillance position and ducked into the alcove to check on the thief. Burke yelled, "Man down!"

Kim twisted her head to look for Burns. He had darted between structures and disappeared.

The first gunshots somehow led to more. The big man didn't have time to go far. Who was doing the shooting?

She counted several shots from multiple guns fired on the north and south sides of the pier away from the lake and closer to the city.

Half a moment later, Chicago Police Department sirens and lights from three directions blasted through the night, headed directly toward the pier. In a matter of minutes, they'd cordoned off the area, preventing the ATM thieves from all routes of escape.

Shouting and gunfire punctuated the continued noise of arriving law enforcement and medical personnel.

"This one's dead," Burke shouted as he left the thief's body on the concrete in the alcove. "The shooter went that way."

Burke took off running toward the lake.

Kim hustled along behind him. She squinted into the gloom and made out the big man's retreating back in the distance with Burke in pursuit.

Burke stopped and raised his gun to shoot.

Kim ran forward and lunged at Burke just before he fired.

She knocked him to the ground. His shot went wide.

He rolled on the pavement, howling with outrage. "What the hell are you doing? Reacher's getting away!" Burke screamed to be heard over the storm.

"He's running eastward. This is a pier. It juts out into Lake Michigan. Where do you think he's going, exactly?" Kim offered him a hand up.

By the time Burke was on his feet again, the police had begun to flood the scene.

Two SWAT weapons trucks arrived. One parked at each end of the pier. Cops jumped out of their vehicles and moved in all directions.

"We got a call of shots fired at this location," the SWAT

leader said as he approached. "Did one of you call us in?"

"FBI Special Agents Otto and Burke." Kim pulled her badge wallet. The last thing she needed was a round of friendly fire. She pointed. "You guys are needed over there."

Another round of gunfire punctuated Kim's point and the officers dispersed without further discussion.

Kim heard a speedboat headed toward the docks. She glanced up to see more police lights and sirens.

The police boat slowed until it abutted the dock, and three officers jumped off to join the others while the driver battled the storm, struggling to pull into the slip.

Kim caught movement in her periphery. She turned her head and narrowed her eyes for a better look.

Pointing ahead through the gloom, Kim shouted to Burke, "I think that's Burns. He has a duffel full of money. He's running in the same direction as Reacher. They must be planning to meet up."

Kim hurried toward the marina.

Burns ran up to the boat and jumped aboard before the fourth officer had a chance to secure it to the dock.

Burns raised the duffel and used its heft to knock the officer into the icy water. He revved up the engines and sped alongside the pier toward the wide-open lake.

Burke raised his weapon again and fired at Burns.

His shots went wide as the boat buffeted in the wind against the churning water.

The big man who had shot into the ATM alcove ran along the pier shouting to the man at the wheel.

The driver slowed the boat and slid closer to the dock's edge.

The big man jumped from the pier and landed hard in the boat.

The driver revved the engines and headed out to Lake Michigan, throwing a churning wake behind.

"Come on! We'll lose them!" Kim yelled into the roaring wind.

"I'll be right there," Burke shouted back, running toward the SWAT truck.

What the hell was he doing?

Buffeted by the wind, the boat wasn't making much headway through the choppy water. She might get lucky. Kim pulled her weapon and sprinted toward the speeding boat.

Burke dashed to the back of the SWAT truck and jumped inside. A few moments later, he emerged holding a fifty-caliber rifle.

He jumped to the pavement and hurried to an open spot closer to the water's edge.

He dropped to the ground on his belly, tripod in hand.

Burke aimed and fired toward the speeding boat, at least a mile from shore now.

Kim realized what he was about to do and ran toward him, yelling, "Burke! Stop!"

He ignored her and continued to fire.

Burke knew his way around guns and how to handle them.

He aimed at the back of the boat and repeatedly fired toward its fuel storage.

The boat was speeding away, weaving and bouncing in the rough waters, making the target harder to hit.

Kim counted the shots as he emptied the magazine and watched the destruction.

The bullets must have been both explosive and incendiary. Did a typical SWAT truck have rifles loaded with bullets like that?

Burke's third shot ignited the fuel.

With the fourth bullet, he succeeded.

The boat exploded.

A ball of fire engulfed the entire boat and flames mushroomed into the air.

Kim knew instantly and instinctively the two men on the boat were dead.

She knew it for sure.

She'd seen such explosions before.

Not survivable.

Not even remotely.

Kim ran toward Burke.

He scrambled up from the ground holding the rifle.

Burke was drenched and so was Kim.

"No one could survive an explosion like that. Not even Reacher," Burke boasted.

Kim stared at the fireball on the lake in horrified shock and disbelief. The capacity for speech had deserted her.

Neagley rushed up behind them from out of nowhere. She wasn't even supposed to be at the pier. Where had she come from?

Screaming curses and epithets like a wild hyena, she shoved Burke onto the pavement and kicked him viciously over and over.

He curled up to protect his belly and covered his head, but Neagley didn't stop.

Kim tried to pull her off before she bashed him to death, but Neagley was strong as steel and hard as woodpecker lips and mad as hell.

Neagley's errant elbow jabbed Kim in the solar plexus and doubled her over.

Neagley didn't even notice.

Her fury did not abate. Burke's body couldn't have even an untouched square inch.

Morrie galloped up, yelling at Neagley, telling her to stop before she killed Burke and landed herself in prison.

She kept on kicking.

The storm's fury did not abate.

Nor did Neagley's.

Morrie said something to her that only Neagley could hear. She didn't seem to care.

Which was when he simply lifted Neagley off the ground and carried her away.

She screamed and swore and kicked and elbowed and twisted viciously, jerking in his arms, but Morrie held her tightly and didn't let go until she finally stopped.

Burke lay bloody on the ground, the rain and wind washing his blood into rivulets on the concrete.

Kim hurried over to him, still holding her sore belly and her breath. She bent to check his pulse. "Burke. Are you okay?"

He groaned.

Burke wasn't dead, but if Morrie hadn't pulled Neagley off him, he would have been.

EMTs were on the scene now.

Kim called out and two rushed over to Burke with a gurney.

After Kim gave them a brief explanation of his injuries, they loaded him up and whisked him away to a waiting ambulance.

Two rescue helicopters, buffeted by the still-raging storm, flew over the burning boat. There appeared to be nothing they could do while the fire continued to burn.

The fire burned so strong even the drenching rain couldn't defeat it.

The wind whipped the acrid stench and heat toward Kim's position on the shore, where she stood staring in continuing disbelief.

Neagley and Morrie came back. Neagley had calmed down. She shrugged. Morrie said nothing.

They stood beside Kim, staring, eyes stinging in the driving rain for a good, long time.

Until finally, the charred boat slipped below the surface and into the deep waters of Lake Michigan, where untold numbers of sailors rested on the bottom for all eternity.

Kim muttered absently, "Hard to believe even ten fifty-caliber rifle shots from this distance could inflict that much damage. That boat was a mile away. Maybe more."

"It's the multipurpose bullets," Neagley said dully. "Probably Raufoss MK 211."

"What's so special about them?"

"Military uses them against helicopters, aircraft, armored vehicles," Neagley replied matter-of-factly as if briefing the Joint Chiefs. "Effective armor piercing. Penetration. Incendiary, high explosive. Those bullets can ignite jet fuel."

"Burke is a good marksman. Multiple hits near the fuel lines," Kim nodded. "Not much chance of error, using ammo like that."

"No," Neagley said quietly, staring into the empty space where the boat had slipped into the cold, dark lake. "The poor bastards didn't have a chance."

CHAPTER FORTY-NINE

Monday, May 23
Chicago, IL
3:30 a.m. (CDT)

WHEN THE CHAOTIC SCENE was finally under control, Chicago PD counted eleven dead. Two on the destroyed boat lost to the lake. Nine on the ground in various locations, dressed in black, their heads and faces covered by ski masks.

When the police lifted the masks, Neagley and Kim were able to identify only one of the bodies.

Doug Jerzekowski, also known as Doug XYZ, was the body in the ATM alcove Burke had found. He'd been shot by the big man Kim and Burke had believed to be Reacher.

But she didn't tell the police as much.

Neagley didn't mention Reacher, either.

The other men who had left with Doug XYZ from the bar in Gaucho on Thursday were Moe Smith, Ray Vance, and Petey Burns. Burns was not among the nine bodies at the scene.

Nor was Jack Reacher.

In all, police recovered four duffel bags filled with cash. Kim guessed there should have been five more bags, but at least one duffel was at the bottom of the lake with the police boat. The fire might have destroyed it.

Crime scene techs would be working here for hours, if not days. Navy Pier wouldn't open today and maybe not tomorrow.

Kim was wet and chilled to the bone. Neagley and Morrie, too.

"Let's head back to my place," Neagley said to Morrie. "Nothing more we can do here tonight."

Morrie offered Kim a lift to her motel and she accepted. She could pick up the SUV Burke had parked on the street another time. Or not. She really didn't care about the 4-Runner. The Boss could figure it out.

The drive out to Lake Forest was faster this time. There was very little traffic. Morrie accomplished it with his usual competence.

He pulled up to the front door of the motel.

Neagley said, "I'll make some calls. Tomorrow, we can talk. Let's meet up at my place at noon."

"Okay," Kim said before she climbed out into the still pouring rain. She trudged upstairs, shed her wet clothes, and stood under the hot shower for a long time.

She managed not to think about Reacher or Burke or even Petey Burns while soot and grime and terror washed from her body and circled the drain.

Her belly hurt where Neagley's elbow had jabbed her. Otherwise, she was remarkably free of physical damage.

When she finally stepped out of the shower to towel off, questions bombarded her from all sides.

Was Burke really trying to kill Reacher?

That's how Neagley took it at the time.

In truth, so did Kim.

But that was a crazy idea, wasn't it?

Surely, Burke couldn't have orders to assassinate Reacher. Where would those orders come from? Cooper didn't want Reacher dead. Neither did Finlay.

Did they?

Neagley could have been wrong about Burke's intentions.

Errant thoughts without pattern kept bubbling into Kim's head.

Burke could have been simply trying to stop the boat and not destroy it. Maybe.

Even in the heat of battle, Burke wouldn't have destroyed that police boat without authority from somewhere. He'd have been fired, for sure and the paperwork alone would have buried him forever.

So he wouldn't have gone rogue like that.

Destroying that police boat had to be about a dozen crimes, not including the death of two people he'd caused.

If they were dead.

Maybe Reacher and Burns had survived somehow.

Search and rescue hadn't found the bodies. Not yet, anyway.

But Reacher had survived worse. Many times.

And Burns was wily. Clever.

They might have made it off the boat somehow.

Which came back to the question she couldn't escape—a question she'd faced before.

Was Reacher alive or dead?

The difference this time was that she knew the answer she wanted, even though her reasons were muddled in her mind and her feelings were all over the place.

Her pride, her career, couldn't absorb such a colossal failure.

Her mission was to find Reacher alive.

He was a wanted man, needed for a highly classified assignment. A matter of national security.

Cooper had been very clear on that point.

She'd risked her life and Gaspar's life to do the job. She simply could not accept that she'd failed so spectacularly.

But that wasn't all.

Reacher had saved her life.

Twice.

She owed him. Simple as that.

If Reacher was dead, someone would pay.

She'd make it so. Or die trying.

She had no idea how she would find answers or fulfill the vow she'd just made to herself.

But she couldn't begin until she had sleep and coffee in that order.

After that, she thought Burke had a lot to answer for, as she succumbed to exhaustion. She slept fitfully as her subconscious relived the battles on the pier. Bleary-eyed, she finally gave up the effort.

Kim ordered a large pot of black coffee from room service and opened her laptop. Hours later, she'd finished her official report and sent it off to Cooper.

She ordered more coffee and, as she always did, wrote a longer, private report next. Because she didn't trust Cooper or Finlay or Burke, for that matter.

She had no idea what was really going on here.

Kim had no intention of being a sacrificial lamb one of these days in a congressional hearing.

At the very least, she'd have a long, accurate, contemporaneous account of everything that occurred. Maybe, just maybe, she could save her own ass.

She drained the second pot of coffee and uploaded the report to her secure server. Paying her insurance premium on a policy she hoped never to use.

With everything that had been swirling around in her head now firmly reported, exhaustion drew her back to bed. Despite mainlining caffeine for the past few hours, she fell deep into oblivion as soon as her head hit the pillow.

When she next glanced at the clock, she realized she was due at Neagley's place in an hour.

CHAPTER FIFTY

Monday, May 23
Near Fort Meade, MD
11:00 a.m. (EDT)

SULLIVAN'S EYES WERE AS dry as toast. He'd been cleaning up the loose ends for hours. The stress and the booze and the long hours had exhausted him. He wasn't a young man anymore.

He was almost finished here.

Earlier, he'd reached out to the two remaining handlers for a full debriefing of the debacle at Navy Pier. Somehow, they had managed to survive.

He didn't care how they'd saved their own asses. Their reports were consistent enough to believe.

He'd sent them both out of the country as a precautionary measure until the official investigations were closed. He'd spoken to them individually and destroyed the burner phones afterward.

The video feeds had recorded the night's events. Sullivan

had rewound and rewatched the situation unfold several times from several angles. Through the process of elimination, he identified the casualties.

Eleven dead.

Chicago PD identified the bodies as four members of Alpha Unit, four members of Bravo Unit, and the leader of Charlie Unit.

All of which was okay.

Although the execution methods were not as clean as he'd planned, the result was good enough.

Four men were not accounted for yet.

By watching the video replays and matching them with satellite imagery, he simply could not identify the two men on the boat. Sullivan had the advantage of knowing all the players.

Which should have made it easier to distinguish Charlie Unit's handler and Moe Smith from Petey Burns and Jack Reacher.

And yet, at this point, Sullivan could not say which two men were on that boat when it exploded and which two were not.

Which was definitely not okay.

Not even remotely.

He had studied the video feeds again and again, looking for the point when the other two men might have escaped.

If he could identify the two who escaped, he'd know which two had died.

The cameras and the angles and the weather all conspired against him. He could not locate two of them on the pier or in the city.

Not yet, anyway.

Sullivan was bone-weary from the effort. If Reacher and Burns were the lucky ones and still alive, they'd surface somewhere soon enough.

Cooper was still looking for Reacher.

If he wasn't dead, he'd turn up eventually. He always did.

Sullivan grinned. Even with the chaos at Navy Pier, Operation Wicked Spider had turned out okay.

He'd lost two handlers. Maybe a third one, too, which was too bad. They were good men.

On the other hand, he now had more than two billion extra dollars to fund global operations. It was a good outcome no matter how he sliced it.

"Not too shabby," he said as he poured another whiskey and downed it in one gulp on the way to his bed. He fell asleep with a smile on his face, happy with a job well done.

CHAPTER FIFTY-ONE

Monday, May 23
Chicago, IL
11:30 a.m. (CDT)

KIM FINISHED HER SHOWER and got dressed. She applied about two pounds of concealer with a trowel to the dark circles under her eyes and stood back to check her appearance.

Her clothes looked like she'd rolled around in the dirt in the middle of a raging storm. Nothing she could do about that.

A quick trip to shops along Chicago's Magnificent Mile would solve the clothing problem. She added the chore of finding clothes to her mental calendar.

She gathered what she needed and locked the rest in the room safe. She'd be here again tonight, for sure. Maybe two more nights if she was unlucky.

The Boss had called three times. Kim ignored his calls and voicemails. She had no energy to deal with him right at the moment.

At least, not until she knew Burke's status. He was still on her team. She was still responsible for him.

She'd heard nothing from Burke since the ambulance had taken him to the hospital and he wasn't answering his phone. She'd tried to check, but no one would tell her anything.

Kim took it as a good sign.

If he'd died, the nurse might have let that information slip.

Still, she wanted to be sure. So she'd texted Gaspar. He'd promised to find out.

A glance through the window revealed that the storm had finally run its course. The grass and parking lot were wet and puddles had gathered everywhere. But she didn't need her slicker.

She slipped all three phones into her pockets, patted her holster to confirm her duty weapon was in place, picked up her room key, and headed downstairs to wait for the car service.

Less than thirty minutes later, the car had dropped her off and she walked up Neagley's driveway. She pressed the bell. Morrie opened the door.

"Good afternoon, Otto."

"Afternoon, Morrie," she said as she walked through and dropped the three cell phones into the black box on the side table. "Is Neagley in the kitchen?"

"Yeah. She's expecting you." He closed the door and followed Kim straight back through the magnificent house.

Neagley was seated with her coffee. A second mug was waiting for Kim. On the table beside Kim's coffee was a large envelope.

"How's your stomach?" Neagley asked, maybe a little sheepishly, which would be rare. Kim had never heard Neagley apologize for anything.

"I've got a big bruise. But I'll live," she replied, seating herself across the table. She tapped the envelope with her index finger. "What's this?"

"Chicago PD identified the bodies at the pier last night. Thought you might like to know," Neagley replied. "A few other things you might find useful, too."

"What else did you find out?" Kim asked, pushing the envelope aside for now.

"They can't say whether anyone was on the boat when it exploded. They haven't found remains yet, either," Neagley replied.

Kim nodded. She'd figured as much.

Neagley said, "We chased down what was going on with those ATMs. All three belonged to Pace & Kent International Bank."

Kim nodded again. She'd heard of Pace & Kent, of course. But she had no specific intel about the bank at her fingertips.

"That's not the interesting part," Neagley said. "At the exact time the ATMs were hacked, Pace & Kent lost a cool billion dollars via unauthorized electronic transfer."

"That's a lot of cash." Kim cocked her head. "Where'd the money end up?"

"Still searching. But it's not likely we'll ever find it. The theft was too sophisticated," Neagley replied. "The ATM thefts were a decoy. I've been on the phone with some of my banking clients. At least one, Racine International, was also hit by an unauthorized transfer. There may be more."

Kim nodded, tapping the envelope with her finger. "You think Cooper's behind the whole bank theft thing?"

Neagley shrugged. "Could be Cooper. Or someone else at that level, given the size, complexity, and sophistication of the operation."

"Doesn't sound like something Reacher would be involved in, though, does it?" Kim said.

Neagley shook her head. "Not even remotely. Reacher has zero interest in money. He would have no idea what to do with a billion dollars."

"But he was there. He's involved somehow," Kim said slowly, running the possibilities through her head.

"Unless he wasn't there," Neagley said.

"What do you mean, unless he wasn't there? I saw him. Burke saw him. You saw him. Morrie, too," Kim replied.

Neagley sipped her coffee without further comment.

Swallowing a heavy lump in her throat, Kim asked, "Are you implying that Reacher wasn't on that exploding boat last night?"

Neagley shrugged.

"Then why the hell did you attack Burke?"

Neagley's cell phone interrupted.

"I need to take this." Neagley shrugged and picked up the call. "Yes?" she said into the phone as she left the room.

Kim stared out the window until Neagley came back into the kitchen a few minutes later.

"That was an NSA source," Neagley said. "Pace & Kent and Racine International were the only two banks they can identify that were hit this morning."

"Good news, I guess," Kim said. "Did your source have any leads on who's behind it?"

"Nothing yet." Neagley shook her head and refilled the coffee. "They'll keep looking. The operation was very sophisticated. It's likely there will be more thefts soon enough."

"Yeah." Kim sat quietly for a minute, giving herself a chance to change her mind. Then she nodded. It was always better to know the truth than flail around in the dark.

She took a breath and held it. Then she said, "Your NSA source is reliable, I assume."

"Meaning?" Neagley said, head cocked.

"Meaning can he be trusted to keep his mouth shut?" Kim replied levelly.

"Tight as a clam."

"Clams open up if you drop them in hot water," Kim replied.

"You've forgotten who you're talking to." Neagley narrowed her gaze. "I wouldn't use him if he couldn't be trusted."

Kim nodded. Neagley was strong as steel. Kim could trust her to keep her word. "Can you have your NSA source check out Burke for me?"

Neagley's eyes widened. "Are you sure you want to go down that road?"

Now that she'd made the decision, Kim didn't hesitate. "Absolutely."

"What are you looking to find?" Neagley asked.

Kim took a breath and held it for a two count. "Everything there is to know."

"I'll see what I can do then," Neagley said, nodding slowly as she considered the implications of Kim's request.

"Thanks," Kim replied. After a moment, she added, "It should go without saying that this is just between us."

"Of course."

For clarity, she said, "Don't tell Reacher."

Neagley said nothing.

FROM LEE CHILD
THE REACHER REPORT:
March 2nd, 2012

The other big news is Diane Capri—a friend of mine—wrote a book revisiting the events of KILLING FLOOR in Margrave, Georgia. She imagines an FBI team tasked to trace Reacher's current-day whereabouts. They begin by interviewing people who knew him—starting out with Roscoe and Finlay. Check out this review: "Oh heck yes! I am in love with this book. I'm a huge Jack Reacher fan. If you don't know Jack (pun intended!) then get thee to the bookstore/wherever you buy your fix and pick up one of the many Jack Reacher books by Lee Child. Heck, pick up all of them. In particular, read Killing Floor. Then come back and read Don't Know Jack. This story picks up the other from the point of view of Kim and Gaspar, FBI agents assigned to build a file on Jack Reacher. The problem is, as anyone who knows Reacher can attest, he lives completely off the grid. No cell phone, no house, no car…he's not tied down. A pretty daunting task, then, wouldn't you say?

First lines: "Just the facts. And not many of them, either. Jack Reacher's file was too stale and too thin to be credible. No human could be as invisible as Reacher appeared to be, whether he was currently above the ground or under it. Either the file had been sanitized, or Reacher was the most off-the-grid paranoid Kim Otto had ever heard of." Right away, I'm sensing who Kim Otto is and I'm delighted that I know something she doesn't. You see, I DO know Jack. And I know he's not paranoid. Not really. I know why he lives as he does, and I know what kind of man he is. I loved having that over Kim and Gaspar. If you haven't read any Reacher novels, then this will feel like a good, solid story in its own right. If you have…oh if you have, then you, too, will feel like you have a one-up on the FBI. It's a fun feeling!

"Kim and Gaspar are sent to Margrave by a mysterious boss who reminds me of Charlie, in Charlie's Angels. You never see him…you hear him. He never gives them all the facts. So they are left with a big pile of nothing. They end up embroiled in a murder case that seems connected to Reacher somehow, but they can't see how. Suffice to say the efforts to find the murderer and Reacher, and not lose their own heads in the process, makes for an entertaining read.

"I love the way the author handled the entire story. The pacing is dead on (ok another pun intended), the story is full of twists and turns like a Reacher novel would be, but it's another viewpoint of a Reacher story. It's an outside-in approach to Reacher.

"You might be asking, do they find him? Do they finally meet the infamous Jack Reacher?

"Go…read…now…find out!"

Sounds great, right? Check out "Don't Know Jack," and let me know what you think.

So that's it for now…again, thanks for reading THE AFFAIR, and I hope you'll like A WANTED MAN just as much in September.

Lee Child

ABOUT THE AUTHOR

Diane Capri is an award-winning *New York Times*, *USA Today*, and worldwide bestselling author. She's a recovering lawyer and snowbird who divides her time between Florida and Michigan. An active member of Mystery Writers of America, Author's Guild, International Thriller Writers, Alliance of Independent Authors, and Sisters in Crime, she loves to hear from readers and is hard at work on her next novel.

Please connect with her online:

http://www.DianeCapri.com

Twitter: http://twitter.com/@DianeCapri

Facebook: http://www.facebook.com/Diane.Capri1

http://www.facebook.com/DianeCapriBooks

Printed in Great Britain
by Amazon

31305316R00209